Wish
I'd Known
You Tears Ago

STEPHEN BLY

Wish
I'd Known
You Tears Ago

BROADMAN
&HOLMAN
PUBLISHERS

NASHVILLE, TENNESSEE

DEDICATION

FOR SHEILA AND VALERIE

● ● ●

Published by Broadman & Holman Publishers

Nashville, Tennessee

ISBN-10: 0-8054-3173-X

ISBN-13: 978-0-8054-3173-5

Dewey Decimal Classification: F

Subject Heading: ROMANCES \ WESTERN STORIES

3 4 5 6 7 8   11 10 09 08 07 06

1

Don't run away!"

The paint filly scampered behind the old weathered barn. Ten-year-old Develyn Upton sprinted after her.

"Come back. I don't want to play hide-and-seek."

With several orange spots dribbled on her white shirt, Develyn paused beside the pine siding, crossed her arms, and peeked around the corner of the barn.

Where is she? Lord, this is a very, very naughty little girl horse. You could make all horses to be well mannered. I think you made a mistake with this one.

The month-old foal bolted into the barn where several missing boards created an undesigned doorway.

"You can't hide in there. I am your friend."

Develyn ducked into the dim light of the barn and waited until her eyes adjusted to the darkness. Sun rays filtered through cracks in the wood siding, making the stale dust sparkle like a golden-brown fog.

"This is a very smelly barn and not a good place for a young girl like you. I'm going to take you back to your mother."

The noise from the corner sounded like a bucket being kicked over.

"I know you're in here."

She spied a flash of color on the other side of the wood pile.

"I see you over there. I promised Mr. Homer I would keep you in the corrals, so you better come back with me right now."

Develyn took slow, baby steps toward the mound of split firewood. "Yes, you are a very pretty black-and-white pony, but you have a lot to learn. I only have a short time to teach you."

She spied another blur of black-and-white.

"OK, enough of this. You are coming with me right now, young lady. I have you cornered. You're pinned against this old barn."

Develyn jogged around the firewood, waving her arms. "You can't run away from me. I am very stubborn, and I always get my way."

The small black-and-white animal turned its rear toward Develyn and hiked its bushy tail.

"No!" Develyn screamed. "I'm not talking to you. Go away."

The skunk hissed.

"Don't you do that!"

"Do what?"

"You know what I'm talking about, young lady."

"Mother?"

Fingers brushed Develyn's blonde bangs off her forehead.

"Mother, are you dreaming?"

Develyn Worrell sat up and sniffed the air. "Delaney?"

"I think you were dreaming."

Develyn stared around at the cabin's shadows.

"What is it you didn't want me to do?"

Silent lightning to the west lit the interior. For a second Develyn could see the sleepy face of her daughter on the thick inflatable mattress next to her bed.

A second voice filtered in from the right. "She always dreams of horses."

Develyn sat up, the sheet dropped to her waist. When thunder rolled, she jerked it back to her neck, even though the cabin was jet black. "Go back to sleep. Sorry to wake you up."

"I don't remember you talking in your sleep at home in Indiana," Delaney said.

Develyn rubbed her neck, then lay down. "I don't remember going to sleep at home. At least, not for years."

"Do you sleep better in Wyoming?"

"I do everything better in Wyoming."

Delaney's voice softened to a whisper. "Mom, I'm glad I came out to see you."

"So am I, Dee."

Develyn could hear Casey's rhythmic breathing. She rolled on her side in the direction of her daughter's mattress.

Lord, I know I've made mistakes. And you and I know Spencer made mistakes. But it doesn't seem fair that our daughter has to pay for them. None of it was her fault. Keep her safe. Tonight . . . tomorrow . . .

The flannel sheets felt good against her legs. She turned the pillow over and nested her head on the cool side.

This time there were no horse dreams.

Or skunk dreams.

"Was that thunder or an explosion?" Delaney asked.

"Did it sound like a shotgun?" Casey inquired. "That could be Mrs. Morton."

"It was like a big balloon popped," Delaney added.

Develyn propped up on her elbow and yawned. "I'm sure it was thunder. Every sight and sound and smell seems to magnify out here. It will blow over quick." She plopped down on the pillow. "We need some sleep. We must have talked until 2:00 a.m."

"Mother, I'm worried," Delaney whispered.

"I know, honey. We'll take you to the doctor on Friday. Let's just trust the Lord. Whatever we have to face, we will face it together."

"No, Mom, I'm worried about that noise. I think it was a bomb."

"In Argenta, Wyoming? Dee, this is a dirt-road town. It's the last place on earth anyone would bomb."

"It shook the windows in the cabin."

"A strong wind will rattle this cabin," Casey said.

"What is that smell?" Delaney asked.

Develyn closed her eyes. "A skunk."

"No, it isn't. I know what a skunk smells like."

Develyn sucked air through her upturned nose. "Sulphur."

"What?" Casey called out.

"It's that sulphur smell like the smoke from a stick match."

"Oh, no," Casey moaned. "Pull your covers over your head!"

The flash of white light and the explosion hit at exactly the same moment. The blast shattered windowpanes and ripped the front door from its hinges. The heavy door slammed down on the front porch. The wind roared like a convoy of semi-trucks, and rain pelted the covers like a barrage of BBs.

"Mother!"

"Delaney, are you alright?"

"Don't get out of bed!" Casey yelled.

The second blast sounded to the north a few feet and the third somewhere in the corrals to the southwest.

"What is it?"

"We got hit by lightning!" Casey shouted. "Don't get out of bed. The residual jolt can kill you."

"What are you talking about?" Develyn asked.

"This cabin is electrified."

"But we are OK."

"The mattresses insulated us."

"Mother, I'm scared."

"What do we do, Casey?"

"Just give it a little time. It will die down quick."

"There's busted glass all over my bed," Develyn announced.

"Everything's getting wet," Delaney whined.

Develyn strained to see in the darkened cabin. "Can I get my flashlight?"

"No, don't touch it," Casey warned.

"Mom, I don't know what to do," Delaney cried. "What is going on?"

"Casey, are you sure?"

"Do you have on your watch?" Casey asked.

'Yes."

"Is it working?"

Develyn pressed the light on her watch. "The light doesn't come on."

"It shorted out," Casey said. "Take your watch off and toss it on the floor."

"Why?"

"Do it."

Develyn tossed the watch toward the open front doorway. When it hit the floor, it snapped and sparked like jumper cables hooked to the wrong post.

"Mother, do something," Dee whimpered.

"Don't get up!" Casey yelled again.

"Do your lips feel funny?" Delaney called out. "I think my lips are burned."

"I'm going to jump over to your mattress," Develyn announced.

"Be careful," Casey cautioned.

"There's some broken glass over here, Mom."

"At the next flash of lightening, I'm hopping over there."

From somewhere near the arena, thunder boomed and lightning flashed.

Develyn jumped to the inflated mattress stretched between the two beds and into Delaney's arms.

"Are you alright, honey?"

"Mother, I'm scared."

"So am I, Dee. Casey, are you alright?"

Cree-Ryder's long black hair tumbled to her shoulders. "Do you smell smoke?"

Develyn sniffed. "Nothing can burn in this downpour."

"Do you smell smoke?" Casey repeated.

"I smell it," Delaney said.

"This cabin cannot be on fire," Develyn insisted. "I will not allow it."

Casey barked the orders. "When the lightning flashes, look for your tennies. If you can reach your shoes without touching the floor, do it."

The lightning was distant but still illuminated the room.

"It's filling with smoke," Delaney cried out.

Casey pulled on boots over her bare feet. "Grab your shoes. We have to get out of here."

"I can almost reach my jeans," Delaney said.

"Jerk on your shoes. Get out of here without touching anything," Casey yelled. "I saw a propane tank blow up once. One more little spark can do it. I don't want to see that happen again."

Develyn plucked up her tennis shoes and slipped them over her cold toes.

"I just have flip-flops." Delaney called out.

"That's OK, just don't touch the floor," Casey hollered. "Grab a blanket for a shawl."

"What if it drags the floor?"

"It won't conduct electricity unless it's wet."

"Mother, I can hardly breathe."

"Hurry."

"Where are we going?"

"Run out to the Cherokee."

"We'll be soaked."

"That's better than being fried!" Casey screamed. "Just hurry."

"I'm scared," Delaney whimpered.

"Let me try it first," Casey called out. At the next flash of lightning, she raced across the smoky cabin wearing short pajamas and cowboy boots. Her long, black hair flagged behind her as she draped a sheet like a superhero cape. "It's OK, come on."

Before Develyn and Delaney made it to the door, the headlights from Casey's truck illuminated the front porch.

"I want my wallet," Delaney called out.

"Dee, the roof is on fire."

"That's my only picture of daddy. You tossed out all the rest."

"I'll get your wallet. You go on out with Casey."

"How can you see in the smoke?"

"Go on."

Develyn shoved her daughter toward the headlights that

reflected off the smoke in the cabin. Develyn could barely see. She squinted her eyes and held her breath.

Lord, this has to be a dream. My daughter hasn't been here six hours. This is crazy.

Smoke-generated tears ran from her burning eyes as Develyn spotted her own purse next to the busted lantern on the counter.

Will it electrocute me to pick it up? This is insane. It's a leather strap; it won't carry electricity . . . will it?

There was a sizzle when she grabbed it and a shock like brushing against an exposed wire on Christmas lights, but she held on and scooped Delaney's beaded purse in her other hand. She coughed her way to the front door and staggered out to the porch. Delaney caught one arm, Casey the other, and tugged her toward the pickup truck.

"The roof's on fire, Mother."

Develyn glanced back at the flames. "Where is the rain when we need it?"

"It left with the lightning," Casey said. "Get in the truck. The Cherokee was locked."

Develyn shoved Delaney's purse toward her. "Casey, I couldn't find your wallet."

Casey tugged the other two toward the waiting truck. "I have it. I always sleep with it."

"Where do you keep it?" Delaney questioned.

Casey yanked open the door and shoved them inside. "With the knife and gun."

"Do we need to call the fire department?" Delaney asked.

Casey piled in behind the wheel. Develyn scooted across to the middle, and Delaney crowded next to the window. The heater blew cold air against their bare legs. Develyn shivered.

"There isn't any fire department. Look at the roof burn." Even from a distance the flames reflected off Casey's brown face.

Delaney hugged herself and rocked back and forth. "Every place has a fire department, right?"

"Welcome to the frontier, Miss Dee," Casey murmured.

"But shouldn't we do something?" Develyn asked.

"Just watch and wait for the scary part."

Delaney's voice cracked. "What scary part?"

"When the tank blows. If it shoots out sideways, it can burn down Tallon's cabin too."

"Coop!" Develyn cried. "I've got to get him out of there."

"How could anyone sleep through this?"

"I have to check. Let me out, honey."

"Mother . . ."

"I've got to do it, Dee. He would do it for me."

"She's right about that. Devy-girl, give me your keys so I can back up the Cherokee," Casey shouted.

Develyn shoved her purse to Casey Cree-Ryder.

"Mother, look at your hand."

A wide red blister crossed her palm. "It must have been the purse."

The wind blasted through Develyn's wet T-shirt and running shorts as she jogged to Tallon's cabin. She circled his truck while watching the sparks fly off the cedar shingles of her cabin.

10

Those sparks could catch the entire prairie on fire. She slammed her clenched palms against the heavy wooden door.

"Cooper! Coop! It's me, Dev. Open up."

The third time she banged, the door slowly swung open. "Coop?"

She eased her way inside the cabin. "Coop? Wake up! We have trouble."

Flames from the roof of her cabin cast a shadowy hue to the room as Develyn inched her way to the back.

Lord, I don't want to wake a man in his own bed. But I will not allow him to lie here while the cabin burns down around him.

But the bed looked empty.

"Coop?"

In the shadows she spotted the man's body stretched out on the floor beside the bed. "Oh, no . . . no . . . no . . . Cooper!"

She grabbed his shoulder and shook it. "Cooper, you have to get up."

He didn't move.

"No, Lord . . . no . . . I can't handle this. This isn't right. This can't be. I want to go home . . . I want . . . I want . . ."

Calm down, Devy-girl. . . . What's the plan? I can't carry him out. I need help. I'll get Casey.

Develyn scrambled out the door toward the truck.

"We're in the Cherokee," Delaney called out.

When Develyn turned toward the Jeep, an explosion like a thousand Roman candles shoved her forward. She stumbled and fell in the shallow mud.

Casey and Delaney pulled her up. She could see their mouths moving but couldn't hear the words.

Casey spun her around, facing the cabin.

There were no flames.

No fire.

Little smoke left.

"What happened?" Develyn called out.

"You don't have to shout, Mother."

"What?"

Casey pointed to the cabin, then spoke slow and loud. "The . . . propane . . . tank . . . exploded . . . straight . . . up . . . and . . . put . . . out . . . the . . . fire."

"It's out?"

"Yes."

"Just like that?"

"Yes!"

"You don't have to yell," Develyn insisted.

"We thought your hearing was damaged in the explosion," Delaney said.

"I think my everything was damaged."

"It's all over," Delaney added.

"Where's Cooper?" Casey pressed. "Did you wake him up?"

"Oh, my goodness, no. . . . I think he's dead."

"What?"

Develyn began to cry. "He was lying on the floor, and I couldn't wake him up. I think he's dead. He must have been electrocuted. Oh, no. . . . "

Delaney hugged her muddy mother.

Casey stared across the headlight-lit yard. "But his cabin wasn't hit."

"He's dead. I don't know why this is happening to me," Dev sobbed. "Of all men, not my Coop."

Delaney grabbed her shoulders. "Mother . . . mother . . . get ahold of yourself."

"You don't understand. Cooper is . . . is . . . is . . ."

"He's standing in his doorway," Casey cried out.

Wearing black boxers and a black T-shirt, Cooper Tallon leaned against the doorjamb and rubbed the back of his neck.

Develyn led the trio to his cabin.

"What do you mean scaring me like that?" Develyn yelled.

He ran his fingers through his gray hair. "What? Miss Dev? What are you . . . Cree-Ryder. You girls will freeze out here in your . . . what's going on?"

"You scared me to death," Develyn sobbed.

"What are you talking about?"

"She thought you were dead," Casey reported.

"Why?"

"You were passed out on the floor, and I couldn't wake you up."

"I sleep on that rug when my back is hurting."

"But I couldn't wake you up."

"I had to take a pain pill to get to sleep. Why did you want to wake me up?"

Develyn sucked in the tears and wiped her face. "Because there was this noise like a bomb, the lightning hit the cabin, the roof caught fire, the propane tank exploded, and we barely got out with our lives."

Cooper stared at her. He rubbed his chin and stared over at the walls of the other cabin. "Am I standing on my porch in my shorts, talking to three attractive women clad in wet pajamas about a cabin blowing up?" He rubbed his forehead. "Or is this a dream?"

Develyn grabbed his hand. "Come and see."

He stared down at her hand. "Not until I pull on some jeans and boots and splash water on my face."

● ● ●

"Where are you now?"

Develyn shifted the cell phone from one ear to the other. "Lily, I'm standing in front of what used to be my cabin."

"And there is nothing left?"

"The walls are still standing, but no roof. Most of the contents were blown to bits and scattered around the yard."

"You're coming home now, right?"

Develyn stared at the paint horse in the pasture. "Why would I do that?"

"You just lost everything and barely escaped with your life. That's a sign to come back to Indiana."

"All I lost was a suitcase full of jeans and T-shirts."

"Dev, I think you are still in shock."

"Everything's OK. Coop borrowed Hank's travel trailer for

himself and insisted that Delaney, Casey, and I stay in his cabin."

"If you lost all your clothes, what are you wearing?"

"Oh, you'd like this . . . I have on a hundred-year-old prairie gingham dress that hangs like a sack to the top of my tennies."

"Where did you get that?"

"Coop had a trunk of old stuff that belonged to his grandmother."

"Just how chummy are you with the gray-haired cowboy?"

"He's a good friend, Lil."

"Who gave you his home?"

"It's his cabin, not his home, and he'd do the same thing for anyone in town. That's just the way he is."

"I still can't believe you aren't coming home."

"Lil, the Lord prompted me to insist that Delaney come to Wyoming. I haven't found out why yet. I'm not leaving here until I know. So what's happening in Crawfordsville?"

"Compared to you, life is totally boring here."

Dev surveyed the yard for Uncle Henry. "And the lawyer?"

"Stewart had meetings in Washington, D.C. Something about Supreme Court guidelines or something."

"Has he proposed?"

"No, but I did."

"What?" Dev choked. "You asked him to marry you?"

"No, I proposed that we go to Chicago for the weekend."

"You what?" A pickup down on the dirt road bounced toward the corrals. She spied a hand wave. She waved back.

"We'll stay at my sister's place."

"Which one?"

"Nancy."

"OK, that works. She's more strict than my mother."

"How is your mother?" Lily pressed.

"She and David decided to go to Florence before they come home."

"How's his arm?"

"In a cast, but Mother is determined that shouldn't slow them down. What about school?"

"Guess who they hired to replace Barbara in first grade?"

"Who?"

"Tammy Givens."

"Tammy? But she . . ."

"She was in your fifth-grade class. Yes, I know, Ms. Worrell. That was sixteen years ago. She's been teaching in Ethiopia."

"We're getting old."

"One of us has been old for quite a while, honey."

"I've got to go." Develyn tugged on the shoulder of the ill-fitting dress. "I'm headed to Casper to buy some clothes for the needy."

"You get a new wardrobe out of this?"

"Of course."

"Hmmmm."

"Don't even think of it."

● ● ●

When Develyn entered the cabin, Casey was by the stove. "How do you like our outfits?"

Delaney stepped out of the tiny bathroom, combing her long, light brown hair.

"Towel skirts and Cooper's T-shirts. Dee looks ready for the beach."

"How about me?" Casey asked.

"With the cowboy boots, you look . . . uh . . ."

"Like a homeless refugee?"

"The thought did come to mind."

"We'll anxiously await your return with some clothes," Casey added.

"I don't know why I'm the one who has to go to town looking like this."

"Simple. You're the only one of us who can fit into Grandma Tallon's clothing," Delaney said.

Develyn looked down at her musty dress. "I feel like I'm in some separatist sect." She let out a slow sigh. "That wasn't very kind. People have the freedom to wear anything they want."

"In that case," Delaney giggled, "Casey and I will go with you dressed in towels and T-shirts."

"No you won't. You won't even go to the door looking like that."

"We want to see what we can find to salvage from the cabin," Casey said.

"Then use safety pins on those towels."

Casey grinned. "Yes, Mother."

"I'm glad she treats you that way too," Delaney said. "Now I know it's not just me."

"Dee, your mama treats every living creature like a fifth-grader. That's the way the Lord made her."

"Even the cowboys?"

"Especially the cowboys."

"I've been here for twelve hours and haven't even met a single cowboy."

Casey put her arm around Delaney. "Sure you did; you met Cooper Tallon."

"Yes, but he's older than my mother."

"Oh, you want a young, eligible cowboy?"

Delaney rubbed her round nose. "It would be nice to at least meet one."

"Casey, isn't a certain swarthy cowboy coming over to see his bronze bombshell tonight?"

Casey strutted over to Delaney Worrell. "Yes, and if she gets within ten feet of Jackson Hill, I'll shove horseshoe nails under her dainty little pink toenails."

Delaney looked down at her toes. "Does he have a friend?"

"While you are out, look for poor Uncle Henry. He must have run off with the explosion. I can't find him anywhere," Develyn said.

"You worried about your boy?"

"It's the first time in eight weeks that he hasn't met me at the front door."

"I thought wild burros were supposed to stray," Delaney said.

"Oh, Uncle Henry is not an ordinary burro," Casey laughed. "He's your mama's baby!"

• • •

Develyn peered over the top of her dark glasses at the man in the gray wool suit. His tie was crooked. "I don't understand this at all," she snapped.

"Just routine security precautions. We'll only detain you for a moment."

"Routine? You bring all your customers into the back room and interrogate them?"

"We asked you to leave the store and you refused."

Develyn noticed the cobwebs in the corner of the ceiling. "I came here to buy several hundred dollars worth of clothing. I spent two hours picking it all out, and you won't let me charge it on my credit card. Then you ask me to leave the store without my goods."

"We won't let you charge it on this credit card. Did you ever tell us your real name?" he questioned.

"You have my credit card, my driver's license, and my wallet. What do I have to do to convince you?"

"Look, lady . . ."

"I'm Ms. Develyn Worrell."

"Whatever. You came in here wearing an old musty dress and tennies looking like a homeless person. You spent $703.46 on clothing and makeup. You filled two shopping carts. . . ."

"Two-and-a-half."

"Then gave us a credit card and a driver's license . . ."

"And my picture is on the driver's license."

"This isn't you, lady."

"That's why I need to replace the clothing and makeup I lost in the fire. So I can look like her . . . I mean me. I've lost some weight since that picture was taken."

"You are much older than she is."

"What's the birth date on the license?"

"Let me see . . ."

"December 10, 1959. I will be forty-six years old next December," Develyn snapped.

"The gal in this picture don't look forty-six. She looks younger."

"I was having a good hair day."

"You don't look forty-six. You look older."

"I am not having a good day."

The man tossed the item down on the desk. "Well, it might get worse."

"How can that possibly happen?"

"I called the police."

Develyn felt her back stiffen. "I committed a crime?"

"You can just leave now, if you'd like."

"Not without my purchases."

"We've dealt with you gypsies before."

Develyn bit her lip. "I'm trying not to get angry. I'm trying to talk myself out of filing a lawsuit for harassment. But you are pressing my patience."

"Look, lady, you don't match the picture. The credit card company says the credit card was issued to some woman in Indiana, but never used. You said you are staying in Argenta, but no one in this store has ever heard of Argenta, Wyoming. And when we called the sheriff's office, they said no structure fires were reported in the past two weeks west of Casper."

"There was no reason to report it. It blew itself out when the propane tank exploded," she explained.

"Were you mixing meth?"

"What?"

"Were you cooking meth? I've read of that blowing up on people."

She gasped. "Am I now being accused of being a drug dealer?"

"I'll leave that to the police."

Develyn rubbed her temples. She rubbed her fingers across the oak table, then looked at the dust on them. "I want to talk to my credit card company."

"They are checking out reports of stolen cards. The police will be here soon."

She shook her head at the framed "Employee of the Month" certificate. "Mr. Donnelly, how long have you worked at Simpson's Department Store?"

He straightened his crisp, tight shirt collar. "Twenty-one years. Why?"

Develyn tried to soften her voice. "Where would you find a job if you were fired from this one?"

He threw his narrow shoulders back. "That's not something I think about."

"You should start. You have left me no alternative but to file suit against you for harassment, discrimination, and unlawful detainment. When that hits the newspapers, I believe sales will dip a tad, don't you?"

He paced around the room. "Lady, don't threaten me. I get lawsuits threatened all the time. Nothing ever happens."

"Would you please contact my credit card company again? I would like to talk to them."

"Do you have any local references?"

"None in Casper, but you can phone Cooper Tallon in Argenta. I have his cell phone number."

"Cell phones are not used for calling references. Anyone can be on the other end of the line."

Develyn pulled out her cell phone.

"What do you think you are doing?"

"I'm phoning my attorney."

"Yeah, right. Play all you want. I won't go along with it."

A lady in a dark blue suit and heels strutted into the room. "The credit card company said they cannot reach Ms. Worrell in Indiana."

"Probably lost her wallet on vacation," the man replied. "That's OK. The police can handle all of that."

Lord, I do not understand what you are trying to teach me here. I just want to get my purchases and leave the store.

"What is the charge against me?"

"Trespassing and failure to pay. When you fail to leave the store, when requested, it's called trespassing."

"Is unlawful detainment called kidnapping?" She shot back. "I believe that's a felony."

"What?"

The woman started toward the door. "I'll go out and wait for the police."

"Quint Burdett," Develyn barked. "Do either of you know Quint Burdett?"

"Everyone knows Mr. Burdett."

"Call him," she insisted.

"Are you telling me he can verify your identity?"

Develyn stomped across the room. "Arnold Schwatzeneggar can verify my identity, but I doubt if you want to call him. Call Quint."

The man in the suit motioned to the lady. "See if you can get Mr. Burdett on the line. This had better be on the level. I've wasted too much time with this charade."

"As have I."

The woman in the suit handed the phone to the store manager. "Mr. Burdett's on line one."

After a muted conversation, he shoved the phone at Develyn. "He wants to talk to you."

"Hi, Quint."

"Miss Dev, what's this all about?"

"Simpson's Department Store decided not to believe my credit card or my driver's license. But don't worry, I'm going to sue them for every penny they have. I've always wanted to own a department store."

"He said you looked like a homeless person."

Develyn explained the previous evening and the present shopping trip. Then she handed the phone back to the manager. "He wants to talk to you."

● ● ●

Develyn arrived at the cabin in Wrangler jeans, a lavender knit blouse with lace at the sleeve, collar, and hem, and fresh Dusty Rose lipstick.

Delaney and Casey jumped up from sitting in lawn chairs on Cooper Tallon's porch and helped her unload.

"You took longer than expected," Delaney said.

"I had an interesting time."

"How much did this set us back?" Casey asked.

"It was free."

Casey choked. "What?"

"The nice manager at that department store decided to give the merchandise to us."

"Out of sympathy for our plight?" Delaney asked.

"Out of sheer fright. When Quint Burdett threatened to buy the store and fire every employee, the manager became quite generous."

"You saw Quint?" Casey inquired.

Develyn shook her head. "You won't believe what happened in Casper."

"You won't believe what happened right here," Delaney replied.

"That's a cowboy grin if I ever saw one. What's his name?" Develyn quizzed.

"Hunter."

"Mr. Hunter?"

"No, Hunter Burke."

"Casey?"

"Don't look at me like that, Dev. I never saw him before in my life."

2

Mom, I'm sort of getting scared."

Develyn turned in the saddle and stared back at her daughter. "Coop's buckskin is a steady horse; but, if you'd rather, you can ride My Maria."

"Shoot!" Casey yelled from the rear, her long black braid hung across her chest like a bullet belt. "If you really want something scary, ride Popcorn. There is no telling when he will blow up. Did I ever tell you what he did at the parade down in Rawlins?"

Develyn studied Delaney's eyes while answering Casey. "I don't think so."

"He bucked me off when the black-powder boys fired off their salute to the flag. I landed right in the cotton candy machine. I was sticky for a month, but I was tasty."

Delaney shook her head. "I don't know what to believe when Casey talks like that."

"If it could happen, it probably has happened to Ms. Cree-Ryder," Develyn laughed. "She delights in living an adventuresome life. Did you want to change horses?"

Delaney pushed back her brown bangs. "No, that's not what I'm scared about."

This time Develyn didn't look back. "Is it about going to the doctor tomorrow?"

"Yeah. Mom, what if I'm pregnant?"

"Then your baby needs a good mama and daddy."

"What if the daddy doesn't want to be around me or any baby?"

"Then, at the least, the baby needs a good mother."

"I'm sorry, Mom."

"Dee, I'm sorry too. You didn't fail me. You failed yourself. My love for you doesn't change. You should know that. But it will change your life forever, that's for sure."

Develyn waited for her daughter to ride up closer to her. "What does the father say about this?"

"I just hinted to him." Her voice dropped lower. "I mean, I can't tell him I'm pregnant until I know for sure."

Develyn raised her thin, light brown eyebrows. "And how did he react to the hint?"

"He said I should have thought about that before I flew off without saying good-bye."

"You dumped him?" Casey rode up beside them.

"He was too nice," Delaney said.

28

Casey tugged her sunglasses down on her nose and peered over the top. "That's a new one."

"Mom knows what I mean."

"He was boring?" Develyn asked.

"He was the kind of guy Grandma would pick out for me."

"Oh, like Raymond LaFines?"

"Exactly."

Casey waved her braid like a wand. "Wait, wait, wait. Who is Raymond LaFines? I've never heard that name before."

"He was the first boy to propose to Dee."

"When was that?"

"In the sixth grade."

Delaney's freckles pinched together when she grinned. "No, I was in the seventh; he was in the sixth."

"Oh, one of those. Drey Miller asked me to marry him in junior high. He said I could break all of his horses and live in the bunkhouse for free if I married him."

"But you turned him down?" Delaney asked.

"No. I told him, heck, yes, I would do it. I thought he would pee in his pants trying to backtrack. Every day for a month I'd tell him that I was coming over to his ranch with my suitcase and tell his mother I was ready to marry him."

"What did he do?" Delaney asked.

Casey shrugged. "He cried a lot."

"He cried?"

"Yeah, I have that effect on men. When they think of marrying me, they cry."

"Twelve years old is hardly a man," Develyn said.

"That might be, but he's the last one to ask."

Casey reached over and tapped Delaney's knee. "So, what happened with you and little Raymond?"

The west wind blew Delaney's brunette bangs into her eyes. "I told him he was too boring. I said for him to go do something adventurous; then I might reconsider."

"Did he do something?"

"He jumped off the roof of his house with a kite and broke his leg."

"Yeah, well, who hasn't?" Casey said.

"Mom, you know when I knew Brian wasn't the right one?"

"When, honey?"

"Right after we, you know, did it."

"I don't know if I want to hear this," Develyn said.

"I do," Casey called out.

"It wasn't just the guilt. But I got to thinking about how you always told me that the right one to marry was the one who brought out the best in me."

When Popcorn started to buck, Casey slapped his rump. "She told me the same thing."

"Right at that moment I knew I was not behaving my best. I'm better than that, Mother. But after that . . ."

Casey spun the Appaloosa around to the left. "He wanted seconds?" Casey blurted out.

"Yeah, something like that. Anyway, that's when I began to realize what kind of mistake I had made."

Casey spun her horse to the right. "I think Jackson brings

out the best in me. But sometimes I wish he didn't. He has the cutest . . ."

Develyn cleared her throat. "Hmmm. I think it's time to change the subject. I can't believe Uncle Henry would run off like that."

"He was scared in the storm," Casey suggested.

"If he was scared, he would come and find me."

"Not necessarily," Delaney remarked. "Maybe he didn't want his mama to know he was scared."

"Are you talkin' daughters or burros?" Casey quizzed.

"Burros, of course."

"Well, he ran off. And he's probably in these trees."

Delaney stood in the stirrup and stretched her back. "Let me get this straight. You have a burro you didn't want. You have no idea what you are going to do with him in three weeks when we go back to Indiana. He's a wild burro and just ran off into the wilderness. Yet you want to go find him and bring him back?"

Develyn laughed. "That's about it."

"Why?"

"Because he'd do the same for me if I were lost."

Casey rode up ahead of them. "She's right about that."

"What do we do when we hit the cedars?" Delaney asked.

"We spread out and comb through the chaparral to the east, looking for Uncle Henry," Develyn reported.

"What do we do if we find him?" Delaney called out.

"Tell him Mama wants him to go home," Casey said.

Develyn picked up the gait. "And if we don't find him, we'll meet at Sweetwater Creek."

● ● ●

It took an hour to comb the scrub cedars north of Argenta. Delaney and Casey waited for Develyn at the creek as she emerged from the chaparral.

"Where now, Mama?" Casey called out.

"He is a very naughty boy. Where do you think a burro goes when he's scared?"

"To his real mother?" Delaney suggested.

"Maybe he headed back to LaSage Canyon," Casey said. "He seemed to like that."

"What do we do now?" Delaney pressed.

"I want to head back," Casey said. "Jackson said he'd come by. I don't want him to show up and see the cabin burnt like that with me not around."

"Maybe Hunter Burke will come back. He said he was looking for Jackson."

"You two go on back," Develyn said. "I'll swing out by Soda Springs."

Casey rode up to her. "Here, you might need this."

"What will I do with a rope?"

"Lead him home. If he's scared of the cabin now, he might need some encouragement."

"I'll be back in an hour or so."

"And if you aren't, we'll get the posse out after you . . . again."

"I'll be back this time. I can follow Coyote Gulch all the way to town."

32

"I'm still not used to calling Argenta a town," Delaney said.

Develyn chuckled. "It takes time."

"How long?"

"About three days," Casey laughed.

● ● ●

Develyn rode east across rolling dry prairie toward trees thick enough to look black on the horizon.

The girls are right, Lord. I don't know why I want to find Uncle Henry. He's used to living in the wilderness. I have to find him a home in three weeks. I just don't want to let him go. He's been the one male that I could figure out in Wyoming. But this is crazy.

I should have gone back and spent some time talking with Delaney. I know she's scared. I'm scared too. I don't know what to tell her. Some part of me, from my mother no doubt, wants to yell out, "This is exactly what I told you would happen." I'm not sure what that accomplishes.

If she's pregnant, that little one deserves a lot of love. That's what I want to give. I want to love that baby and give it the best it can have under these awkward circumstances.

Lord, you hold Delaney responsible for any sin she committed.

I'll hold the baby and make up for any love it will miss.

Mother will be petrified.

I wish Dewayne lived close. Dee would do anything for Uncle Dewayne.

The bray was distant but distinct.

33

Develyn stood in the stirrups. "Uncle Henry?"

She prodded My Maria to a canter on the second bray. When she crested the rise near Soda Springs, she spied the burro in the mud.

"What are you doing out there, baby? Get out of the mud and come here."

The burro brayed again and tugged at its front legs.

"Are you stuck? Oh, Uncle Henry, no wonder you couldn't come home. You got scared, ran out here, and sank in the clay gumbo. You have more mud than Cooper Tallon last week. I could hardly tell it was you."

Let's see . . . rope him and pull him out.

That is, if I knew how to rope.

What did Renny say? Either "tie the rope to the saddle horn first," or "never tie the rope to the saddle horn first." I can't remember.

She rode the paint mare up to the water's edge.

"Your face looks funny all covered with mud, baby. When we get home, I'm going to give you a bath."

Develyn slipped the rawhide hondo back until she had a large loop in the blue nylon rope. Then she tied the other end to the saddle horn.

"OK, so far so good."

My Maria turned her head and stared at Develyn.

"Don't you laugh at me, young lady. Let's see, how do they do it in the rodeos? Hold the coil in my left hand, twirl the rope in my right and . . ."

The medium-hard 5/16th rope slapped against her head and

34

dropped around Develyn's neck. "OK, I proved that I can rope me. Now I'll just try that again."

The second loop tumbled across My Maria's neck.

The third dangled off the stirrup. The fourth hit the water two feet away.

The burro brayed again.

"Don't hurry me, young man. You are the reason I'm here. If you had walked out of there, I wouldn't have to make a fool of myself."

I could ride down and get Casey, but what if she has gone off with Jackson?

Maybe Coop is at home.

But I am a Wyoming cowboy girl. I have it in my soul. I can do this.

Six more tosses and all she had was a muddy rope.

My Maria pranced.

The burro brayed.

Develyn fumed.

"I'm not going back without you. I need to get closer, but I'm afraid My Maria will get stuck. And if I hike out there, I might get stuck. I do not want to be rescued again."

If I hold onto the rope . . . then I can pull myself out. I just need a few steps in that direction.

"Uncle Henry, you are a pill today."

Develyn pulled her feet out of the stirrups and reached down and untied her tennis shoes. She pulled them off and shoved the socks inside. After she tied the laces together, she draped them over the saddle horn.

She slid down from the saddle to the muddy ground next to the spring. Cool clay squished between her toes as she rolled up the legs of her jeans.

If it gets halfway up my calves, that's deep enough.

Holding the tethered coil in her left hand and a big loop in her right, she inched closer.

The burro stared off to the north.

"You could show a little more enthusiasm in your rescue, young man."

My Maria looked bored on the other end of the rope.

"Do you have a better idea?" Develyn called out to the paint mare. "I didn't think so."

Of the first five tosses, two splashed in the water in front of the muddy donkey. The other two bounced on its back. Each time the animal flinched, but remained planted in the mud.

"I am not going back without you," Develyn mumbled.

The sixth toss circled the burro's neck and drooped like a necklace.

"Yes!" Dev shouted.

The animal shook it's head. The rope tumbled to the water and mud below.

"No!"

She coiled the muddy rope again. "I can't believe you did that. After all I've done for you. You were headed for the glue factory when I took you in. I feed you nummies out of my hand. I let you sleep on the porch. Now I'm going to throw this around your neck one more time. If you toss it off, that's it. I'll leave your miserable carcass to rot in the mud until the buzzards make supper out of you. Do you understand me?"

The burro stared north.

Of course he doesn't understand me. What am I doing? Lord, I could use a little help here. I'm supposed to get back and talk to my daughter, not spend the day toying with some auction burro.

The loop circled the donkey's neck.

Once again the muddy animal flung it off.

"OK, that's it. Nice to have known you, Uncle Henry. Hope you have a nice life. But I'm not going to waste any more time here."

As she began to coil the rope, the burro snapped its teeth around it.

"Turn loose of my rope."

The harder Develyn pulled, the more the burro pulled back.

"Oh, you think that's funny? We'll see if your teeth are as powerful as My Maria."

Develyn sloshed out of the spring and wiped her feet on the tall green grass that clumped by the water's edge. She shoved her bare foot in the cold rawhide-wrapped stirrup and swung into the saddle.

"We are getting Casey's rope back, even if we have to pull Uncle Henry's teeth out."

With knee commands, Develyn inched the horse forward. When the rope stretched taut, she prodded the horse again.

The burro did not turn loose.

But it did take one step out of the mud.

Then another.

"Yes, we will pull him out by the skin of his teeth." *I wonder where that saying came from?*

She kept My Maria at a slow walk until the burro was well out on the prairie. She tugged at the rope.

"Turn loose now, Uncle Henry."

The burro continued to clutch the rope.

"Honey, you can walk home on your own from here. Turn loose."

She yanked the rope; the burro jerked back.

"You are being impossible. I should spank your big, brown . . . but it's covered with mud." She slid out of the saddle. "I'll show you who's boss. You'll have to come home on a lead rope. How do you like that?"

She marched up to the burro, who promptly shook his head, and dollops of mud peppered Develyn's face.

With both eyes squinted, she grabbed Uncle Henry's ear and bent it sideways.

The burro dropped the rope.

"Oh, you don't like that? Well, what do you think of this?"

She slipped the loop over the animal's head and cinched it up to its neck.

"We're all going home now."

Develyn mounted the paint mare but left her shoes hanging across the pommel of the saddle. The burro resisted the tug of the horse for a moment, then gave in and trailed behind.

"We did it, girl. We found him. We roped him. And we

brought him in. If that isn't a Wyoming cowboy girl, I don't know what is."

Develyn kept My Maria at a slow, steady walk. The burro kept the rope taut.

● ● ●

When she spotted the one remaining cabin, she stopped, leaned forward, and patted My Maria. "Honey, Uncle Henry might not want to come back to the cabin. The noise frightened him last night. He might try to run away again, so I'm going to turn him out into the pasture with you and Popcorn. But don't annoy him, or his braying will keep us awake all night."

As she got closer, she could see Delaney leaning on the tailgate of Cooper Tallon's pickup. *Who's she talking to?*

When they plodded around Tallon's corral, she spied the gray-haired cowboy standing on the other side of a burro, who, on spying Develyn, trotted right out to her.

"He missed his mama," Coop called out.

"Uncle Henry?" She looked back at the muddy animal at the end of Casey's blue rope.

Uncle Henry leaned against her leg, and she scratched his ears. "But . . . who do I have?"

Cooper and Delaney strolled over.

"I see you brought Uncle Henry a friend," Coop grinned.

"I thought he was Uncle Henry covered with mud."

"She," Cooper corrected. "You have a female burro there."

"She?" Develyn said. "No wonder she didn't want to come with me."

Coop winked at Delaney. "You'd think a mama would know her own children."

"She was covered with mud, and I . . . didn't look very close, did I?"

"You just captured a wild burro out on the prairie. I'm impressed," Cooper said.

"She was stuck in the mud."

"Yes, well, from time to time we all are."

"What am I going to do with another burro?"

"Maybe she'll run off." Cooper slipped the rope off the burro. She meandered over to Uncle Henry. "OK, maybe she won't."

"Uncle Henry, don't you sidle up to her. She's no good for you, honey. She's very stubborn and self-willed and quite untidy, as you can see."

When the female burro trotted toward the corrals, Uncle Henry followed.

"Oh, no you don't, young man. You get over here right now."

Uncle Henry paused but didn't turn back to Develyn.

"I said, right now!"

Head slumped, the burro returned to Develyn.

"Wow, Mom, I'm impressed," Delaney said.

Develyn scratched Uncle Henry's ears. "Where did you find this naughty boy?"

"Mrs. Morton brought him home," Cooper explained.

"Mrs. Morton?"

Tallon waved back toward town. "She was very apologetic. She said that during the storm Leon had locked Uncle Henry in their outhouse, and she didn't discover it until this morning."

"How do you get a burro in an outhouse?"

"It's a two seater," Cooper explained.

Develyn climbed off My Maria, carrying her shoes. "This is more information than I want to know."

"What are you going to name your new burro?" he asked.

"She's not my burro."

"Of course she is. You roped her and brought her in."

"Doesn't she belong to the government?"

"Nope. She's yours, Devy-girl," Tallon insisted.

"Let's name her Aunt Jenny," Delaney offered. "But I refuse to call their offspring my cousins."

"Oh, they wouldn't. I mean, they can't . . ."

Cooper chuckled. "Sure they can. They aren't mules. They're donkeys."

"I will have no talk of that," Develyn huffed.

Delaney wrinkled her nose beneath a wave of faded freckles. "I don't think you have much say in the matter."

Cooper Tallon sauntered to his travel trailer. "Don't be sure of that, Miss Worrell. Never underestimate your mama's will."

"Are you calling me stubborn?"

"Focused, Miss Dev. You are the most determined gal I ever met. And I assure you, I mean that as a compliment. It's a part of your attraction."

"You see, Dee, this is the type of smooth talkin' cowboy I warned you about. He just called me stubborn and inflexible in such a charming way that I feel good about myself."

Cooper mumbled to himself as he entered the trailer.

Develyn and Delaney led My Maria to the pasture.

"Mr. Tallon is a nice man," Delaney offered.

"He can be abrupt and opinionated. Probably about as stubborn as me. But he has the most generous spirit of any man I have ever met. Hard working to a fault, and yet a very caring heart under that tough cowboy exterior."

"Is he the one for you, Mom?"

Develyn peered at her daughter's soft, pale green eyes. "Dee, my focus is on you now. Everything else can wait."

Delaney slipped her hand in her mother's. They continued to lead the paint mare to the pasture. While her daughter perched on the fence rail, Develyn pulled the tack off My Maria and brushed her down. After a handful of feed, she turned the paint out.

"Mom, you do that like you're a Wyoming lady."

"That's me, honey . . . a Wyomin' cowboy girl."

"How did you learn all of that?"

"From Ms. Casey Cree-Ryder." Develyn closed the gate and stepped over by Delaney. "By the way, where is that bronze bombshell?"

"She and Jackson went to Casper for supper. Mother, he is so totally cool."

"And he's polite, honey. His mother's a schoolteacher, you know."

Delaney brushed her brown bangs out of her eyes and pushed her sunglasses up on her nose. "They make quite a pair."

"Casey is like a sunflower in a strawberry patch. She stands apart from everyone. She might be the most unique gal I've ever met in my life."

"She made me cry," Delaney admitted.

Develyn slipped her arm around her daughter's shoulder. "What did she do?"

"She said you were the most gracious, loving, fun woman she ever met, and she would give anything to have you as her real mom."

"Did you cry because I'm not that way for you?"

"No, Mom, just the opposite. I know you are that way. I cried because for the first time I realized how much Daddy hurt you."

"Dee, that's in the past. I let go of that. I failed your dad lots of times too. I can't survive if I clutch to my failures, or to others' failures."

Delaney's voice lowered. "I wish Daddy were still alive."

"You know what, honey? For your sake, so do I."

"Do you ever miss him, Mom?"

"Don't hate me, baby, but I don't miss him at all."

"Was it that bad for you?"

"Someday maybe I can tell you. Not now. But for several years I would fall asleep at night hoping the Lord would take me home before morning. I just couldn't handle the rejection and pain. I was scared to death of what the next day would bring."

Delaney hugged her mother. "I'm sorry, Mom. I never knew it was that bad. Why didn't you do something earlier?"

"I thought if I bore all the pain and anguish myself, you wouldn't have to. I was wrong. You had to bear so much. Besides, I kept praying for a miracle."

"And it never came?"

"Maybe it did, Delaney Melinda Worrell. You and I are standing in a dirt-road town in the middle of Wyoming hugging and crying. That's a miracle to me."

"Yeah, I know. Mom, I was thinking. Maybe we aren't so different. Maybe we are a lot alike."

"You think so?"

"Except I don't look anything like you."

"You have the same little upturned nose seldom seen in girls over twelve."

"Yes, we have the same nose, but the rest of me looks like Uncle Dewayne. With my round face and full figure, the best I can hope for is to look cute. But you, you doll yourself up and have that head-turning, heart-stopping, cowboy-melting glamorous look."

"Where in the world did you get all of that?"

"From Casey."

"I think you two had too much time to talk."

"She told me how it was at that big ranch barbecue."

"Honey, I'm a middle-aged mama. I think the Lord allowed me that one time just to cheer me up. If you could have seen the disdain the manager at Simpson's gave me this morning, you would think I'm ready for the rest home."

"I can't believe he said those things to you."

"The Lord has ways of keeping us humble, Delaney."

"I know, Mom. I know what you are saying." Delaney stepped back. "But we are going to make it, aren't we, Mom?"

"Even if you are pregnant, you mean?"

"Yeah."

"We all face sin, failure, repentance, and forgiveness. Making right decisions now will always stop a cycle of wrong decisions in the past. The Lord and I were talking about you when I was out looking for Uncle Henry."

"What did he say?"

"He said to love any baby you have with all the love I have for you."

"What did you tell the Lord?"

"I told him I would do it because I love you with more love than anyone on the face of the earth."

"Really, Mom? You said that to the Lord?"

"Yes, I did."

Delaney slipped her hand into her mother's. "Sometimes I wish I hadn't been such a pill this summer. We could have gone to Maine together."

"I think I was supposed to come out here."

"Do you think, maybe, I was supposed to go to South Carolina?"

Develyn studied her daughter's face. "Perhaps."

"Oh no, oh no!" Delaney moaned. "Tell him I'll be right out." She sprinted to the cabin.

"Tell who? Delaney?" Develyn glanced over the rim of her sunglasses toward Argenta. A white Ford pickup made its way up the drive.

Develyn waited at the back of the Cherokee.

The dimples in his cheeks were so perfect they seemed painted on. The lanky, tanned cowboy in a long-sleeved shirt sauntered toward her. "Evenin', darlin. What happened to that cabin?"

"It was hit with lightning last night."

"Look at that mess. Was anyone hurt?"

"No, we got out before the fire."

"You a roommate of Miss Delonie's?"

"Her name is Delaney. Yeah, I'm one of her roommates."

"I'm Hunter Burke."

He didn't release her hand when he shook it. "Say, you aren't her sister, are you?"

"No." Develyn tugged her hand from his warm, firm one.

"That's good because . . . I . . . well. Say, who would have thought two fine-lookin' gals would be bunked up in this little shack?"

"It's a cabin, and there are three fine-lookin' ladies here. Casey has gone with Jackson to Casper."

"I missed him again? This is getting to be a routine."

"Can I take a message for him?"

"This is a business thing. He's still working a pack string up in Glacier, isn't he?"

"As far as I know."

"What time will he be back?"

46

"I have no idea. It could be late."

"Maybe I should wait," Hunter suggested.

"Certainly. There's a bench in front of Mrs. Tagley's store."

"No, I meant here."

"I don't think so. We don't have room to entertain guests, and we don't know when they might return."

"Are you nervous? Some ladies get nervous when I'm around. Why do you think that is?"

"I don't have a clue. I'll tell Jackson you are looking for him."

"Could you tell Delonie I'm here? I'd like to speak to her."

"Her name is Delaney."

"I know. But it wouldn't be polite to stop by and not say hello. My mother taught me to be polite."

"Delaney knows you're here."

"What's she doing, then?"

Making herself cute, no doubt. "I'm not sure."

"Of course, you and me could sit in the truck and visit until she comes out." He raised his eyebrows.

"I think you should leave," Develyn snapped.

"You are nervous, aren't you? It's OK. Once you know me better, them butterflies in your stomach will disappear. What did you say your name was?"

"I didn't."

Delaney strolled out on the deck, then paused. "Hunt? Well, hi!"

She strolled over to where they stood.

"I hear I missed Jackson again."

"I'm glad you didn't miss me."

"I was just visiting with your roommate, wondering how two pretty women can be in one cabin."

"Oh, good, you met my mother."

"Your mother?" he gasped.

Develyn pushed her sunglasses up on top of her head and flashed a pasted grin. "You are surprised?"

"Oh, no ma'am."

Your eyes lie, Mr. Hunter Burke.

"I was thinking of walking down to the store and buying a Pepsi. You want to go for a walk, Miss Delonie?"

"He always calls me that," Delaney giggled.

You've only met him once. What do you mean he always calls you that?

"Anything we need at the store, Mom?"

"A quart of 2 percent milk would be nice, now that we have a cabin with a propane refrigerator."

Develyn watched as Hunt and Delaney strolled out to the road.

Well, at least they aren't holding hands. There is something wrong here. How can she be carrying one man's baby and giggling down the lane with another?

"Your Delaney has a friend already?"

Develyn turned to Cooper. "She just met him. I think he's a friend of Jackson's. His name is Hunter Burke. Do you know him?"

"Nope. But that doesn't mean much. Are you worried?"

"Why do you say that?"

"Your face looks worried."

Develyn stood straight and slapped a wide grin on her face. "There, is that better?"

Cooper laughed. "You can't hide it, Miss Dev. Ever'thing shows on your face."

"Everything?"

"Yep. Even the mud from bringin' in Aunt Jenny."

"Oh, dear." She rubbed her cheeks with her fingertips. "Is that better?"

"Not really." Cooper reached over, brushed his calloused thumb across her left cheekbone. "There."

"Thank you, Mr. Tallon."

"I've got some business down in Cheyenne and didn't want to get in you gals' way, now that there is only one cabin. But I'm hoping we can ride up to the springs soon, so I can show you that homesite I found."

"I'm planning on it, Coop. I still grieve over the loss of the cabin. I feel like a jinx or something."

"You gals being safe is the only thing that matters. These cabins aren't worth insuring. I'll tear this one down if I build a log home back at the springs."

"Oh, leave it up if you can. It will remind me of my two best summers."

"Remind you? You aim on coming back, don't you?"

"Cooper Tallon, you contracted me at no pay to be the interior decorator of your log home. Have you forgotten so soon? Of course I am coming back."

"You mean, if I build the house, it's a guarantee that you will come back?"

"That's what I mean."

A wide grin broke across his leather-tough, tan face. "That's the best news I've heard since they put cabs on backhoes."

Develyn stared at him.

"That's a compliment. An old construction joke."

"I must admit I don't know many construction job jokes."

"It's a good thing, Dev. Most should never be repeated."

"Can we ride up to the springs on Monday?"

"Sounds good. I'll pack us a picnic."

"No, you won't."

"I won't?" he replied.

"I'll furnish the picnic. It's my treat."

"You can't do that. It's my invite and . . ."

"Coop, let me do something for you. Last week you fixed me a wonderful supper, so it's my turn."

"I reckon you won't bend on that."

"Remember, you said stubbornness is a part of my charm."

He pointed to the road. "Here comes your girl, Mama."

Develyn and Cooper watched Hunt and Delaney amble up the dirt driveway. When they got within thirty feet, Delaney sprinted to the cabin.

"I've got to write down my cell phone number for Hunt," she called out.

The lanky cowboy leaned against the door of his white pickup and folded his arms. "It's been a long time since a gal's mother and father waited for me in the yard."

Tallon cleared his throat. "I'm not . . ."

Develyn slipped her arm in Cooper's and interrupted him. "You know, Hunter, we are concerned for Delaney. She has some things in the past to deal with before she thinks about the future."

"I know. She told me everything."

Develyn felt her neck stiffen. "Everything?"

"Yep."

"Then you understand why she will need some space for awhile."

"Don't know anything about space. But I do know she wants me to have her phone number."

Delaney bounded out of the cabin.

"Here!" She shoved the white note in his hand. "You promise to call me tomorrow?"

"Sweet Dee, I'll phone, that's a fact."

He leaned closer until his face was only a few inches from Delaney's.

"Drive careful, Hunter," Cooper boomed.

Burke jerked his head back.

Develyn marched over to them. "And we'll tell Jackson you're looking for him."

Hunter climbed into the truck and closed the door. "I'll talk to you tomorrow." He spun the pickup toward the corral and raced out to the road.

"How old is he?" Cooper asked.

"He must be Jackson's age," Delaney reported. "They went to school together."

"That's at least ten years older than you."

Delaney waltzed over and slipped her arm into her mother's. "Isn't he dreamy, Mom? No wonder you like it out here. I think coming to Wyoming is the best thing I've ever done."

3

The first thing Develyn spotted when she stepped outside the next morning was Uncle Henry in the pasture alongside Aunt Jenny.

"How did you get in there?" She marched over to the fence. "All summer long you hated that pasture like a prison, and now you sneak in? You come here right now. I will not have a disobedient watch-burro."

The second thing she viewed was Renny Slater's red Dodge truck bouncing up the driveway.

Renny parked in front of the burned-out cabin.

"Looks like you brought the house down, Devy-girl."

She strolled over to the mustang breaker. "I still shudder when I look at it. Coop's going to bring one of his rigs in here and haul it all off. How did you hear about it?"

"Well, I was sittin' around by the phone, pinin' for my Indiana schoolteacher, and . . ."

She slugged him in the arm. "You were not."

"OK, I was in Bridger helpin' a pal shoot coyotes."

"Why?"

"They were eatin' his sheep. Livestock men are funny that way. They just don't cotton to feedin' coyotes."

"You didn't answer my question."

"Well, I did get a phone call."

"From who?"

"I thought it was 'from whom.'"

"Are you correcting the teacher?"

He grinned like the first-place winner at a spelling bee. "No, ma'am."

"From whom did you get a phone call?"

"Burdett asked me to make a delivery. He told me about the cabin and said you were in need of a few things."

"What kind of delivery?"

Renny pointed to two huge cardboard boxes in the back of his truck. "I reckon about half the clothes Miss Emily ever owned."

"He sent me her clothes?"

"That's what Lindsay told me."

"But I can't take them, Renny. They belong to Miss Emily. Doesn't matter how long she's been gone; they will always be called Miss Emily's."

"I sort of reckoned that's what you'd say. But I didn't want to interfere."

"You'll just have to take them back."

"That's where it gets complicated. I've got an appointment tomorrow morning bright and early. I need to keep heading west to be there on time."

"Where?" she asked.

"Twin Falls, Idaho."

"Are you going to check out that rodeo coach position at the college?"

"I figured it wouldn't hurt to know what I'm turnin' down."

"I'll pray that the Lord will lead you."

"I sort of figured you would. I'm not in a hurry. I took to heart what you told me. I know there are a lot of people to help around here. I need to know how much time off they'd let me have."

"Ask to see a sample contract and study the details. Make sure everything they promise is down in writing."

"Yes, ma'am. I'd have you go with me and check it out, you know, if circumstances were different."

"You mean, if I weren't too old for you?"

Renny laughed and gave her a hug. "I don't reckon I will ever live that one down, will I?"

"I would go with you anyway, but Delaney is here. We have some things to work out."

He pointed to the burned cabin. "That's quite a welcome you gave her."

"It was so bizarre. It seems like a dream."

"It don't look like a dream." Renny turned toward the truck. "What do you want me to do with these clothes?"

"Will they fit in my Jeep?"

"Does the back seat fold down?"

"Yes. I'll take them back to Quint myself."

"There's another problem. The reason he didn't bring them down himself is that he and Lindsay are flying to Austin this afternoon. He needed to do some maintenance on her plane."

"She's going to take that job at the University of Texas!"

"Is she coachin' rodeo too?" Renny grinned.

"Not hardly. Director of communications, or something like that. When are they leaving?"

"He said around 2:00 p.m."

Dev rubbed her nose and looked at her watch. "If I headed up there now, I could get to the ranch by ten and be home by noon or so. That might work."

"You got some cowboy waitin' for you at 1:00?"

"Delaney has a doctor appointment at 3:00 in Casper."

"Is she sick?"

"Eh . . . it's a . . ."

"A female thing?"

"Yes."

"Well, don't tell me. I might get squeamish."

"Renny Slater, squeamish?"

"Did I ever tell you about the only time I fainted?"

"I can't believe that."

"I was visitin' some friends in the hospital, Barry and Barb Greenfield. They got that nice place east of Kaycee. It was their first baby, and I was in town. So I bought the little guy a pair of cowboy boots. I sauntered over to St. Joseph's to give my congrats. I had been workin' outside all day. It was July hot outside and air-conditioned cool inside. Anyway, I joked with Barry in the hall and stepped in to tip my hat at Barb.

"She said, 'Come here, Renny, and look at the first pictures of little Cody.' Well, I figured it would be an insult not to look at the photos, so I stepped over and she shoved a stack of pictures at me. They were the first ones of the baby, alright."

"What do you mean?"

"She was naked from the waist down and strapped into some harness thingy, and the baby is halfway out of the womb, so to speak."

"Oh, my."

"I said somethin' a little stronger, right before I blacked out. When I came to, I was on the cold linoleum floor with a uniformed nurse lookin' down at me."

"What did she do?"

"Nothing. She just looked at me and said, 'The same thing happens to me all the time,' then walked off."

"You did recover?"

"Yeah, but I promised myself to steer clear of delivery room pictures and female problems."

The cabin door opened, and shorts and T-shirt clad Casey Cree-Ryder waltzed out to the yard. "Hi, Renny!"

"I like your hair down, Miss Casey. Are you ready to dump that Hill kid and ride off into the sunset with a real bronc buster?"

Casey turned to Develyn. "It's pathetic when they beg like that."

"Oh, darlin', you are turnin' down the chance of a lifetime."

Casey laughed. "Jackson Hill is my chance of a lifetime, and I'm not letting go."

Renny hugged Casey's shoulder. "Jackson is a lucky cowboy."

Casey studied his eyes. "Thanks, Renny. I know you mean that." She turned toward his truck. "What are you hauling?"

"Sequined blouses and designer jeans, I reckon."

"You just peddling them out of the back of your truck, or are you headed to the thrift store?"

"They are all for you and Devy-girl, I reckon. A present from Quint Burdett. They are for all three of you," Renny said.

"I can't fit into anything Miss Emily ever wore. I was bigger than that when I was eight."

"It doesn't matter. I'm hauling them back. I want to choose my own clothing," Develyn said.

"You just going to dump them in his yard, or what?"

"Of course not. I'll just say . . . I'll . . . I'll think of something."

The cabin door banged open, and Delaney emerged with cutoff jeans and a gray sweatshirt turned inside out and her hair pulled behind her in a short ponytail. She padded across the dirt yard barefoot.

"You must be Delaney. I recognize the toes."

Delaney curled her toes in the dirt. "Don't look at them. Do they look like Mom's?"

"I wouldn't know. Your mother always curls them just like that and forbids anyone a glance. I recognized you from the picture in your mom's wallet. One time, in a fit of generosity, she let me look at your picture."

"You must be the mustang breaker."

He tipped his hat. "Yes, ma'am. Renny Slater. How did you guess that?"

"You look exactly the way my mother described you."

"Delaney," Develyn cautioned.

Renny grinned. "And just how is that?"

"I think her words were . . ."

"Delaney!"

"Renny's a short, thin, blond-haired, weak-eyed young Robert Redford with dimples that will melt your socks."

Casey burst out laughing.

Develyn's face flushed as if she had been drinking Tabasco with a straw.

Renny shook his head and sidled up to Delaney. "But now that you've seen me in person, you figure I'm much better lookin' than your mama described?"

"I think she overrated things."

"Listen," Renny said, "I'll unload these boxes in the Jeep if that is what you want. I've got to get on down the road."

"Are you going to a rodeo?" Delaney asked.

"No, I'm looking into a college teaching job in Idaho. You want to come with me? We can swing down to Wendover, Nevada, and get married on the way."

"Wha . . . what?" Delaney stammered.

"Am I rushin' things a bit?"

"Slater!" Develyn cautioned.

"But I just got here." Delaney recovered her smile.

"Your point is?"

"She needs time to look around, Renny," Casey chuckled. "She could probably do a whole lot better than you."

"No, that's not it," Delaney stammered. "I just have never . . ."

"That's alright, Dee-Darlin'. Concernin' runnin' off and teachin' college, I was just teasin' about that one."

"Which one, about me running off with you, or teaching college?" Delaney probed.

"You are a lot like your mama," Renny laughed.

"No one has ever told me that."

"Toes and nose and tease—you are practically twins."

Develyn looked her daughter over. "Twins?"

"Devy-girl, do you look like your brother?"

"Not at all."

"And you are twins, right?"

"I get your point," Develyn grinned. "Dee and I are like nonidentical twins that are twenty-five years apart."

"Yeah, that's it."

Develyn raised an eyebrow. "Only I'm too old for you, and Delaney is too young,"

"Hey, don't look at me," Casey protested. "I already turned him down once this morning."

"I'm not all that young," Delaney demured.

"Are you changin' your mind?" Renny said.

"She is busy today, cowboy," Develyn added. "We are going up to the Burdett Ranch this morning."

"We are?" Delaney asked.

"Yes, and we had better hurry, because we need to get you to Casper by 3:00."

Delaney shrugged at Renny. "Yeah, I need them to check . . ."

Slater held up his hands. "I don't want to know. Whatever it is, I wish you a speedy recovery. But I don't want to know."

● ● ●

The gravel road north had just enough moisture to hold down the dust. But the brief rain hadn't melted the washboards. Develyn had to keep it under forty miles per hour.

Delaney clutched the handhold above the door. "This is the only way to some big, fancy ranch?"

"It is rather remote."

"No, Argenta is remote. This is fifty miles past remote. Now, you are not going to marry this rancher guy back here?"

"No, I'm not."

"Mom, how do you know the one *not* to marry? All my life I've been trying to learn how to tell which one to marry. But I don't know squat about which one not to marry. I mean, I know not to marry a self-centered, woman-beating jerk. But beyond that, how do you tell?"

"Honey, that's something I've been trying to learn this summer. I think it has more to do with knowing yourself than knowing the man."

"What do you mean?"

"We need to discover what life the Lord has planned for us. Then we know who fits in."

"But you are old. You know what your life should be. I mean, you're not that old, but you know what I mean."

"If you don't know where the Lord is leading you, you'll have a tough time finding the right guy."

"What have you learned this summer, Mom? Who are you? What does the Lord have in store for you?"

"I'm an Indiana schoolteacher. That's who I am. That's who I will always be. If the Lord ever brings a man into my life on a permanent basis, it will fit well with that calling."

"Are you saying I need to choose a career first?"

"No, Dee, it's more than a career, it's . . ."

"Was Daddy the right one for you when you married him?"

"I was convinced of it at the time."

"Do you regret marrying him?"

"Never, babe. You are the wonderful reason I married your father. I regret the way it all turned out, that's all."

"Whoa, is that an antelope?"

"Yes."

"It's beautiful out here, Mom."

"Wild, empty, and breathtaking."

"Like some men."

Develyn laughed. "I love the way you blurt things out. We haven't spent nearly enough time together during the last two years."

"Can I drive? I just realized that I've never driven down dirt roads like this."

"Sure, but you have to take it easy. With the loose dirt and gravel, the rig will slide on the corners."

Delaney took the wheel and eased back onto the dirt road heading north through scattered scrub cedars. "This is the third time I've gotten to drive your Jeep."

"You've driven it more than that."

"No, the first time was when I hit the planter. The second time I locked the keys inside, and you had to phone AAA."

"You always had the car your father bought you."

"I like this Cherokee."

"It's worked well out here."

"Have you had to use the four-wheel drive?"

"On several occasions."

"How much farther?"

"We are about halfway there, I think."

"Wow, I can't believe anyone in America lives this remote."

"Slow down a little on the curves. If it's muddy in the shade, we can slide."

"This is fun, Mom, like explorers. We can have pretend adventures. Like we did in the summers when I was little and you and I would spend the afternoon in the hallway under the cooler. Remember all those stories we made up?"

"Yours were always about being at the beach."

"And yours were always about horses. Hey, did I tell you I got an "A" in my creative writing class?"

"No, you didn't. I think when you got grades we were on a not-speaking-to-each-other jag."

"I pulled a 3.37 grade point average this term."

"That's wonderful, honey. Would you believe that Casey is a straight-A-type student?"

"Really? That's so cool. She is so . . . so . . . you know, out there." Delaney put on the brakes. "What's that?"

"A piece of recap tire off a truck, I suppose."

Delaney motioned to the side of the road. "Should I go around it?"

"It's steep to my side. It won't hurt to run over it. The Jeep is tough."

"Oh . . . no!" Delaney swerved at the last moment. It was a muffled explosion and the Jeep slid to a stop at the road's edge.

"Did we get a flat tire?" Dev asked.

"It was a kill strip," Delaney moaned.

"A what?"

"One of those things the police put across the highway to blow out tires and stop a chase. The reality police shows always use them."

"No one would put a kill strip way out here." Develyn stared at the flat front right tire. "It's flat, alright."

Delaney hiked back to the dirt road and dragged the rubber mat behind her. "Look at the spikes. We are lucky to only have one flat. Why would anyone have this out here?"

"Maybe it fell out of a sheriff's vehicle. Anyway, we have a flat to change."

"Did you ever change a flat?"

"No, but I watched AAA do it several times. The spare and the tools are under the floor in the back."

"It's steep over there. I didn't want to pull any closer. You would think they'd have guardrails."

Develyn opened the tailgate. "Let's pull out these clothing boxes and put them over on that level spot. Two Worrell women are as strong as one mustang breaker, right?"

"Yeah," Dee mumbled, "I guess."

"I'll take the steep side. Work your fingers underneath, and we'll lift it down."

The gals staggered back with the huge, heavy cardboard box. Develyn felt her right heel catch on a rock.

"No . . ."

As she tumbled to her backside, the box slipped from Delaney's hands. Eighty pounds of clothing slammed against her chest and face. Develyn shoved the brown cardboard box, and it somersaulted over her head and down the embankment. She leaped to her feet. "No!"

On the second rotation, the folds of cardboard untucked and broadcast the contents into the dirt and mud of the hillside.

"Oh, no . . . no . . . no," Develyn moaned. "This is absurd."

"Most of them are, but that green one looks nice."

Develyn turned to her daughter, and both ladies burst out laughing. They hugged each other and watched the box lodge against a sagebrush.

"Mother, what are we going to do?"

"Retrieve the clothing, change the flat, and go to Casper. We'll take them all to the dry cleaners. What else can we do?"

"That hillside is steep."

"We'll strap our belts together or something."

"Mother, I believe we're building a memory."

"I have a feeling for the rest of our lives we will say from time to time . . . remember when we dumped all those sequined blouses off a cliff in the middle of Wyoming?"

"It's not exactly a cliff."

"Oh, it will be twenty years from now when we retell it."

"I like that, Mom. You know, thinking about you and me laughing and giggling at the past, twenty years from now."

"I do too, honey. And the sooner we get this mess cleaned up, the better."

Develyn found the dirt and rock on the side of the hill loose but soft. As long as she jammed her foot down and leaned into the mountain, she could scoot to any place she wanted.

She stationed Delaney about ten feet below the gravel roadway. As she retrieved a garment she tossed it up to her daughter, and Delaney tossed it up at the remaining cardboard box.

"I like this one, Mom." Delaney held up a mauve short-sleeved top with a silver sequined armadillo.

"That's horrible."

"But it came from Rodeo Drive."

"Then it's expensive and horrible. It should crawl back home."

"Maybe we should leave it here on the mountain."

"Oh, no . . . somewhere there is an inventory of Miss Emily's clothing. I'm just sure of it."

"Maybe you can tell the guy at the cleaners that you are doing this for a friend."

"I'm thinking of leaving the cardboard box down there. It's tough to get to."

"Do you think there are any left in it?"

"Oh, rats. You might be right, baby. I'll go down. Here . . . catch this."

"Did you look at this one?"

Develyn shaded her eyes and stared back up the hill.

"You can see right through it. Whoa, this is like something they wear to the Academy Awards or something."

"I'm sure Miss Emily wore a discreet blouse under it."

"Why do you think that?"

"Because I want to. I'll go get the box."

"What do you want me to do?"

"Fold everything and set them on the back seat for now. We'll stuff them in the box after we change the tire."

"Is this a good day, Mom?"

"It's an adventure—a mother-daughter adventure."

Digging in one heel at a time, Develyn inched her way down the hillside. Ten feet above the box her right heel struck rock and provided no traction. Her left foot staggered forward. To prevent tumbling forward, she plopped down on her rear and began to slide. Before she could get her heels speared into the hillside to break her slide, she crashed into the empty cardboard box.

The box launched into the air. Develyn's flailing right hand clutched the box and yanked back. She slammed against the mountain. The big box swallowed her like Jonah in the big sea.

She tried to catch her breath.

OK, that was cool. I don't hear Dee dying of laughter. Maybe no one saw it. Maybe it didn't happen. Perhaps I am as classy and together as everyone thinks.

Sorry, Lord. You and I know better, don't we? Do things like this happen to other people and no one ever discusses it? Did Miss Emily slide halfway down a mountain once and look like a complete idiot?

Develyn tipped the box over and sat up.

"OK, that's enough fun, class. Recess is over. Time to go back to the classroom. Devy Upton, you make sure you wash up before you come to class."

Wouldn't my class have loved to see that scene? Well, too bad, boys and girls. Nothing but smooth moves from now on.

"I have no idea why I wanted to save your life, Mr. Empty Box, but I've come this far; I intend to rescue you, whether you want me to or not."

She couldn't carry the box in front of her and still keep her balance leaning into the mountain. With her hands over her shoulders, she held it on her back. Taking short, sure steps, she plodded up the hill.

Lord, this would be a great time for Coop to drive by and change my flat. No, not Coop. He's rescued me enough already. Maybe Cuban or Tiny, or one of the other boys from the ranch.

She could see the top of the Cherokee when she heard voices. Delaney was talking to a man.

Develyn stood straight up. "Dee?" But her center of gravity shifted when she stood, and she tumbled back into the cardboard box. When she tried to scramble out of the box, it began to slide down the hill.

"No!" she hollered.

Backward in the box, she could only see where she had been. Delaney appeared at the edge of the roadway with a tall, lanky cowboy next to her. She waved and screamed, "Mother?"

Develyn waved back.

That's it? That's all I did? I'm sliding down the mountain to my death, and I just wave?

She tried to peek over the edge of the box at where she was headed, but the box began to tip over.

No . . . no . . . She pulled herself back into the box. *I will close my eyes and pretend that I'm riding the whip with Dewayne at the Montgomery County Fair. I'll wake up from a dream, or I'll wake in the hospital, or I'll wake up in heaven. It doesn't matter. No, it does matter. I want to be with Dee. Lord, I need to spend time with . . .*

The box brushed against a low, gray sage, spun around three times, then stopped in the middle of a dirt road. With deliberate caution she crawled out of the box and stood. She brushed dirt off her new jeans and stomped her tennies on the roadway as if that would magically clean them.

She surveyed the upper roadway but couldn't see Delaney or the lanky cowboy.

"Mr. Box, you and I will take the road back up to the Jeep. I am going to load you up and carry you home. Then tonight I will slowly slice you to pieces and burn each scrap in the fire. Nothing personal, of course."

Her thighs burned by the time she hiked the mile up the winding road. She spied a white Ford pickup, the Cherokee, and Delaney wearing a red sequined jacket, buttoned at the neck.

As she approached, the tall cowboy finished tightening the lug nuts on the wheel.

"Hi, Mom, that looked like fun. Did you have a nice ride? Isn't it so cool that Hunter just happened along? I think he was God sent, don't you?"

"What are you doing with Miss Emily's jacket? It's too tight on you."

Delaney's voice softened to a whisper. "Don't ask, Mom. I'll explain later."

Burke sauntered over to them. "There you go, Mrs. Worrell. It's all fixed. I just put the flat in the back by the clothes. I reckon you'll want to get that tire fixed. You'll need a new tire, of course."

"Hunt offered to haul off the kill strip."

"Thank you very much, Hunt. We do appreciate the help. What were you doing way out here?"

"I got lost. I was headed to Brady Fetter's place. You don't happen to know where it is, do you?"

"I never heard of him."

"Where does this road go, anyway?"

"Follow it south and you'll end up at the corrals in Argenta. But that's about twenty-five miles back. To the north it leads past the headquarters of the Quarter Circle Diamond ranch."

"Thank you, Mrs. Worrell. It's what I get for headin' out without directions. Kind of like a Sunday school class without a Bible, I reckon."

Delaney listened to Hunt like a woman who wants to make sure the man feels good about himself.

"Delaney Melinda Worrell, we had better get back to town ourselves. I want to clean up before we go to Casper."

"We will have to visit the Burdett ranch another day."

"Are you headed to see the Burdetts?"

"That was our destination before we had a flat."

"Their place is only four-and-a-half miles from here."

"Yes, I know, but we must get back. Again, thanks for your help."

He tipped his straw cowboy hat. "You're welcome, ma'am. Think I'll mosey up the road another mile or two. I'd hate to come this far and not see my old pal, Bradley."

"Bye, Hunt. You promised to call, remember?" Delaney insisted.

His dimple caught the sunlight. "Hunter Burke keeps his promises."

Develyn loaded the box and the rest of the blouses into the Cherokee as Delaney walked Hunt back to his pickup. She was combing her short blonde hair using the side-view mirror when the Ford roared on up the road.

"Is that so cool that he came along? Mother, something is happening here."

"I agree with you, honey. There are some unanswered questions."

"Like what?"

"What was Hunter Burke really doing on this road?"

"He was looking for a friend."

"Don't you find it strange that he just happened along?"

"I thought it was marvelous. Why are you so suspicious?"

"I'll answer that if you'll answer why you are wearing that red sequined jacket that's way too tight for you."

"I didn't know he was going to drive up. While I waited for you, I wanted to try on one of Miss Emily's blouses. But I didn't want Hunt to see me in it."

"He saw you in the jacket. What difference does it make?"

"It's, you know, the see-through blouse."

"But that won't fit you."

"I know," Delaney grimaced.

She unzipped the red jacket and tossed it in the Cherokee. "See?"

Develyn turned her head. "Delaney, you get some clothes on right now."

"But you didn't see . . ."

"I saw everything you were born with. Get dressed. I am positive that Miss Emily wore a shirt under that thing."

They were headed south back to Argenta when Delaney asked, "Why were you suspicious of Hunter?"

"He said he was lost and didn't even know his way back to town, but he knew the Burdett ranch was 4.5 miles on up the road. Don't you find that strange?"

"I never thought about it."

"Then he said he was looking for an old pal, Brady. But later on he called him Bradley. All this property is the Burdett ranch. There isn't anyone else living up here."

"Mother, you are making too much of this."

"I just want you to be cautious."

"I can't believe I've been here two days, and you are doing this to me all over again."

"Doing what?"

"Dissing any guy that I am interested in."

"I'm just asking the questions you should be asking."

"That's what you said about Troy and Peter and Chip and Johnny. Well, Johnny was a jerk; I'll admit that. Every boy I ever brought home to visit, in your eyes, had some big character flaw. It never fails."

"Dee, that's not true. I just want to make sure . . ."

"It is true. Name one boy that I ever dated that you liked."

"I'm sure that . . ."

"Name one."

"Delaney, this is not . . . how about the foreign exchange student?"

"Jerold?"

"Yes, he was very nice. How come you only dated him once?"

"Because I didn't like being groped in the movie theater."

"You never told me that."

"Did you tell Grandma everything when you were in high school?"

"Of course not."

"You criticize every guy I want to date, Mom. You always wanted me to be more discriminating, but no matter how much I tried, you could find fault. I gave up trying to please you."

There was silence for several miles.

"Honey, I'm sorry. Never once in my heart did I want to make your life miserable. I was hoping for your happiness."

Delaney reached over across the front seat and took her mother's hand. "I know. That's just the way you are. Grandma gets on your nerves. You get on my nerves. And someday I want to have a beautiful daughter who looks like Grammy Dev, and I'm sure I'll get on her nerves. It's a family tradition."

"Grammy Dev, huh?"

"It sounds good."

"Yes, it does. And if that's what happens, I will embrace it without regret. But if it's alright with you and the Lord, I'd just as soon wait a few years to be called that."

"I won't mind waiting a while to be a mommy either."

"Honey, if you are going to have a baby, he or she must be your focus. You'll have to learn how to be a single mom. For the first year or two, I don't think it would be wise for you to be dating. Maybe when the baby is here, the father will be more interested. You have to give the little one that option."

"But what about my needs?"

"It's not about you. Life is about that baby."

"And what if I'm not pregnant?"

"Then you can search for your man."

"And you?"

"I think I'm giving up the search."

"Why?"

"Because life isn't about me either, sweetie. I'm a single mother, and I have a daughter. Until you are settled into God's plan for you, I don't want to complicate things."

"I've never heard you say that."

"It took a dirt-road town in Wyoming to teach me that."

"So, if I'm not pregnant, you'll let me date Hunt?"

"You are twenty years old. I can't tell you whom to date or not to date. But I can give you my opinion. I'll tell you what: if you're not pregnant, you date whomever you and the Lord agree on, and I won't say one word."

"Not a word?"

"Unless you ask me."

"I can't believe you said that, Mom."

Neither can I, honey, neither can I.

Not one word was spoken the entire trip back from Casper.

The few times Develyn glanced out of the corner of her eye, Delaney gazed out the window at some distant horizon. Develyn felt tightness in her neck and shoulders. Her stomach cramped as if she had eaten a green chili burrito from the mini-mart.

When she glanced at herself in the rearview mirror, all she could see were her narrow, crow's-feet-framed eyes hiding behind dark glasses.

You look old and worn out, Develyn Gail Upton Worrell. In some ways this summer has been a great deception. Cowboys compliment, and you believe them all. But they flirt with every woman. You are middle-aged and getting older by the minute. Look at those eyes,

WISH I'D KNOWN YOU TEARS AGO

Devy-girl. This is the best you are ever going to look. It only gets worse, honey. Someday soon, all the makeup in the world won't cover those age creases. So are you going to be a gracious old lady or a bitter old lady? Those are your choices. Either way, you will be an old lady.

I have some goals in this life, Lord.

And I don't know if I'm achieving them or not. I want to finish a career of teaching elementary children. That is one passion that has never faded. I want to be a good mother. Delaney is my only shot at it. And right now, I feel like I'm going down for the third time.

She sucked in a deep breath and glanced at her daughter, who sat with hands in her lap, jaw clenched, eyes turned away.

For two weeks, Lord, I couldn't wait for Dee to come out and be with me. Everything would be fine then. I would mother her, and she would need me. In two days we've gotten to the not-speaking-to-each-other stage. How can I try so hard and be such a miserable failure?

It sounds like my marriage.

Something inside of me needs to be fixed, and I don't know what it is. I thought I got things right this summer. Dee was sort of the test. Did my journey to a dirt-road town really change me?

Another glance at her daughter, then Develyn slowed to turn at the Waltman/Argenta Road.

Change? This is like most weeks since the divorce.

As long as I'm chasing windmills, Lord, I'd like to know that I can love a man right and keep him loving me. I suppose that means I want to get married again. But I'm not even sure of that. I just want to know that I can do it.

Without glancing at her daughter, she wiped the tears from the corner of her eyes.

She made a quick turn by the cottonwood tree and parked the Cherokee in front of the grocery store. "I'm getting an orange Popsicle. Do you want one?"

Delaney leaned against the window, eyes closed.

"I'll assume that means 'No, thank you, Mother.'"

Develyn paused on the front porch and rubbed her fingertips across her brother's initials carved into the wagon seat bench.

Dewa, so much has happened since we were ten. Lots of it painful for you and for me. You loved your wife like crazy, and she died in your arms. I tried to love my husband, and he spent most of his life in others' arms. It hurts, Dewa. I know it still hurts you too.

I don't want any more failures. Any more pain. I don't know how to be the mother Delaney needs. She's all I have. Dee and you. I need you, dear brother. I'm a forty-five-year-old little girl who misses her brother.

Develyn wiped her eyes on her blouse sleeve.

And I need an orange Popsicle . . . bad.

●　●　●

The living-room store smelled of a blend of cinnamon rolls and menthol rubbing cream. Develyn strolled past the rack of Little Debbies to the large chest freezer behind the counter.

"It's just Devy-girl, Mrs. Tagley. I need my Popsicle."

The older woman's voice filtered out from the back room. "I'm just finishing my soaps."

Develyn paused at the doorway between the store and the living quarters in the back.

Mrs. Tagley didn't take her eyes off the television screen. "You look tired, honey."

"It's been a long day already."

"She's pregnant, you know."

"What? I mean . . . how do you know that?" Develyn questioned.

"Devy, if a woman gets drunk at a party wearing a dress that plunges down to her navel, she's likely to wake up pregnant."

"Who are you talking about?"

Mrs. Tagley pointed to the screen. "Misty."

"Oh, yes, well, a seductive dress does get results, so I hear."

"Don't they teach young girls anything in school these days?"

"Sometimes they do, but the girls don't listen."

"I don't think she will be a very good mother."

"Perhaps she will learn."

"Some women never do, you know."

Develyn took a lick on the orange Popsicle and glanced out the front window toward the Jeep. "Yes, I know."

"This will break her mother's heart."

"Whose mother?"

"Misty's. Remember that horrible boating accident that left her mother a widow? Misty is all she has. What will the Brownsvilles think?"

"Brownsvilles?"

"Misty's mother's neighbors who own the pineapple

plantation in the Philippines. And how will her dear mother tell all her friends at the yacht club?"

"Children do present challenges."

"And grandchildren."

"So I hear."

Mrs. Tagley turned and looked at Develyn. "They took away her shotgun."

"Whose?"

"Mrs. Morton's. The deputy came by and took away her shotgun."

"That might be best."

"Well, it's best for Leon, that's for sure. They gave her a trumpet instead."

"Does Mrs. Morton know how to play a trumpet?" Develyn asked.

"No, but what does that matter?"

"What's the trumpet for?"

"A warning signal that Leon's on the loose. That's what the shotgun was for. It was to warn all of us that Leon was out and about."

"And now we will listen for a trumpet?"

"Yes."

"I didn't know that was a warning signal."

"Did you think she was trying to shoot him?"

"The thought did cross my mind."

"You've been back east too long, honey. You aren't going to stay away another thirty-five years, are you?"

"I will be back next summer, that's for sure." Develyn waved the frozen treat. "You'll need to stock up on orange Popsicles." Develyn felt a drip of cold liquid splash on her chin. When she looked down, it slid off her chin and onto her blouse.

● ● ●

Delaney wasn't in the Cherokee when Develyn stepped outside. Develyn surveyed the one dirt road and dozen buildings of Argenta.

She must have walked back to the cabin. I don't blame her.

I'm sure I treated my mother the same. Maybe not when I was twenty, but when I was sixteen.

Dev drove slowly up the drive to the cabin.

She rolled down her window when met by a burro.

"What are you doing out of the pasture, honey? There's Popcorn. Where's Aunt Jenny and My Maria? Did they run off? We'll find them, baby. Now, come on up to the cabin."

Dee wouldn't purposely leave the gate open, would she? No, the gate's closed.

When she pulled up to the cabin, she noticed Cooper Tallon cinching her saddle on My Maria. His buckskin gelding stood saddled next to the mare.

"Hi, Coop, what's happening here?"

"I didn't have to go all the way to Cheyenne after all. So I thought about riding out to the springs and trying to dig my digital camera out of the rocks. When I saw you pull up to

82

Mrs. Tagley's, I took a chance that you wanted to ride a little today and fetched My Maria from the pasture."

"Yes, well, I didn't expect to get back from Casper so early."

"Miss Dee hiked into the cabin a few minutes ago. I take it you two had a tiff. Not that it's any of my business."

"We spent the last hour not talking to each other."

"That's what I figured."

"What happened to Aunt Jenny?"

"When I swung the gate open to lead out your mare, that she-burro broke for the open ground and bolted to the north. I closed the gate on Uncle Henry, assumin' you didn't want him to leave home just yet."

"But he got out?"

"He got frantic when she left and galloped down to the creek. If he lays down in the water, he can roll under the wire down there."

"And he didn't try to follow her?"

"He trotted back to the cabin and turned north just as you drove up the drive. When he spotted you, he spun around and plodded your direction."

"He chose me over Aunt Jenny?"

"Never underestimate a mother's pull." Cooper nodded at the cabin.

"You talking burros or daughters, Mr. Tallon?"

"Both, Ms. Worrell."

She stroked Uncle Henry's nose. "We'll go look for her, baby. But we will not drag her back here again. If she wants to run off, there is nothing we can do. Besides, I don't think she was right for you."

"You want to ride out to the springs with me, then?"

"I'd like that. But I might dump a bunch of mother-daughter things on you. I need to get some things out."

"I can listen, Miss Dev. A bachelor my age has spent most of his life listenin', not talkin'."

"Thanks, Coop. I'd better let Dee know where I am headed. Casey didn't get back yet, did she?"

"Nope."

Develyn carried her purse to the cabin and laid it on the counter. Delaney was stretched out, face down, on the lower bunk. Dev grabbed her new University of Wyoming sweatshirt.

She paused by the bed.

"Honey, I'm going to ride out to the springs with Coop and help him recover his digital camera."

There was no reply.

"Dee, I'm sorry I lost my cool at the doctor's office. I know I embarrassed you. We need to talk some on what to do next. I know that. But you need a nap, and I need a ride. I'll be back in an hour or so; is that alright?"

Still no reply.

"I love you, honey. Sometimes, I know, I'm not showing that in a way that you need. But I have loved you since the moment I found out I carried you in my womb. Now get some rest."

As Develyn reached the open doorway, she heard a muffled voice.

"What, honey?"

"I love you, too, Mom."

● ● ●

Without much effort, Develyn swung up into the saddle.

Cooper handed the reins across to her, then nodded at the cabin. "Ever'thin' alright in there?"

"We'll get through it, Coop. Some days I think the only thing I know how to do is teach fifth-graders. I'm sort of a failure at everything else."

He took the buckskin to a trot. She pinched her knees against My Maria and rode up beside him. Develyn glanced over her shoulder at Uncle Henry. "Come on, baby. We'll go look for your pal."

"Dev, it isn't any of my business, so don't feel like you've got to tell me."

"You want to know what happened at the doctor's office?"

"It would help me pray for you and Delaney. Is she pregnant?"

"I don't have a clue."

"The doctor couldn't tell?"

"I'm sure he could have, but we never got that far."

"But that's why you drove to town."

"I know. It's rather. . ." She sighed, her shoulders slumped.

"You don't have to tell me."

"Yes, I do. I have to tell somebody, Coop. It's eating me up."

"OK, you went to the doctor's and didn't get to see him."

"The clinic lobby was crowded. We're just tourists from out of town. All I had told them was my twenty-year-old daughter needed a checkup."

"Not high on the priority list."

"I could tell Dee was getting more nervous by the moment."

"Well, the results do change your life forever, I reckon."

"There were a couple of sick, crying babies in the waiting room. That didn't calm us down much."

"Did they ever call you?"

"Yes, Dee wanted me with her, so we waited another thirty minutes in the tiny exam room. She started chewing her tongue like she does when she's near panic. I think it was hitting her all at once. She didn't want to talk."

Dev paused and bit her lip. She waited for him to say, "You don't have to say any more." He didn't say anything but led them single file down to Cougar Creek.

She rode up alongside him when they came up on the prairie on the other side. "After a half-hour a young man who looked like a college freshman, with a name tag that read Dr. Jeremy Dierkens, came into the room. He apologized that Dr. Marguerite Sievers was called to the hospital over a shooting injury. He was taking her afternoon appointments. Dee just stood there with her mouth open.

"He glanced down at the information form we had filled out, then grabbed stirrups out of the drawer and shoved them into the exam table. He said something like, 'Please disrobe completely from the waist down, and hop up here on the table.'"

"To which Delaney replied?"

"'I most certainly will not!' Her voice cracked, and she wrapped her arms around herself. He looked surprised, then glanced down at the clipboard. "'You wanted a preg check, right?'"

"'Not by you,' Delaney sobbed. 'I want a lady doctor.' I tried to comfort her. I told her, 'Honey, we can't be too choosy today. I'll stay in here with you.'"

"But that didn't help?" Coop asked.

"She bolted out of the exam room and into the crowded waiting room. When I grabbed her arm, she was headed to the front door. I said, 'Dee, you need an exam.'"

"'Not from him!' she shouted. I tried to get her to lower her voice. I told her, 'Honey, he told me he graduated from the University of Arizona med school, class of '03. He's twenty-nine years old.'"

"It takes a brilliant young man to get through that young," Cooper said.

"A fact that was lost in the circumstances. I was still holding her by the arm. She yanked it away and stumbled into an older man with a walker. By now everyone in the room was staring at us. With as quiet a voice as I could muster, I said, 'Delaney Melinda, let's go to the back room and get that exam now.'"

"I don't reckon she gave in, huh?"

"She yelled at me, with a horrible, angry voice. 'Mother, I am not going to strip buck naked from the waist down, jam my feet into those metal stirrups, and let some kid doctor stare inside of me."

Cooper pushed his hat back but didn't look at Develyn. "I surmise you two don't intend to go to that clinic again."

"I've been considering whether I have the nerve to show my face in the city of Casper again."

"So she stomped out, and you stomped out right behind."

"I was frozen in place long enough to read all the faces in that room."

"What did the faces say?"

"'There is one spoiled brat and her terrible mother."

"You read all of that?"

"Yes."

"Your girl is scared, Mama."

"Of course she is. But we need to find out the facts so we know what to do next."

"Dev, I don't know squat about daughters. I don't know anything about raising children. It's a fact that causes me grief if I ponder it."

"You wanted to have children?"

"Yeah, a wife, kids, and a quiet country home. I wanted that since I was twelve."

"But why didn't you . . ."

"Miss Dev, that story is for another time. I want to talk about horses."

"Horses?"

"You told me that last week Renny showed you how to tame a wild horse."

"Yes, he did."

"What was the basic, underlying principle when working with an unbroken horse?"

"She's scared to death and will always try to do what seems safest to her."

"You learn quick."

"Thank you."

"About horses."

"Are you saying daughters are like horses?"

"It seems to this old bachelor that Dee is so scared of being pregnant, of being a single mommy, of disappointing her mama and her Lord that she will always bolt for anything, and maybe anyone, that offers her safety. She spied daylight at the gate, and she ran. Don't get mad at her for being so scared."

"I'm not mad at her. I'm mad at me. I didn't handle it very well." Dev let out a deep breath. "OK, I am upset with her some."

"It's OK to be mad. You just got to turn it loose. It will eat away at your soul if you don't. I don't need to know anything about your divorce. But you've got to turn that loose too."

"You have lots of advice today, Mr. Tallon."

"Yeah, I don't know what's got into me. When he was sixty-one, my daddy had a stroke. He was in and out of consciousness for six weeks. When he was awake, he had such anxiety. I don't know if his kidneys were failin' or what, but he hallucinated some. So my mama and me spelled each other off sittin' by his side, tryin' to comfort him when he came to."

"Did your brother help out?"

"Porter was in a Mexican jail that year."

"That must have added to the stress."

"It was toughest on Mama. She figured she was losin' him, and she just knew she couldn't survive a day without her man. She got married when she was sixteen, and he was everything to her. But this night, about three in the mornin', his eyes opened up, and he recognized me. 'Butch,' he said . . .'"

"He called you Butch?"

"I had short hair back then. He always called me Butch. Anyway, he signaled for me to lean closer. 'You got to forgive me for sellin' Brownie.'"

"Your dog?"

"My horse."

"You had a horse named Brownie?"

"Yeah, not much of a name, was it?"

"I rode a horse thirty-five years ago named Brownie."

"Yeah, it's a common name. It was a common horse. I had forgotten all about it, actually. When I was twelve, I came home, and Daddy had sold my horse."

"That must have been quite a blow."

"I got mad and yelled and screamed and called him horrible names that I would never repeat to you. I took off that night."

"You left home?"

"I was back by chore time the next morning. Anyway, I was forty-two years old and sittin' by my dyin' father's bed when he asked me to forgive him for that. I told him I had forgotten all about it. He said it nagged at him almost every day of his life. He explained that he had been so worried about groceries that he took an easy way out. Then he told me to fetch his wallet out of the hospital dresser."

"He wanted to pay you back?"

"I tried to dissuade him, but he would have no part of it. He shoved a twenty dollar bill in my hand and said, 'Butch, for my sake you have to take this money.' So I took it. I still have that twenty. I'll carry that to my grave, I imagine. After that night Daddy had two peaceful weeks until he slipped into heaven. I promised myself never to carry guilt that long. The reason for this long, windy story is to encourage you to get this settled up with Delaney before it becomes a habit."

"So what do you think I ought to do?"

"Let me get back to horses. When you want a scared horse to do something, you have to wait until it sees your option as the best thing it can do for itself."

"You mean, forget the doctor's visit?"

"For now. Just buy her the cutest little baby outfit you can find."

"What? But I can't . . ."

"Get her a fancy maternity blouse."

"But we don't know if she's pregnant."

"Pick up a cute book of baby names."

"I'm not getting this, Coop."

"Sooner or later she'll say, 'The only way I'm going to stop Mother from embarrassing me like this is to go to the doctor.' Then let her go by herself."

"What if she invites me?"

"Then you can go. Sit in the waiting room unless she wants you in the back room."

When they reached the cedars, they dismounted and walked the horses. Uncle Henry trotted up next to her.

"You are amazing, Coop."

"I'm just an ol' cowboy who's been operatin' backhoes most of his life."

"I was married almost twenty years. Spencer, Delaney's father, and I raised her together for seventeen and a half years. Never once in those years did we ever have as meaningful a discussion about how to treat her as you and I just did." She shook her head. "How come you weren't in Indiana in 1980?"

"That's about the nicest thing anyone has ever said to me. I don't think I ever met anyone I'd like to have known earlier in my life as much as you. I was in Alaska repairing a pipeline in 1980, making more money than I had ever imagined."

They mounted up and rode east through the scrub cedars.

"I have a couple of questions for you, Mr. Tallon."

"Shoot."

"No reason for that. I don't carry guns and knives like Casey."

He shook his head and grinned. "It's a lame joke, but you're right, we needed a break. It's been kind of somber conversation. What do you do for fun, Ms. Worrell?"

"What?"

"Back home in Indiana, what do you do for fun?"

"My friend Lily and I go to rodeos and concerts."

"No foolin'?"

"It's our thing. Although, now that Lily found herself a nice lawyer, I might need a hobby I can do by myself. How about you, Coop? What do you do for fun?"

"I make it to a rodeo or two. I always make it to the NFR."

"You've gone to the National Finals Rodeo?"

"I've had season tickets ever since they moved to Las Vegas from Oklahoma City. Two seats in the Plaza section down by the ropin' boxes. How about you and your Lily pal usin' them this year?"

"You have to be kidding me."

"Think about it. They're yours."

"They must be worth a fortune."

"Maybe, but you'd have to take them for free, or I won't give them to you. But my real fun has been collecting old Winchester rifles. If I get a chance, I'll buy some historic old gun. That's about it for fun."

"This summer has multiplied my fun."

"Mine too, Miss Dev."

"Are you trying to avoid my questions?"

"No, ma'am. Ask away."

"How did your mother get along after your father died?"

"Mama was always a frail lady, especially after the babies. She lived nine lonely months and died of a heart attack right before Christmas. I just don't think she wanted to face the holiday without Daddy."

"Oh, Coop, that must have been difficult."

"I don't mind tellin' you, Miss Dev, I shed a tear or two. Porter was still in jail when she died."

"You said your mom lost some babies. Do you mean miscarriage?"

"I forget the medical term. It's too long and complicated to memorize. But Mama had a genetic defect. She could have boys but not girls."

"I've never heard of that."

"Neither had she. She lost two girls between me and my brother. After he was born, she got her courage up. She was determined to have a daughter. She carried six little girls to eight months, and then they died in the womb. Every one of them stillborn."

"What a heartbreak."

"Every loss took a little more out of her. The docs didn't figure it out until she lost the sixth one. By then I was sixteen. They gave me, Daddy, and Porter all the tests too, trying to figure it out. That's when they discovered that I carried the same problem as Mama."

"Is that why you never married?"

"At first it was. I felt it wouldn't be fair to put any woman through what Mama suffered. What would I tell a lady: 'We can have boys, but all the girls you will carry for eight months, and they will die in your womb'? I just couldn't do that."

"But I have several friends that have good, happy marriages without children. Wasn't that an option?"

"In the sixties and seventies, all the women I met were wantin' families."

"So you threw yourself into your work?"

"Yep. I was one of those who said, 'If the Lord has someone for me, it will be his timing and his leading. But the years turned to decades, and no gal appeared."

"Some things I will never understand. There are child-abusing fathers all over the country who never should have had children. And you would have made a wonderful father. It doesn't make sense to me."

"Miss Dev, I have a suggestion. For the rest of this ride, we have to talk about pleasant things and leave the moping behind."

"That means I can't talk about your horse, Brownie, being sold?"

"You can talk about good horses. That's a pleasant theme."

"Oh, goodie. Did your family live in Argenta when your horse was sold?"

"No, Daddy was trying to make a go of things on some range property over by Riverton that was owned by my uncle's first wife's family."

"It didn't work out?"

"The cow business has always been tough."

"So you came home, and your dad sold your horse. Did you ever see him again?"

"We were close to the Wind River Reservation. Several of the men off the Rez would ask to cut through our place to go huntin' up on the ridge. If they drove across our place, they could pack the meat out in pickups instead of on their backs. They were a polite bunch. They kept us in elk jerky, which at times was our main meal for the day."

"He sold your horse to them?"

"Brownie wasn't much to look at. Dirt colored and real slow movements. At first I thought he was retarded. He wasn't working out at the feed lot, and ol' man Pinkham gave him to me. He was the most sure-footed, loyal horse anyone could ever own. He took care of me and taught me all about cows. All I had to do was hang on, and he went to work. I got him when he was seven and had him five years."

"When did your dad sell him?"

"About the time you were two, I guess. Let me tell you how loyal he was. I took my dad's coyote gun out hunting one time. I didn't tell him, but I grabbed his Winchester 1894, 25-35 carbine. I was about ten years old, and I wanted to shoot a bear that had killed one of our calves. Of course, that gun wouldn't kill a bear very easy, but a ten-year-old didn't know that.

"When we got to the chaparral, I had it cocked and lying across the saddle. I decided to get down and take a bathroom break. I carried the carbine with me on the dismount, missed the stirrup, and crashed to the ground. The gun went off, and I shot ol' Brownie in the ear. I mean, I punched a round hole in his ear. He flinched, shook his head at the dripping blood, but never took a step."

Develyn put her hand over her mouth. "I don't believe it."

"It was mighty dumb, but the Lord looks after fools and kids."

"No, that's not what I meant. It was the right ear, wasn't it?"

"You know, that's what I never could figure. I got off on the left side of the horse, and shot him in the right ear. He must have cocked his head sideways. Wait a minute, how did you know it was the right ear?"

"I don't believe this, Coop."

"What's goin' on that I don't know about?"

"Was the Indian you sold Brownie to named Mr. Homer?"

"Mr. Rooster Homer. What's going on here? Do we know the same man?"

"We rode the same horse!" Develyn shouted.

"What do you mean?"

"Remember I told you I spent two weeks here when I was ten?"

"Yeah."

"The horse I rode was named Brownie."

"And I said lots of horses had that name."

"But the man who allowed us to ride the horses was Mr. Homer, and Brownie had a scar in his right ear that the owner said was a bullet hole he got as a young pony. I imagined he was a veteran of some historic western battle."

"Wait, are you saying you rode my horse, Brownie, when you were ten?"

"Brownie was in his early twenties then. I rode him for two weeks. I've dreamt about him for thirty-five years. Those dreams are the reason I came out here this summer."

"You rode Brownie? You really did?"

"Yes, is this incredible or what?"

"I can't quite believe this."

"If he shied away, I'd sit on the ground with my back toward him. He'd sneak up and droop the reins over my shoulder."

"I taught him that," Cooper claimed. "That way, I didn't have to picket him around a campfire. As long as I had my back toward him, he would hover near me and not wander off."

"I don't know what to say. This is . . . this is so wild. I mean, it's almost like we are related. Brownie has been an important part of my dream life since I was ten."

"I haven't thought about Brownie in years and years."

"I haven't dreamt about him since the night before last."

"It does make us seem a little closer friends, doesn't it?"

"Me and Mr. Tallon?" Dev drawled. "Why, we were ridin' the same horse thirty-five years ago."

"Kind of fun to think about," he added. "I don't think I ever pondered much who were all the other people who rode this horse or that one. I think about it with my old Winchesters, wonderin' which cowboy carried them and what he pointed it at. But I never thought about a horse. We do have a mutual friend, Miss Dev. I like that. Maybe that's why the Lord allowed him to get sold out from under me, so that a ten-year-old girl from Indiana could learn to ride."

"Well, thank you for all the fine training, Mr. Tallon. Brownie was a very good horse, even as an old man. He was about the plainest looking horse I ever saw. But oh my, he was smart."

"Miss Dev, this has certainly turned out to be a great day. That's the springs up there."

"We're here already? Time flies when you're having fun."

"It wasn't all fun. Time flies when you're with a good friend."

Develyn trailed behind him as they crossed the creek and broke into the clearing. "We have become good friends, haven't we? Are these markers the corners of your house? I love the location."

"Actually, that's my shop. The house is marked by those rocks up there. Do you think I should move the house down here?"

"It's a better view."

"That's why I put the shop here. I figure I'll spend more time in the shop than the house."

"That all depends, doesn't it?"

"On what?"

"Whether you are living alone or not."

He stared at her until she glanced down at the creek.

"You can put the house anywhere you want," she said.

"I've decided to put the house down here. The driveway will come in up above, and the shop needs to be near the roadway."

They dismounted and tied the horses to a cedar.

"Let me show you what it looks like up here. I'm thinking a two-story house would be nice. You know, have a better view."

"Yes, definitely, a log house facing the southwest. You'll need a forest green metal roof, white lace curtains on the dormer windows, and green shades that match the color of the roof."

"You are something, Miss Dev. I don't reckon I've ever gotten to know anyone so quick as I have you."

"That's easy to explain. We rode the same horse."

"That must be it."

"Coop, I have one more question for you."

"Is it a sober one, or a fun one?"

"I'm not sure. The other night after that wonderful supper and visit, you walked me back to the cabin."

"And shook your hand?"

"Yes. Did you do that because of this deal with the babies and just not wanting to get too close to women?"

He began to laugh. "No, it was because I was just scared of you."

"Scared?"

"You are a pretty lady, Miss Dev, and I'm an old man."

"Age doesn't have anything to do with this."

"Well, if that's the case, if given the chance, I do not intend to repeat that same mistake. If that's alright with you?"

"It's alright with me," she murmured.

D o you plan to have much company?"

Cooper pulled off his cowboy hat and scratched his head. "What do you mean?"

Develyn shoved her sunglasses to the top of her head. "When you get your big, beautiful home built back here, do you plan to entertain much?"

He dragged the point of his boot across the soft dirt. "I don't think so."

"Hmmm."

"What's that 'hmmm' about?"

"You need people in your life. You can't retire and crawl into a cave."

He shoved his hat back on. "Perhaps I should enroll in a charm school."

"Yes, and an Arthur Murray dance course. Some cooking classes at a local college." Develyn plucked up a three-foot stick from behind a small sagebrush.

Cooper Tallon's gray eyes widened. His jaw dropped.

Develyn grabbed his hand and towed him across the clearing. "You are the only person in Wyoming who is easier to tease than me."

He laughed and patted her hand. "Good, for a minute there, I felt on the edge of a cliff about to tumble to my death. You have no idea how terrifying such things sound."

With both hands on the stick, she began to draw a line in the dirt that connected the corner markers of the proposed house. "You don't have to do any of those things. You are quite charming in your own, ol'-cowboy-hard-working-construction-boss gruff way."

"Thank you, ma'am, for that wonderful compliment. It was a compliment, wasn't it?"

"Of course."

"Are you drawing out my house?"

She stood and wiped the back of her hand across her cheek. "Yes. I need perspective. I insist that you build your house to entertain guests. You'll need a quality road back here that's accessible year-round by people who might not be used to Wyoming winters."

"Perhaps Indiana schoolteachers?"

"I am certainly going to check on you from time to time. Someone has to make sure you're eating your vegetables."

"What?"

"I love it, I love it, I love it. I have someone to tease. I've
been the object of so many jokes for these months. Now I have
someone to tease."

He erased part of her dirt line with his boot and drew two
slashes. "This is the front door, don't you reckon. Building a
good road back here will be the easy part. I've been doing that
kind of construction for years."

Develyn put the line back in the dirt with her stick and
pointed eight feet to the left. "The door must be there. It's
important for those who drive up to the house to see the front
door. Now let me tell you why you need to build a home fit for
entertaining. First of all, be optimistic. The Lord might lead you
to a wonderful person to share this home with."

Develyn glanced up to see if Coop was grinning, but his
gaze looked distant. "You will want a place that is large and
comfortable and doesn't give her cabin fever. Right, Coop? Are
you listening to me?"

He nodded.

"Now, here's a second reason for a big place. The charming
Mr. Tallon, even if he chooses to remain single, will have company from time to time. This part of the state is so isolated and
remote, they will need a place to stay. So plan for overnight
guests with plenty of space for everyone. That means nice guest
rooms and extra baths. You are planning on having indoor
plumbing, right?"

Tallon nodded as if answering a lengthy survey.

She etched out one-foot-by-one-foot squares in the dirt.
"It's your terra-cotta tile entry." She shuffled her feet. "Don't

103

you just love tap dancing on tile? OK, now here's a third reason for the big, spacious home. This home will outlive you. Someday it will belong to someone else. Part of your legacy to them is to provide a home that will be comfortable and useful for others as well. I'm talking more than resale value, although that is a factor. Does that make sense?"

"Yeah," he murmured.

"So putting those ideas together, I vote—that is, if I had a vote—for you to build a large, spacious home. I know that is a lot of house to clean, but perhaps you could hire someone to come out from Casper once a week and do housework. What do you think?"

He drew his boot toe across the dirt.

"Coop? Did you hear anything I said?"

He took the stick from her hand. "You know, Dev, it's funny. I learned how to keep so busy 24/7 that I never had to think about myself. And I didn't have to ponder about the future. Those words pierced me to the soul."

"Which words?"

He outlined the living room in the dirt. "Share the rest of my life with someone."

"I didn't mean for them to disturb you."

"No, no, I just—this sounds crazy—but I gave up thinking about someone to share my life with so many years ago that it doesn't even enter into my thinking. Kind of sad, isn't it?"

"It does sound rather lonely."

He began etching odd-shaped circles in the south end of the

room. "But when you said that, it dawned on me that maybe you are right."

"Right that the Lord might have someone for you to share your life with?"

"No. Right about the indoor plumbing."

"What?"

The wink preceded the smile. "Dev, I'm not the only one easy to tease."

She slugged his arm.

"I like what you said about the size of the house." He pointed at his artwork in the dirt. "This is the river-rock fireplace."

She rubbed her hands and held them out as if warming them by the fire. "I take it I was getting a little too personal?"

"You know what I think, Develyn Worrell?"

"What, Mr. Cooper Tallon?'"

"I believe the Lord brought you to Wyoming this summer to challenge me to open up things that I put on the shelf thirty years ago."

"Is that good or bad?"

"I'll let you know as soon as I figure it out."

Develyn tugged the stick out of his hand. "In the meantime—she pointed at the blue sky—you'll want a vaulted ceiling here in the living room. I just can't decide whether hardwood floors and area rugs or wall-to-wall carpeting."

"Flooring? I have to have flooring?"

"I will ignore that crude attempt at humor. If terra-cotta tile at the doorway catches the mud, then hardwood floors and area rugs might be best. Perhaps you want to stick with a buckskin brown and forest green décor. What do you think?"

He took the stick back and drew two huge squares in front of the outline of the fireplace. "I think we need to sit down in these big leather chairs and write everything down. I won't remember any of this."

"Do you have pictures of this location?"

"If I can retrieve my camera out of the rocks."

● ● ●

Develyn balanced on a boulder and peered down between the crevices. "How did your camera wind up way down there?"

"It may have to stay there. I can't believe I got my arm stuck for hours trying to retrieve it. I tell you what, Dev. You promise never to tell another living soul about that, and I'll give you credit for one secret of yours."

"That's a deal, Mr. Tallon. I'll just have to think about it for awhile to decide which secret to tell you."

"You got a lot of them?"

She studied his leather-tough face.

"Coop, it seems like my life is crammed with things I could never tell another living soul. I've had Lily to talk to. And that helps. But I know I have to be guarded in what I tell her."

He lifted a boulder the size of a basketball and splashed it into the creek bed. "Sometimes I think how good it would be to sit back in a big, old leather chair in front of a rock fireplace next to someone who held your trust and your dreams and just blurt it all out—every pain, every failure, every joy, every fear. To know that nothin' you said would change how they felt about you. Wouldn't that be somethin'?"

Develyn tried to pluck up a boulder but found it too heavy. "It sounds wonderful. But I wonder if people could stay friends knowing that much about each other?"

Cooper laughed. "Now, that's the question, isn't it? And I don't have a clue. Maybe it's not a good thing. But when you've spent a lifetime holdin' things in, it sounds like a good thing."

"How are you ever going to get those big boulders moved enough to get your camera?"

He raised one about six inches, than dropped it with a crash. "I didn't reckon this arm was still so sore. There was a day when I could have plucked that up like a grapefruit."

"Don't hurt yourself more."

"If my arm weren't so fat, I might be able to reach down there."

"Cooper Tallon, I punched your arm. I can tell there isn't one ounce of fat. I bruised my knuckles bouncing off your muscles."

"Either way, I don't aim to get stuck again in front of a purdy lady."

"Why don't I try to retrieve it?"

"No, it's not your problem."

"Nonsense. Let me try." Develyn lowered herself to her knees.

Tallon grabbed her shoulder. "No, Dev, I can't let you do that."

"What in the world are you talking about? What is this chauvinistic thing where I'm not allowed to do anything for you?"

"It's just the way things are out here."

Still on her knees, Develyn clutched her arms across her chest. "You know what, Mr. Cowboy Man? I don't believe that."

"What are you talking about?"

"I'm talking about allowing a woman to dig in the rocks to help a friend. Your great-grandparents came out here and claimed this land, right?"

"Yep."

"Do you think your great-grandmother ever got on her knees to help Greatgrandpa clear a garden or dig out a stump? Do you think he put her up on an immaculate pedestal and made her stay there?"

"I reckon she'd do whatever needed to be done."

"OK. There's the real western tradition. The woman worked alongside the man, willing to do whatever it took to get the job done. So when I'm down here grubbing through the rocks to help you, I'm being more like the pioneers than you are."

"Well, if you're lookin' to shame me, you succeeded."

"Good."

"But there is one difference between you and your greatgrandmother."

"Besides clothing, hairstyle, and uncalloused hands?"

"Yeah. She was married to the man she dug in the dirt with."

"Ha. You aren't going to let the lack of a marriage license keep me from doing this, are you?"

He threw up his hands. "It surely will keep us from doingsome things, but digging isn't one of them. You are the most . . ."

"Stubborn?"

"*Persistent* woman I've ever met."

"That's only because you haven't met many women."

"That's true. OK, I'll swallow my cowboy pride and let you get down there and grub for my camera."

"Goodie." Develyn sprawled herself across the hard, cold granite boulder and snaked her arm through the crevices.

"Are you havin' any luck there?"

"It's deeper than it looks, isn't it?"

"I might have to wait until my arm heals up and dig the rock down a little farther."

Her cheek up against a rock, she glanced up at him. "I've got good news and bad news. My arm fits through the crevices fine, but it's about six inches too short to reach it."

"Thanks for trying anyway. Let me help you up."

"Now, now, just wait. You are talking to the most stubborn woman in Indiana and Wyoming, so I'm not giving up."

"You figure on levitating the camera, or just growin' a longer arm?"

"What I need is for you to hold onto me and lower me over this boulder so I can reach a little farther."

"I don't understand."

"If you lowered me down there a little, I could reach your camera. Grab hold of me."

"Where?"

"Are you blushing, Mr. Tallon?"

"Pretend you didn't see that. Where do you want me to grab you?"

"My legs."

"Your legs?"

"Oh, my, looking embarrassed looks good on you. Let's see. Is it acceptable for a cowboy to grab hold of a friend's sock-covered ankles and lower her over this rock?"

"OK. But you make sure I'm doing this right."

"The only thing you could do wrong is turn loose."

She felt the viselike grip circle both ankles. "Good. Now lower me down a little." Develyn's fingertips brushed against the top of the camera. "Just a little more."

"I can't unless I pick you straight up by your ankles."

"Then do it."

"Are you sure?"

"You have more hesitancy than a new student on opening day of class."

He swung Develyn up and over. "Are you alright?"

"Lower me down, cowboy." She felt around the rough granite rock, then clutched the cold, silver camera.

"Got it. Up, please."

"What floor?"

"The penthouse!"

She giggled as she dangled when she heard the roar of a small engine.

"Hey," a voice shouted. "I don't know what you two are playing, but it looks like fun."

She cocked her head sideways at the lanky man in a new straw cowboy hat. "Hunter Burke?"

He sauntered toward them, then bent his head down to his waist as if looking upside down. "Mrs. Worrell? I didn't recognize you in that position." He tipped his hat to Cooper Tallon. "Mr. Worrell, how are you? I didn't mean to be buttin' in on somethin'."

Tallon lowered Develyn to the dirt.

Develyn struggled to her feet. "Most folks call him Coop." She put her hand on Cooper's arm, than held up the silver camera. "We had to retrieve this. It had fallen down among the rocks."

"Yes, ma'am."

"Did you find you friend Brody?" she quizzed as they walked back up to the house site.

"Yes, he's a hunting partner of mine." Burke studied the lines in the dirt. "Say, is this your property?"

"Yes, it is," Cooper said.

"Is that chaparral on the east side of the ridge BLM land?"

"All the way to the highway. Why?"

"My friend . . ."

"Brody?" she asked.

'Yeah, good ol' Brody wants to scout that land so we can hunt it come fall. We hope to be out there a few days, riding four-wheelers all over. So I was thinking of chaining a can of gas to one of the trees over there, you know, for some extra fuel. But it might be a little safer if I chained it over here on your place. We will haul it off in the next few days. We won't drive over here, just keep the gas can, if it's alright."

"That's fine," Cooper said.

He tipped his hat and winked. "Thank you both. Now I reckon you can get back to your game."

He sauntered back up the hillside.

"Hunter," Develyn called out. "Wait. Say, as long as you are here, can you take a picture of me and Coop up here at the springs?"

"Surely, ma'am."

She handed him the camera. "We'll pose over by the creek."

Develyn grabbed Cooper's arm and tugged him toward the narrow stream.

"What's this all about?" he said through clenched teeth.

"Play along with me," she whispered.

She snuggled close. "Now, honey, smile big for Hunter."

"Yes, darlin'," he droned.

When the shutter clicked, Develyn retrieved the camera. "Now I need to get a picture of you, Hunter."

"Oh, no. I never take good pictures."

"Nonsense. We'll let Cooper take a pic of you and me."

"No, really, I don't think . . ."

She shoved the camera at Cooper and grabbed Hunter's arm. "Come on, Hunt, I'll pose with you. Delaney would be livid if I visited with you and didn't bring a picture back."

"Mrs. Worrell, really, I should be getting back. My pal . . ."

"Brady?"

"Yeah, Brady is waiting across . . ."

"Go ahead, dear. Press that big ol' silver button."

"I know how to operate the camera. It's mine, remember?"

She squeezed Hunter's arm. "A Father's Day present."

● ● ●

Develyn and Cooper waited until the sight and sound of Hunter Burke had dissipated.

"Now are you going to tell me what that was all about?"

"Well, Mr. Worrell . . ."

"Doesn't that deception bother you?"

"A little. But dear Mr. Hunter Burke is deceiving as well."

'You mean how he allowed you to change the name of his friend?"

"There isn't any friend. That's why he can't remember his name."

"Maybe he can't admit he doesn't have a friend. I can relate to that. I take it you wanted a picture of him, and it has nothing to do with Delaney."

"I'm just suspicious. He keeps showing up where I am. It feels creepy."

"You have any ideas?"

"No, but I keep thinking about your brother and his pal rustling Quint Burdett's cattle."

He led her down to the cedars where the horses were tied. "A lot of guys survey new hunting ground before they go out."

"I know. Still, I feel uneasy." She studied the sleeping Uncle Henry. "There's one that's not worried about a thing."

Cooper tightened the cinches on the saddles. "He's having Aunt Jenny dreams, no doubt. Dev, are you sure the deal with Burke isn't just that you don't like some cowboy sniffing around your Delaney?"

"That's a rather graphic way of putting it."

"Sorry."

"You might be right. I just don't know what he's after with Dee. I mean, he was hitting on me when he first drove up. But one look with the sunglasses off cured him of that." She rubbed My Maria's front right leg, and when the mare lifted her hoof, Dev glanced at the frog. "Anyway, I have his picture, just in case. And a nice picture of us."

"I'm glad to get a picture of you and me out here. I'll frame it and put it over the mantle. 'My first visitor.'"

"Too bad Hunter didn't snap one of me dangling by my heels from your hands."

"Yeah, I could've labeled it, 'Too small, I had to throw this one back, but you should have seen the one that got away.'"

She started to slug his arm but rubbed her knuckles instead.

"Too small? Watch it, cowboy. There are things I don't take teasing about too well."

"I was talkin' about your weight, of course. You are so light, I could hold you up with one hand."

Develyn continued checking My Maria's hooves. "Are you sure you were just talking about my weight?"

"What did you think I was talking about?"

She glanced at her arm as if she wore a watch. "My, is it that late? We'd better ride back to town."

Cooper stepped up in the saddle. "I don't know what's on your mind, but laughing like this feels good. It's what friends ought to do."

They chatted nonstop during the hour-long ride back to the cabin. When they rode into the yard, Develyn spotted Jackson Hill's Dodge truck parked where her Cherokee had been.

Casey and Jackson perched on the porch bench.

"Where's my Jeep?" Develyn called out.

"Delaney took it. She said she wanted to go for a ride."

"Where?"

"She didn't say. She just wanted to think some things through."

"But she doesn't know her way around here."

"She headed for the highway, Mrs. Worrell," Jackson called out. "She can't get lost if she stays on the blacktop."

They dismounted. Cooper took her reins and led My Maria to the pasture.

Develyn marched to the porch. "Did she leave me a note or anything?"

"No, but she told us about the visit to the doctor, how she walked out and all."

"I suppose she mentioned the two of us getting in a big shouting argument in the middle of the waiting room that left the people shocked and both of us in tears."

Jackson glanced at Casey and then back at Develyn.

"No, ma'am. She didn't tell us that part."

"Oh," Develyn murmured.

"Devy, I like Delaney," Casey said. "She'll be OK. She just needs some time to think. Some people think best when they are driving."

"Did you have a nice ride?" Jackson asked.

"Yes, I needed some fresh air."

"To think?" Casey slipped her hand in Jackson's.

Develyn slapped her hands on her hips. "Yes, but I told her I was riding with Coop. I just wish Delaney had said, 'Tell Mom I'm driving into Casper. I'll be home in three hours' or something like that."

Jackson pointed to the clear Wyoming blue sky. "It's a nice day to do some thinking."

"Are you changing the subject?" Develyn snapped.

"Just lookin' for common ground."

Develyn plopped down on the edge of the uncovered porch and stretched her feet across the dirt yard.

"Yes, it was a nice ride. We were able to retrieve Coop's digital camera. He had dropped it down between some boulders. While we were there, a guy . . . Jackson!"

Hill sat straight up and dropped Casey's hand at the sound of her shout. "Yes, ma'am?"

"Do you know a guy named Hunter Burke?"

"No, I don't think so. Is he in rodeo?"

"I don't know, but he claims to know you. He stopped by here the other day and asked if you were around. Then Dee and I ran into him on the road up to the Burdett ranch. He showed up on a four-wheeler out near the springs today."

"He says he knows me?"

"Says he wants to talk to you."

"What did he look like?"

"Tall, lanky like you, but not wide in the shoulders. More weak rounded. Of course, he has pathetic white skin. He was . . . wait . . . I have picture of him on Coop's digital camera."

"You took a picture of him? Why?" Casey asked.

"To show Jackson. I'll be right back."

"Can we hold hands while you are gone?" Jackson asked.

"Yes, of course."

"Can we smooch too?" Casey called out.

"No, you may not."

● ● ●

Develyn stared down at the camera. "Now, which is the button I push to preview the pictures?"

"The one in the middle," Cooper instructed.

"Nothing is happening. I'm a total klutz with technology."

Cooper took the camera and pressed the silver metal button. "Don't blame yourself. The battery's dead."

"Have you got another one?"

"No, do you?"

She stared at the ruins of the cabin. "Not anymore. I'll go down to Mrs. Tagley's and get one."

"It takes two," he called out.

She marched back to the porch where Jackson and Casey whispered.

"I got to go down to Mrs. Tagley's and get some batteries for the camera."

"You want to drive my truck?" Jackson offered.

"No, I'll walk. I need some time to . . ."

"Think things through?" Casey asked.

Develyn stuck out her tongue. "Countess, I just hate it when you are right."

"Countess?" Jackson questioned.

"It's a long story. Listen, Mr. Hill, I need you to identify this guy. Don't go running off."

Casey threw her arms around Jackson's neck and clutched him tight. "Don't worry, Dev, I'll make sure he doesn't get away."

● ● ●

Uncle Henry meandered beside her as Develyn strolled down the dirt driveway. He brayed when she patted his mane. "I know you are missing your Aunt Jenny, honey, but this is different. Delaney is my daughter. She doesn't know her way around Wyoming. I know she needs time to think, but she's

118

had weeks and weeks to consider it. Yes, I know I can be intimidating. I know she always thinks she can't live up to my image of her. I don't make unreasonable demands. I just want her to have the best life possible. I want her to be all that the Lord created her to be. For Pete's sake, Uncle Henry, doesn't she know that I'm on her side?"

The burro paused, and she stopped beside him.

"You know what's scary, Uncle Henry? I just realized that my mother could give that same speech about me. This is crazy. I spend weeks fuming over my mother and then treat my daughter the same way. I have to be different. I'm not really like my mother, am I?"

Uncle Henry brayed, then spun around and trotted back to the cabin.

Develyn watched him run away. *I'll take that for a yes. What got into you? I thought you wanted to go for a walk. Did you smell Aunt Jenny?*

"Where did your Shetland pony go?"

Develyn turned back to see Leon Morton jog up to her.

That's why Uncle Henry ran away.

"Hello, Leon." Develyn continued toward the road. "My burro ran off because you were mean to him."

"No, I wasn't! I saved his life."

"How do you figure that?"

"There was lightning all around. He could have been fried like when you drop wingless flies on a bug zapper. I saved him by shutting him in the outhouse. Have you ever heard of an outhouse gettin' hit by lightning?"

"No, I don't think I have."

"See? I saved his life."

"From the burro's point of view, you locked him in a smelly place where he didn't want to be. I'm sure you can understand his anxiety."

"Sort of like being locked in a file drawer in the principal's office, I reckon."

"Someone locked you in a file drawer?"

"No, I did it myself. How was I to know it had a self-locking door?"

"I'll bet you were scared."

"Not as much as Mrs. Plouver."

"Why was she scared?"

"She came into the principal's office a couple of hours later and pulled open the drawer."

"Did you yell at her?"

"No, I just asked her for a sandwich. She screamed and fainted dead away."

"Yes, well, having students hide in the file cabinet might do that." Develyn turned east on the main dirt road.

"Where are you going?"

"To Mrs. Tagley's."

"You goin' to buy yourself an orange Popsicle?"

"Perhaps."

"Is that the only thing you buy at the store?"

"No, but I do buy a lot of Popsicles, don't I?"

"That's OK. I know the reason."

"You do?"

"Yeah, you are great with child."

"What? Why did you say that?"

"Grandma said that she ate lots of Popsicles right before my daddy was born. So she said you were great with child."

"Do you know what that means, Leon?"

"You're pregnant. You know, you had . . ."

"That's enough, Leon. I'm not pregnant. I'm way too old."

"You are? But you can still . . ."

"Leon, I do not want to talk about this with you."

"Then why do you always buy orange Popsicles?"

"I liked them when I was a little girl and haven't had them since. I love how cold they are."

"You know what I liked when I was a kid?"

"I'm almost afraid to ask."

"Bananas."

"Oh, that's nice."

"Black bananas."

"Black? I don't think I've ever seen those."

"Sure you have. They all turn black sooner or later. Yep, you can just stick a straw in them and suck their guts out."

Lord, I will never complain about Dougie Baxter again.

She heard an out-of-tune blast from a brass instrument.

"I've got to go. Grandma thinks I'm hidin' under the porch waiting to scare the dog."

"Oh, dear, poor dog."

"He's the one who taught me that trick. Good-bye, pony lady."

"Good-bye, Leon."

"Hey, you'll get a free Popsicle."

"Why's that?"

"The old lady that runs the store is dead."

Develyn grabbed her arms and hugged herself to keep from shaking. "Mrs. Tagley is dead?"

"I went into the store for a package of Lil' Debbies and couldn't find the old lady. I looked in the back room, and she was sprawled out there on the floor as dead as a goldfish in an ice-cube tray."

"Oh, my word, did you call the sheriff?"

"Nah, I just took a pack of Lil' Debbies for free. I figured she won't need the money now."

"She's still in the back room?"

"I reckon so."

● ● ●

Develyn's side cramped as she sprinted to the general store. The screen door slammed behind her as she dashed to the back room.

Mrs. Tagley was sprawled face down, next to her sofa.

Lord, no . . . no . . . no . . . no!

She dropped to her knees on the worn carpet. "Mrs. Tagley?" Develyn rubbed the bony shoulder. "Mrs. Tagley? Oh, please say something. You have to be OK. It's your Devy. Talk to me, Mrs. Tagley. Oh, please talk to me."

With great care she rolled the elderly woman over on her back and pressed her wrist. "Mildred, I need you, so don't you dare die on me."

There's no pulse. Lord, I can't find a pulse!

Develyn's eyes searched the room as if expecting para-medics to be standing by.

"Calm down, Ms. Worrell. You can do this. Get a hold of yourself."

That's it! There it is! A pulse. Thank you, Lord!

"Mrs. Tagley, you just keep that heart pumping. I'm going to call for EMTs. They do have EMTs, don't they?"

● ● ●

Develyn sat on the floor with Mrs. Tagley's head in her lap for forty-five minutes until the EMTs and an ambulance arrived.

When they rolled her out through the front of the store, Develyn trailed along. "Can I ride in the ambulance with her?"

"Are you her daughter?"

"No, I'm just a friend and neighbor."

"Only family in the ambulance."

"Are you taking here to St. Joseph's in Casper?"

"Yes, but we'll need to contact the family. Do you have some phone numbers?"

"Mrs. Tagley has no family left."

"Then we will need you to give a report to admissions. Can you bring IDs, Medicare cards, health insurance records?"

"I'll look around and bring what I can."

● ● ●

On top of a cluttered oak desk, Develyn found Mrs. Tagley's purse. In the second drawer to the right, there was a metal box labeled "Personal Documents." She grabbed both. On her way to the front door, she plucked the store key off a nail and turned off lights as she went. She jogged back toward the cabin.

My Cherokee . . . Dee has my Jeep! I'll have to take Jackson's truck, or he can give me a ride. But I need to be here when Delaney gets back. Lord, this is out of control!

With labored breath and aching legs, Develyn slowed to a walk back up the driveway.

Cooper Tallon stood beside the porch talking to Casey and Jackson. He spied her and marched over.

"What happened down there?"

"Mrs. Tagley had a heart attack. They rushed her to the hospital in Casper. I've got her documents and have to go to town."

"I'll drive you," he offered.

"No, I'll just . . ."

"I'm driving you to town, Dev. That's settled."

She bit her lip and nodded.

"What can we do?" Casey called out.

"Wait right here for Delaney. The moment she pulls in, hop in my Cherokee and drive her to the hospital. I have to talk to her."

She shoved Mrs. Tagley's purse and metal box into Cooper's hand. "Put these in your truck, honey. I have to run a comb through my hair and put on some lipstick. I'll grab my purse and be right back."

He stepped in front of her. "Dev, are you doing OK?"

"I'm scared, Coop."

"About Mrs. Tagley or Delaney?"

"About calling you 'honey,' and neither one of us flinched."

Develyn leafed through the yellowed papers in the small metal box as she sat in the corner of the emergency waiting room.

"Oh, dear." Develyn unfolded a stiff document. "She lost a son in the war, didn't she?"

Cooper's voice was soft. "I heard she lost both boys."

"Oh, poor dear. No wonder she adopts everyone who comes through the door."

"I don't reckon Mrs. Tagley latches on to ever'one like she did you, Dev."

"I suppose there aren't a lot of choices in Argenta." Develyn stared at the swinging double doors. "I don't know why they make me wait out here."

"You should have told them you were her daughter."

"I have a tough time lying. You can thank my mother for that."

"But you told Hunter that I was Mr. Worrell."

"I most certainly did not. He assumed it, and I didn't correct him. That's different. I'm trying to solve a mystery about him."

"I wonder what would have happened if ol' Hunter hadn't showed up about then?"

Develyn studied Mrs. Tagley's purse. "I wonder what would have happened if I hadn't gone to the store?"

"You're right. We ought to change subjects."

"And I wouldn't have gone to the store if your camera didn't need batteries."

"It must have been left on while it was down in the rocks."

"And we wouldn't have needed batteries right away except to show Jackson a picture of Hunter. So in a way, the Mr. and Mrs. Worrell thing led to finding Mrs. Tagley."

"Are you saying the end justifies the means?"

"I'm saying the Lord can use anything to achieve his purpose."

"Yes, ma'am, I reckon he can." Cooper stared down at his Wranglers. "Dev, where were you on March 24, 2002?"

She studied his blue-gray eyes. "That's a very leading question, Mr. Tallon." *Am I finally going to learn something about his past? He's not really asking me. He wants to tell me something personal, and he's working up his nerve.*

"I suppose I was teaching fifth grade in Crawfordsville, Indiana. What is the significance of that date to the mysterious

Cooper Tallon?" *Lord, I hope it's something I can accept. Don't let him be a sex offender or a . . .*

"I don't think I've ever been called mysterious before."

Don't lose your nerve, Mr. Tallon. Tell me, straight out. I can take it. "Mysterious or not, what happened on March 28, 2002?"

"March 24."

It must be something big. He's really nervous about it. "Yes, what happened, Coop?"

"I have no idea."

Develyn felt her shoulders tense. "What?"

He pointed to the *Field & Stream* magazine lying on the oak end table. "That issue is over four years old. March 24, 2002. Why don't they have current issues? For all the money it costs to come to the hospital, you'd think they'd have better magazines."

"Do you mean to tell me this is all about a magazine?"

He tapped his finger on the date. "See?"

"You set me up. I thought this was important."

"No need to snap at me like that."

"I didn't snap at you."

"Of course you did."

"Mr. Tallon, I did not snap at you."

He stared at his feet. "Let's ask that elderly gentleman with a cane over there if you snapped at me."

She tugged him back down, then whispered. "I was startled, that's all. I do not snap at anyone."

He patted her hand. "Not even at the fifth graders?"

"Not even them. Well, perhaps I may have half snapped at Dougie Baxter once or twice."

"That's probably it. I overreacted. You merely half-snapped at me."

"Mr. Tallon, we were involved in a spiritual conversation about how the Lord uses our failures to accomplish his purposes, and then you lay an arbitrary date on me. I thought there was some connection."

"I can see that. Maybe there is."

"In what way?"

"I was ponderin' the results if I'd met you in the spring of 2002."

"It would have been awful. Coop, my divorce was just about final. Delaney was running wild. I cried myself to sleep every night, if I slept at all. The only time I liked myself was in the classroom and going to rodeos."

"Rodeos helped you?"

A large, redheaded lady rushed through the room with a crying baby in her arms. "Get Dr. Draymn right now!" she hollered.

They watched her bang through the double doors.

"You were talking rodeo?" he said.

"It was an escape. I could get lost pretending to be something I wasn't. It gave me some relief. You did not want to know me that spring. I was a pathetic mess."

"That's tough to believe."

"Trust me, Mr. Tallon, the Lord was gracious to spare you from knowing me then. How about you, Coop? What did you do in the spring of 2002?"

"You want to hear something really pathetic?"

"I think so," she murmured.

"I can't remember 2002."

"Can't remember?"

"That year, 2002, was just like 2003 and 2001. They all run together, Dev. One day is like the rest; one week like the other. The years blend together. Work hard all week. Go to church, nap, and do the laundry on Sunday. Then repeat it over and over and over. I don't have any other memories. Just a blur where I am tired and busy."

"That sounds sad."

"It gets worse. I can't remember any distinction in 1992 or 1982 either. It's like I grew up, went to work, and suddenly realized most of my life is past. I think I was wondering what it would have been like to know you back a few years."

"Well, 2002 was not my best."

A short, bald man crossed the waiting room to the counter, a towel draped over his left arm. When he pulled the towel back, there was a toaster stuck on his hand.

"Oh, Mr. James, not again," the registrar said.

Develyn turned to Cooper. "Again?"

"I reckon we've all done dumb things. But I've never seen that before." He patted her knee. "Dev, when were your best years? When were those times you can point to and say, 'Those were the best years of my life.'"

"Sometime when Daddy was still alive, when Dewayne was still around."

"Your brother?"

"Yes, I miss him. There's a special bond that twins share."

"Would you go back, if you could?"

"Sometimes I think about it. Sometimes I try to remember what it was like before the tears began."

"When was that?"

"It was on a Saturday, about 4:00 p.m., four months after Delaney was born."

"That's getting exact."

"I was sitting on the brown tweed sofa, wearing a soft orange blouse that I had made myself. I was nursing Delaney. Spencer burst in after playing golf and stared at me. I think his words were, 'Good grief, Develyn, when are you going to wean that child? I don't intend to stay married to an overweight milking machine.'"

"He said that?"

"Oh, yes. Then he went out and didn't come home until daylight the next morning. I cried myself to sleep that night. I had a tough time getting my weight back down after Dee was born."

"But you are so slim."

"Thank you, Mr. Tallon. Your flattery is gratefully accepted."

"You didn't cry every night for twenty years, did you?"

"No, but that's where the tears began. How about you, Coop? When did your tears begin?"

"I don't reckon I've cried much in my life, but there were plenty of 'tears of the soul.'"

"I like that phrase, 'tears of the soul.'"

Cooper stared across the emergency waiting room. "I think my golden years were my late twenties."

"That's not what I asked, Mr. Tallon."

"Let me ponder the other."

"OK, why were those your golden years?"

"I was startin' my own business. All my dreams were up ahead. There was nothin' I couldn't do, and everything I was missin' I knew would come around in its time."

A woman with a wrinkled white blouse, carrying a baby in her arms, led a toddler of two out of the emergency room. The little boy trotted over to Dev and Coop. "Look," he said as he held up his cast-covered arm, "I broke my arm."

"Does it hurt?" Develyn asked.

"No. I didn't even cry. Mama cried, but I didn't cry."

Develyn glanced up at the mom. "And Daddy will cry when he gets the hospital bill. Come on, Captain Jack."

When they made it through the automatic doors, Develyn turned to Cooper. "Captain Jack?"

"I believe that mama will be back here again."

"We were talking of golden years."

"Yes, when were your golden years, Dev?"

"Not counting this summer?"

He stared at her until she turned away. "You too?"

"It's been a good summer, Coop. I can't remember so many days in a row when I enjoyed being me. I don't want to sound too negative. I've had a lot of good times . . . good months . . . good years. I loved college. It was my first time on my own. I was out from under my mother's constant supervision. Taking courses I enjoyed. Trying out new things."

"What new things?"

"Diet Coke and disco dancing," Develyn giggled. "Mother was sure diet soda would cause cancer. And dancing, well, needless to say, it was not acceptable behavior for an Upton girl."

He shook his head, then grinned.

"What's the matter, can't you imagine me doing disco? I was pretty good. Spencer was better. That's how I met him, at a dance at Purdue. He showed up without a date and wanted to enter the contest. My friend Beth and I hunkered in the corner, sort of dancing by ourselves and watching. He marched right over and said, 'I guess you'll have to do.' Then he tugged me out on the dance floor."

"Not exactly enthusiastic?"

"I suppose that's how he always thought of me: 'I guess you'll have to do.'"

"How did you two do in the contest?"

"We won first place. So he walked me out to the parking lot. When we got to my car, he said, 'Looks like we'll have to go out next week and defend our title.'"

"Did you love him, Dev?"

"Of course I did."

"Did it feel good to love him?"

She studied the tanned, deep lines on Tallon's face. "It felt good to know someone was thinking about me all day. That someone wanted to be just with me. That someone thought I was attractive." She patted his hand. "Are you saying that you don't know what it feels like to be in love?"

He pulled off his black cowboy hat. His graying brown hair

kept the hat curl. "Were your college years the only golden ones?"

"And my first trip to Wyoming, but that was only for two weeks. I enjoyed raising Delaney. I liked going back for my master's degree."

She studied as a man rushed a very red-faced, pregnant woman across the waiting room. "Oh, dear."

For a couple of moments, no one spoke.

Cooper broke the silence. "November 1995."

"Are you talking about another magazine?"

"That's when the tears of my soul began."

"Mr. Cooper, you aren't real good with transitions, are you?"

"You need to know one thing. I have already talked to you more than I've talked to any lady in my life. So, if I'm not very good at it, you'll have to school me."

"OK, here's the first lesson. Don't leave me hanging. Tell me, right now, why the tears of your soul began in the fall of 1995."

"I had a big contract to lay an oil line from Rock Springs south to the Utah border. It was quite a deal. About the middle of June, a guy walks up with a backpack. Says he wants a job. He'd hitchhiked down from Ethete, an Arapaho town over on the Wind River Reservation."

"He was Native American?"

"Yeah. Miles was skin and bones. Looked like a poster image for a concentration camp. I didn't figure he could do a whole day's hard work. But he begged me for a job. Said he had a

family to support and needed the work. I put him on tempo-
rary and let him bunk in the toolshed, since we didn't have any
other place for him to stay."

"Was Miles a good worker?"

"He would do anything I told him. He didn't talk much.
Come payday, he asked for cashier's checks so he could send
them home."

"So you kept him on?"

"He didn't know how to operate anything more complicated than a shovel when he hiked up. But I'd teach him how
the rigs worked, and he'd catch on fast. So I let him work until
the job was done."

"When was that?"

"November of '95. We got the job done and were packin'
gear. He pulled out his sleepin' bag and duffle and said he
would hitchhike back up to Ethete. I told him I was headed
here to my cabin at Argenta, and I'd give him a lift."

"Is this going to be a sad story? Are you trying to prepare
me for something sad happening to him?"

"Just the opposite."

"But you said this is where the tears of your soul began."

"Yep, that happened when . . ."

"Is there a Devy here?"

Develyn glanced up to see a nurse in a pale green uniform
standing in the doorway to the emergency rooms. She and
Cooper both stood.

"I'm Develyn."

The nurse motioned her toward the open door. "Your mother wants to see you."

"Actually, I'm . . ."

Cooper squeezed her hand. "How is Mother Tagley?" he asked.

"We think she is past the worse part. She said her daughter brought her in, and she wanted to talk to her Devy."

"Dear, you go on in and see your mom. I'll wait here."

"Your husband can come too."

"No, I'll wait here."

"He's a little squeamish in emergency rooms. The last time he was in one, he fainted straightaway," Develyn said.

The hallway reeked of disinfectant and medicine. Her tennis shoes squeaked on the highly polished linoleum floor. Each bed in the large room was circled in curtains. The nurse tugged some back and ushered Develyn in.

"I'll go find you a chair."

Develyn scrutinized the gray-haired lady tucked under the covers with an IV in one arm and a breathing tube down her nose. She reached over and stroked Mrs. Tagley's age spot-covered hand.

"Hi, honey. How are you?"

One eye opened then the other. "Devy girl, do you have my purse?"

"Yes, it's out in the waiting room with Coop. Do you need something?"

"My makeup. If I'm going to meet Jesus, I want to look my best."

"How about me getting your makeup and you postponing heaven a few more years?"

"Why?"

That's a very good question, Lord, and I'm not sure I have the answer. "Because Argenta needs you."

"I've run a store in that town for over seventy years. I think it's time to quit."

"You can quit the store, but you have some more good years."

"My life is that store. I'm tired."

"I know you are. Get some rest while you are in here, and we can talk about it when you come home. Do you want me to run the store for you?"

"I couldn't ask you to do that."

"That's what daughters do. Didn't you tell the nurse I was your daughter?"

"She wouldn't let you bring me my makeup unless you were my daughter."

"Well, for the next few weeks, let's just pretend I am. I can get Casey to help, and we'll keep the store open if you like."

"I'd like that. There's a binder under the back counter. It tells you what to buy and when."

Develyn rubbed her arms. "You always order the same amount of everything?"

"Most of the time. This summer I've had a rush on orange Popsicles."

The emergency room nurse breezed back to the bed. "The doctor said that she's stabilized enough to move her up to

CCU. If you'll stay in the waiting room, I'll come get you when we have her situated."

"You're not moving my mother one inch until she gets some makeup on," Develyn said.

Mrs. Tagley squeezed her hand.

● ● ●

Cooper Tallon stretched out his long legs in front of the chair. "So they think it was a mild heart attack?"

"They're still mulling its magnitude. She will be in the cardiac care unit for a few days."

"And the store?"

"Casey and I will keep it open for her."

"You are quite a lady, Ms. Worrell. You've only known Mrs. Tagley a few weeks."

"I feel like I've known her since I was ten. Every daydream I ever had about Wyoming included Mrs. Tagley and her store. She was the one fixture in all of them. I can't remember any of the local kids we played with or anyone else. But I never forgot her. Who else does she have? Every mother should have a daughter."

Cooper leaned back and rubbed his square jaw. "I think you are a bulldog, Ms. Worrell. I mean that as a compliment. What's the plan for the rest of the evening?"

"I want to make sure she's tucked in her new room and that the nurses have my cell phone number. Coop, if you need to get back, I can hitch a ride with Casey and Jackson when they bring Delaney to town."

"What if your daughter doesn't come back right away?"

"She has to." Develyn sighed. "You don't have to sit here, Coop. I'll be fine."

"I drove you here; I'm driving you home. You take home the girl you brung to the dance. It's an old cowboy rule. And I'm an old cowboy."

"Enough of that 'old' talk, Mr. Tallon. But I will accept your offer. All of this doesn't sound so confusing, having you here with me."

A nurse scooted over to them. "Mrs. Worrell, the doctor is in with your mother. Just give them a few minutes and you can go up. She's in CCU Room 220. Mr. Worrell, it's a nice, cheery room. I believe you could go up too. Just remember if the voices grow distant or your vision starts to close in on you, put your head between your knees and breathe deep."

He shoved his hat back on. "Yes, ma'am, I'll remember that."

The nurse looked at Dev. "They have a few more papers for you to sign."

She stood but motioned for Cooper to stay seated.

"What can I do to help you?"

"Wait here for Casey and Delaney. And promise you will finish your story about Miles, the Arapaho worker."

"I'll wait here. You take care of Mama."

● ● ●

Develyn had a long wait at the elevator. She folded her arms and glared at the light that seemed to be stuck on 4. *Lord, I know you bring the right people into our lives at the right time, but it doesn't always seem that way. Why is Mrs. Tagley now in my life? Why is it you needed me to wait this long to meet Casey and Quint and Renny and dear Coop? And why did I call him "dear Coop"? Sometimes he seems so sad. I don't think I know all of his story. He had a lonely life isolated from people, and I have had a lonely life surrounded by people. It doesn't matter, does it? It's not the people. It's our perception. We allow loneliness to cling to us like a virus that we can never shake. It's always there, sapping our energy. Is loneliness ingratitude toward you? It must seem that way at times. Lord, I'll be so happy to be in heaven where I finally get it all right.*

"Lady, are you going up?"

Develyn stared at the uniformed maintenance man. "I certainly hope so."

● ● ●

It took more than an hour to get Mrs. Tagley's makeup on and settle her into her new room.

"Mildred, it's time for me to go. Here's the remote. Your soaps will be on channels 4 and 6, and channel 26 has classic soap reruns. Your water is right over here. I told the nurse that you wanted your makeup on first thing in the morning. My cell phone number is by the telephone. You have them phone me if you need anything. I'll be back tomorrow, but I don't know what time. We'll get the store open for you. Is there anything else?"

The elderly woman held out her hand.

Develyn held it tight.

"Now I know why the good Lord had me live so long. He wanted to allow me to know what it feels like to have a daughter looking after me."

"How does it feel?" Develyn asked.

"Wonderful. So good, in fact, I think I should stick around a while longer and enjoy it."

"Now, Mother, that's what I like to hear. I'll see you tomorrow."

"I know, honey. I know."

Develyn recognized Casey's voice from the far end of the hall. When she got to the waiting room, Coop, Jackson, and Delaney sat in chairs while Casey stood in the middle of the room laughing at her arm that dangled down from her extended elbow.

"Did I miss something?" Develyn asked.

Delaney shook her head and grinned. "Casey was demonstrating what she looked like the last time she was in this emergency room."

"I busted my arm steer wrestling."

"You come here often?" Develyn chided.

A security guard stuck in his head. "Casey, you don't have any guns or knives this time, do you?"

"Nope. You wantin' to frisk me, Tony?"

He rested his hands on his duty belt. "No, ma'am."

"How's Mama?" Cooper asked.

"She is resting comfortably, but she looks so tired."

"Are we ready to go?" Casey asked.

Develyn studied the crew. "Let's see, we have my Cherokee and Cooper's truck. . . ."

"We came in my truck," Jackson said.

"Why don't you and Delaney take my truck?" Cooper offered. "I can ride shotgun with these two."

"Thanks," Develyn replied.

"Mother, are you ticked at me for driving off?" Delaney blurted out.

"I was worried, honey. I know this is a tough time for you, and I haven't been much help. Don't you think we should talk some?"

"Yes. But I don't care if your Coop comes along too. Casey and Jackson were thinking of going to a movie."

Develyn turned to Cree-Ryder. "I thought you went to a movie night before last."

"Mother!" Casey faked a whine.

"You see, Mr. Tallon, if it isn't one daughter, it's the other. OK, you two go to the movie, but don't stay out too late. We have to run Mrs. Tagley's store in the morning."

"We do?" Casey asked.

"I promised her I'd keep it open for a few days until we see how this is going."

"I used to work at a store," Jackson offered. "I worked at Albertson's in Sheridan in high school and junior college."

"Jackson and I will run the store," Casey blurted out.

"We will?"

"You're the stock boy, and I'm the cashier."

"What? It's such a small store, we'll both be sitting around with nothing to do."

Casey grinned. "And your point is?"

"You'll sit out on the front bench," Develyn said.

Casey shook her head at Delaney. "Mama's on a roll tonight. See if you can soften her up. You want to tell her, or do you want me to?"

"Tell me what?"

"I'll tell her," Delaney said.

"Tell me what?" Develyn repeated.

The five of them meandered out to the parking lot.

"Mr. Tallon, did you ever get a feeling that these ladies are saying a lot more to each other than our ears can 'cipher?" Jackson asked.

"Sometimes it's like being in a foreign country and not knowing the native language," Coop said.

"Men," Develyn sighed.

"Totally," Casey concurred.

"Why do they assume communication has to be verbal?"

"Or logical?"

● ● ●

Cooper drove with Develyn in the middle and Delaney by the window. When they turned west off of I-25, he cleared his throat. "Ladies, if I'm in your way, I'll just pull over and hitch a ride."

"Dee, I'm sorry about the scene in the doctor's office this morning. I'm really ashamed about how I acted."

The tires whined on the blacktop during the silence.

"I know you are, Mother. Why do we do that?"

"Bring out the worst in each other?"

"Yes, I don't understand."

"Honey, I don't know. This morning I think I was as scared as you were."

"You worried about what Grandmother Upton will say?"

"No. Mother will deal with it in her own 'why me' way."

"You were worried about what people at your school will think?"

"To tell you the truth, Dee, none of that is important. I'm worried about you. Being pregnant changes your life forever. I want the changes to be for your good. I'm not the important one in this; you are."

"No, Mom, the baby is the most important one."

Develyn slipped her arm around her daughter. "You're right, honey. Is that what you needed to think about?"

"That's why I drove all the way to Riverton and back."

"What did my daughter decide?"

"If I'm pregnant, it's not the baby's fault. She should get all the love she deserves."

"Or he," Cooper broke in.

"Isn't that just like a grandpa. They always want a grandson," Develyn blurted out.

"Grandpa? Is there something going on here I don't know about?" Delaney pressed.

"Just a little game," Cooper said. "The emergency room nurse called me Mr. Worrell. No offense. I'm sorry for intruding. Here, take the wheel."

He raised his hands and grabbed the door handle. "I'll wait outside."

Develyn clutched the black steering wheel. "No, you won't, Mr. Cooper Tallon. Not when the truck is going sixty."

She turned back to her daughter. "You are right, honey. If you have a baby, we'll love her with everything we've got."

"I decided that under no circumstance would I get an abortion."

"I'm glad, Dee. You know that would break my heart."

"It would break mine too. You know what is ironic, Mom?"

"What, Dee?"

"We just did it once. We had a picnic by the river, and it cooled off when it got dark, and the breeze was blowing. It was so peaceful and sweet, just like something out of a Jane Austen novel. It seemed so natural for . . ."

"Wait!" Cooper called out, then drove over to the side of the road. "This is where I get out."

"What's the matter?" Delaney asked.

"I think we embarrassed Coop."

"Ladies, mothers, and daughters should have the freedom to talk about anything they want. But fifty-five-year-old bachelors shouldn't listen in."

"You're fifty-five?" Delaney gasped. "And never married?"

"Yes, but that's my story." He turned off the engine. "You see that cabin up there? I'm thinking of buying it. You two wait here while I go up and inspect it."

"It's leaning so much the next wind will knock it down," Develyn insisted.

"Just a little work, and it will be good as new. You two go ahead and talk about anything you want. Honk when you want to go on."

He sauntered up the hill.

"Mother, I like your Coop."

"He's a good friend. And that's all for now. I feel relaxed when I talk to him, and he has good advice."

"He looks very strong, you know, for an older gentleman."

"Those arms are solid muscle."

Delaney giggled. "And how does Ms. Worrell know he is solid muscle? Just friends?"

"I only have energy for one focus at a time, and right now you are it."

"I know, Mom. I've never felt that more than the past two days."

"Now I'm a schoolteacher, and I can't survive without a lesson plan. What's our lesson plan for you and the little one, you know, provided you are pregnant?"

"I'm going to the doctor tomorrow."

"I'll call and get an appointment."

"I already called. Casey knew a lady doctor in Lander. I'm going over there."

WISH I'D KNOWN YOU TEARS AGO

"But, if you got an appointment in Casper, we could stop by afterward and see Mrs. Tagley."

"Mother, I really do love you."

"I love you too, honey."

"But I don't want you to go to the doctor with me."

"You don't? But . . ."

"I asked Casey to go with me."

"You hardly know her."

"She's like a sister, remember?"

"But . . ."

"I'll be twenty-one my next birthday. I'm responsible for my actions. I have to take care of this myself. It's important to me, Mom. I have confessed my sin before the Lord, and now I'm ready to accept the consequences. Please let me do it my way."

"You are absolutely right, Dee."

"I am?"

"Yes."

"You mean that, don't you?"

"Yes, I do, honey. Remember, I'm your mother. That means I am always on your side, and I am ready to help you any way I can."

"Will you be ashamed of me if I show up at Target in Crawfordsville with a tummy bigger than a basketball?"

"I will not be ashamed of you. But I will not pretend you did nothing wrong. I want my daughter to have a husband and my grandchild to have a father. That's the way God intended it. But I accept your confession, and I know the Lord does as well.

We all make mistakes. Some have broader consequences than others. There are no perfect people."

"You know what, Mom? You have always been the most perfect person I've ever known."

"How can you say that? I wasn't very perfect this morning at the doctor's office."

"I didn't say you were *perfect*. You're the *most* perfect. I've compared you to my friends' mothers and to other women. I'd like to be like you, Mom."

"I think I'm going to cry."

"Me too."

For several moments Develyn and Delaney hugged and wept. They sat straight up when a pickup with several cowboys honked at them.

"We are a sight, I suppose. Two grown women sitting in a pickup alongside Highway 20, in the middle of Wyoming, hugging and crying."

"Mom, I'm sorry for all the pain Daddy put you through. When Brian got mad at me and wanted nothing more to do with me, I said to myself, 'This must be the way Mom felt.'"

"I don't think it could ever have worked out for your father and me to get back together. But I could have learned to be gracious, kind, and generous to him again. I'm sorry for how my pain and bitterness made your life difficult. I don't understand why the Lord took him when he did. I had just decided to change my attitude, and he was gone."

"I spent several years trying to deny that Daddy did those things. I knew you were right, but I didn't want it to be true.

I think I had this fairy-tale view of how a family was supposed to be, and I couldn't accept that we weren't that way."

"We're sinners saved by grace, baby. That's all that we are. But we can love each other."

"Are we going to cry and hug some more?"

Develyn grabbed her daughter and hugged.

The driver's door swung open. "Did you two honk for me?" Cooper asked.

"No," Delaney cried.

"Is everything OK?"

Develyn gulped air to try to catch a breath. She blurted out through the tears, "Everything is perfect."

"Perfect? You two look like the dog died."

Develyn wiped Delaney's eyes with her shirtsleeve. "Men. Why can't they tell when we're happy?"

"Do you want me to go back up and hide in the cabin?"

"No, drive us home, please," Delaney said.

"Are you telling me everything is OK?"

"It's wonderful," Develyn sobbed.

Cooper started the engine and eased back onto the road. "Now, you know that I've never had a wife. And I've never had a daughter. So I'm a little more confused than the average man. You'll cut me a little slack if I seem bewildered."

Develyn dug through her purse for a tissue, then blew her nose. "Sorry, Coop, it's a mother-and-daughter thing. If you talk to us, we'll probably stop crying."

"Do you want me to bore you to sleep or talk about something interesting?"

"You are going to finish the story about Miles the Arapaho."

He glanced over at Delaney.

"Stop the truck. I'll go up on the hillside and wait for you to honk the horn," Delaney said.

"Oh, no," Cooper grinned. "Me and your mama don't talk secrets."

"We do too. Cooper Tallon, I expect some of the things I told you never to be repeated."

"You do?"

She jabbed her elbow into his ribs.

"Oh, like the time you rode buck naked across the meadow and jumped the three-rail fence?"

"What?" Develyn gasped. "I . . . I . . ."

Delaney burst out laughing. "That's the funniest thing I ever heard. My mother would never do that in a million years."

"I know," Cooper said. "But I reckon that's the kind of thing I was to keep quiet about."

"I can't believe you said that about me."

"I wanted to divert the attention away from your addiction."

"What addiction?" Delaney pressed.

"Yes, Mr. Cooper, what addiction do I have?"

"Devy-girl, you are obviously still in denial. It's quite sad."

"I said, what addiction?"

"I believe she snapped at me." Cooper leaned forward and glanced over at Delaney. "Did your mama just snap at me?"

"I did not snap at you."

"She snapped at you," Delaney nodded. "On a scale of one to ten, I'd rate that snap as a seven."

"Seven? I figured it was more like an 8.5."

"Oh, no. An 8.5 will stand the hair on the back of your neck stiff. Trust me on this."

"Are you two through dissing me?"

"We're teasing you, Mother."

"Mr. Cooper Tallon, would you please tell me what is my addiction? There, was that the right tone?"

"Was that a whimper?" he asked.

"Not a very good one," Delaney giggled. "No more than a five."

"That's what I thought."

"I'm so happy you two get along so well. You'd make a delightful team at the comedy club in Indy."

Delaney bounced up and down on the pickup seat. "And now sarcasm? She's multitalented. I'd rate that about . . ."

"Don't," Coop warned. "You've got to know when to hold 'em and know when to fold 'em. Now's the time to fold."

"Thank you, Mr. Tallon."

Cooper stepped on the accelerator and passed a Fed Ex semi pulling three trailers. When he swung back in the right lane, he put the truck on cruise control. "Orange Popsicles," he blurted out.

"What about them?" Delaney asked.

"Your mother is addicted to them."

"I'd never seen her eat one in my life until I got to Wyoming."

"She probably tried to hide it from you."

"You mean she was a closet orange Popsicle addict?"

"Sounds sticky, doesn't it?"

"I can give them up any time I want," Develyn insisted.

"That's what they all say."

"But you don't understand," Develyn sighed. "I need my orange Popsicles. They calm me down and help me get through the day."

"Oh, sure. First it's one a day, then two. Where will it stop?" Delaney jibed.

"I tried to get her to go on *Oprah*," Cooper said.

"I am not as bad off as those people. I'm just a recreational orange Popsicle eater."

"Don't worry, Mother, I'll stick with you and help you lick this."

All three burst into laughter at the same time.

Develyn finally caught her breath. "Dee, reach back there and grab Coop's carbine."

"Why?"

"I'm going to have to shoot him if he doesn't finish the story about Miles, the hardworking Arapaho."

"Leave the gun. I'll finish the story. Anyway, it took another day to get the yard cleaned up and the rented equipment shipped back, so Miles and I took off early the next morning. He'd been working for me for six months and only went home twice during all that time.

"Drivin' north I was calculatin' all my bills and trying to figure the profit I made on that job. I couldn't wait to sit down with my briefcase full of invoices and my calculator and tally it up. I was guessing around one hundred grand."

"For your profit?" Delaney asked.

"Yep. Anyway, I was countin' dollar bills in my mind, and Miles was napping when we pulled into Ethete. He sat straight up like an alarm went off, then directed me down a dirt road. Kind of leanin' out in the sage at the end of this trail was a faded green single-wide, and a couple of busted cars. A big, tall one-eared goat was munchin' on an empty dog food sack. An old tricycle and a broken lawn chair lounged in the dirt yard in front of the house.

"I stopped the truck, and Miles hopped out. He hadn't taken six steps when a little girl, about five, wearing nothin' but underpants, skipped out on the porch and shouted, 'Daddy's home!'

"A thin lady with a long, black pigtail flew out of the house and sprinted toward Miles. She leaped into his arms and wrapped her legs around his waist. They danced like that, and she kissed him as if he'd been five years to war.

"The little girl is joined on the porch by a brother, slightly older. He's only wearing jeans, and the two of them run out and hug Miles's legs.

"I tipped my hat to Miles, and he waved back. Then I drove over to the cabin in Argenta. I thought about that scene all the way. Who was the rich man? Who was the pauper? When I drove back down the drive and trudged to the cabin, I knew the answer to that. I didn't bother countin' profit that night. No matter what I made, it wouldn't balance what Miles had.

And that, Ms. and Miss Worrell, was the night I first felt the tears of my soul."

Develyn hugged his arm and leaned on his shoulder.

No one talked.

The sky turned from charcoal gray to black. The headlights glared as the tires hummed.

Cooper broke the silence. "Did you tell Dee we ran across Hunter Burke today?"

"You did? Where?"

"Near the springs where Coop wants to build his log home."

"He said he was going hunting or something. He has a gun rack in his truck, you know."

"I didn't know that," Develyn said.

"Did Hunt mention that we have a date for tomorrow night?"

"But you hardly know him."

"How will I get better acquainted unless I go out with him?"

"This is crazy, Delaney. You are going to the doctor with Casey tomorrow, remember?"

"That's in the morning."

"Dee, there is something about this Hunt that . . ."

"His eyes. Aren't they dreamy?"

"His eyes? Until I figure out why he lied to me, you are not going out with him."

"Mother, you just said I can make my own decisions."

"You might be carrying some other man's baby. Doesn't that make you pause in the dating process?"

"Why should it? The Lord forgives me. Do you mean I can never have any fun again?"

"Using a hyperbole to make a point doesn't impress me much. There are times for fun. This isn't one of them. First things first."

"Mother, if I want to go out with Hunter, I will do it."

"Coop, do you believe this?"

"That you two are squalling at each other? Yep, I can believe it. I can handle this. It's that cryin' and huggin' that threw me for a loop."

7

"Hurry up, this might be our last ride."

"Brownie and I have no intention of making the ride shorter. I don't know why Daddy won't let me ride Brownie home. I'm sure I could be there by September."

Dewayne leaned his hand on the rump of his buckskin gelding and waited. "I thought you said October."

"Whatever. Brownie wants to go home with me."

"How do you know that?"

"We talk a lot."

"You mean, *you* talk a lot. All he ever does is snort and say 'neigh.'"

"Yes, but it's the way he says 'neigh.'"

"I'll race you down the mountain."

"I will not race you."

"Are you chicken?"

"I don't want to get sweaty."

"What?"

"Girls don't like to get sweaty. Didn't you know that?"

"Sweat doesn't hurt anyone."

"It messes up my clothes."

"You've got orange Popsicle drops splattered across it. What difference does sweat make?"

"The cliff is steep down by those cedars. It's not a good place to race."

"I was right. You are chicken."

"I am prudent."

"Well, prudy-girl, I'm racing. I'll take a nap and wait for you under a shade tree."

Develyn plodded along the narrow trail. The slick, worn leather of the saddle seat rubbed her thighs and knees. "He just wants to show off. I don't know why boys are that way. I'm glad you aren't that way." She leaned forward and patted the brown mane of the brown horse. "And you're a boy. Daddy said you were 'sort of' a boy, whatever that means."

She watched her brother gallop toward the narrow part of the trail. "Look at him race. That is not very smart."

Dewayne's buckskin stumbled, then turned and righted himself, then stumbled again.

"Dewayne, you should . . ." Develyn's shout was halted by her brother's scream.

"Devy, I'm falling!"

She dropped the reins, and her hands went to her quivering chin as she watched her twin brother, still in the saddle, plunge over the cliff.

"No, no!" When she leaped from the horse, she twisted her ankle, then slammed her bare knees into the granite rocks. She could feel the warm blood trickle down her legs as she sprinted to the cliff.

"Dewayne! Dewayne!"

She jumped back when she got to the edge. Instead of the sage and grass incline she remembered, there was a vertical rocky cliff that descended for several thousand feet. Develyn felt her body quiver all over, and she tried to hug herself to keep from shaking.

She watched as her brother and the horse cannonballed into the wide brown river below.

"Dewayne, you come back right now," she sobbed. "I need you."

She waited for his head to surface above the turbulent water. Instead of seeing the horse or her brother, the water of the river quieted, and suddenly it was still, just a pool, a pond. Beside the pond under a willow tree, she thought she spied someone sitting on a blanket.

"Come on, Devy."

"No, Dewayne, no. You scared me."

The voice was soft, persistent. "Come on, Devy, let's mount up and ride."

"Come back, Dewayne," she whimpered.

"Come on, Mama, you're dreaming again."

"I am not," Develyn snapped.

One eye popped open. A black braid swished across her nose.

"Casey?"

"How about a ride? We need to talk."

Develyn sat up on the bed. The damp sheet dropped to her waist. "My jams are soaking wet. It must have been hot last night. I perspired through the sheets."

"It wasn't that hot unless you were dreaming of cowboys. Now, come on. Dee's still asleep."

"I dreamed of Dewayne."

"What was your heroic brother doing this time?"

"He died. He plunged his horse over some steep cliff and dropped into a roaring river a thousand feet below."

"Well, that's not around here unless he was over at Wind River Canyon. Dreams are crazy. There's no explanation."

"I'm troubled, Casey."

"About the dream?"

"Yes. Twins have a close connection, you know. It's like we can sense something internally about each other."

"You said your brother's in the Persian Gulf aboard a ship. What does that have to do with riding horses?"

"I don't know. I wish I could call him right now."

"Let's go ride and talk about it."

Develyn staggered into the tiny bathroom. She emerged, wearing jeans and a red T-shirt with yellow scrolled words, "Genuine Cowboy girl," across the front.

"Cute. Where did you get that?"

"Lily found it in Greencastle and mailed it to me. She was afraid I'd be dressed in thrift store clothing after the fire."

"Did she marry that lawyer yet?"

"She promised to wait for my approval. I think she's in Wisconsin with her grandkids now. What's the hurry about a ride?"

"We haven't been on a ride for a while."

"I went out with Coop."

"Yes, and I went out with Jackson two days ago. That's my point, you and I haven't gone out for a while."

Dev tugged on her tennies and shoved her straw hat down on partially combed blonde hair. "Why so early?"

"Because Jackson will be here at eight to help run the store, remember?"

"Oh, yes. Poor Mrs. Tagley."

When they stepped out on the porch, the dust in the wind swirled like miniature confetti. "This isn't a good day for riding," Develyn said.

"There's no such thing as a bad day for riding. I've got them saddled. Come on."

Uncle Henry sauntered up to Develyn, and she scratched his ears. "I know it's early, honey, but the bronze bombshell has something spinning in her mind." The burro plodded along beside her toward the paint mare. "Does anything ever spin in your mind? Besides Aunt Jenny? Casey, why are you dragging us around so early?"

Cree-Ryder pulled herself into the saddle and clutched My Maria's reins while Develyn mounted. "This is going to be a crazy day. I want to get focused before it gets out of control."

Develyn rode up beside Casey. "Ms. Cree-Ryder wants her life focused?"

"You see, you are rubbing off on me."

"I don't know, you are still the bronze bombshell."

"I don't mean that pathetic white skin. Actually, you are so tan now you could pass for a . . . a . . . Nevadan."

"Is that good?"

"As long as you stay out of Vegas and Reno."

"Where are we going?"

"It doesn't matter."

"You want to see the springs where Coop is going to build?"

"Sure."

Develyn buttoned her long-sleeved denim shirt like a coat and tugged down her new hat. She led the way when the trail dropped down to the tiny creek, then back up on the sage and brown grass prairie. Uncle Henry shuffled along about twenty feet behind.

"Now, will you tell me what this is all about?" Develyn asked.

"You and I need a private talk. I figured this would be a good excuse."

"What's the subject."

"First, me."

"You? Could this be about you and Mr. Jackson Hill?"

Casey's thick lips broke into a wide grin. "Yeah. He asked me to marry him."

Develyn spun My Maria around to face Casey. "And you waited until now to tell me?"

"You and Dee were asleep when I came home. I mean, I don't have a ring yet. We just sort of agreed to get engaged."

Dev turned back for the cedar ridge to the north, and the ladies rode side by side. "How did that come about?"

"Well, we were parked in front of the cabin last night, making out, and Jackson's hand slipped into . . ."

"I don't want to know this. That's too much information. What I want to know was how did he propose?"

"That's what I'm getting to. His hand . . ."

"Casey, I don't want to know where his hand was or your hands were, your lips or . . ."

"Relax, Ms. Worrell. His hand slipped into his pocket, and he pulled out a poem he had written and read it to me."

"A poem?"

"Yes, Mother, a poem about a search for someone to share a life with and a future with children, horses, and a '65 blue Mustang convertible."

"Jackson has a '65 Mustang?"

"No, but he doesn't have a wife and kids either. It's what he wants. Then he asked if I'd be the one to help all those dreams come true."

"That's sweet."

"He's wonderful, Dev."

"So what did you tell him?"

"I said, 'Heck yeah, I'll marry you.'"

"But you didn't say it that way." Develyn paused. "You did say it that way?"

"Heck yeah, I did."

"OK, but you know what I am going to tell you."

"That we've only known each other a couple of weeks? That's why we want to get engaged. We figure it will accelerate our relationship, and we'll find out what we are really like."

"So you aren't getting married right away?"

"Of course not. We want to wait until the fifteenth."

"Of what month?"

"August."

Develyn choked. "That's ten days from now!"

"You see, I said we were willing to wait. I'm just teasing you, Mama. I told him I would not marry him until ten months after he gives me a ring. That makes it next June."

"Why ten months?"

"Because I don't want anyone thinking he's marrying me because I'm . . ." Casey's hand went to her mouth. "Sorry, Dev."

"That's OK. Delaney has her trail to hike. You have yours."

"Anyway, Jackson wanted us to focus on really getting to know each other for a while."

"How's that going to work out with him working up at Glacier Park?"

"He's moving to Casper."

"When?"

"He's going to call his boss today."

"But he doesn't have a job."

"He said he'll find one. He loves me, Dev. He wants to be

164

with me all the time. You and Jackson are the only two people I've ever known that like to be with me, day after day. Not even my mother could stand it every day."

"I'm very happy for you."

"Good. Will you talk to Jackson?"

"Why?"

"I told him I could not agree to marry him until he talked to Mama."

"But, I'm not . . ."

"Please, Dev."

"What do you want me to say to him?"

"Pretend that you really are my mother. What would you want to ask him? I need to know that someone smarter than me asked all the right questions."

"What makes you think I'm smarter than . . ."

"Please talk to him."

"OK, Casey. I'll visit with your man. I want to find out if he is worthy of the sweetest, kindest, most tenacious half-breed on the planet."

"You forgot the bronze bombshell part."

"That goes without saying."

"Go ahead and say it."

"The most tenacious bronze bombshell on the planet."

"Thank you."

"When am I going to have this visit with Mr. Jackson Hill?"

"Today. When I go to Riverton with Delaney, you and Jackson can talk." Casey stared at the landscape. "Where is Cooper going to build his house?"

"Up in those cedars. You want to race?"

"Remember the first race we had this summer?"

"I remember I sailed right over My Maria's head and landed in the dirt."

"How many times have you been bucked off this summer?"

"Six or seven," Dev replied. "Who's counting?"

"You've toughened up on the outside. How about on the inside?"

"Now you are getting personal. Are we going to race or not?"

Casey slapped Popcorn and shouted as she galloped toward the distant mountain range.

My Maria bolted after the Appaloosa, and within a couple of minutes had pulled into the lead. Develyn's backside pounded leather until she found the paint mare's stride. Then she transferred most of the jolt into her knees and legs. The strong crosswind cooled the left side of her face and brought early morning chills to her arms.

This is what I will miss most of all, Lord. Oh, how I love to gallop like the wind. Why is that? It's on the verge of being reckless. On the edge of danger. One step away from being slammed to the dirt. It's like my life had become so routine, so safe, so predictable I could go through every day, every week, every year without a thought. I existed in such a rut, it takes so little of my mind or body or soul. I shoved myself out into a mental swamp and coasted for years. Finally, this summer, it's as if I came to a dead stop and learned how to paddle all over again.

I like it, Lord.

I like feeling alive. Maybe I was right. Maybe that day when Dee was a baby was the day I stopped really living and just tried to survive.

No more.

Develyn reached the creek at the bottom of the cedar ridge and turned My Maria north along the bank. She slowed the mare to a canter, then to a trot, and waited for Casey Cree-Ryder to catch up.

"You two are getting faster every week." Casey reined up beside Develyn.

They dismounted and let the horses drink the gurgling water.

"I like running the prairie, but I still get nervous winding through the trees," Develyn admitted.

"You think we should turn back?"

"Let me show you our . . ."

"Our?"

"I don't know where that came from."

"Your heart?"

"This has been a strange summer, Casey. For years I have not given any man more than two glances, and now . . ."

"You have them waiting in line."

They mounted and rode up the creek.

"No, they aren't waiting in line, but I've learned a lot about myself from each of them."

"It's been a good summer for me too."

"Well, it was the Lord's leading that brought four special men into my life."

Develyn heard a familiar bray from far behind them.

"Five," Casey laughed.

"Poor dear." Develyn watched as the burro approached. "Those short legs get tired so fast."

"So where are you and Coop going to build your house?"

"Coop's house. But I get to decorate it. It will be fun."

"So you do plan on coming back?"

"Are you kidding? I was promised that I get to be matron of honor."

"Only if you keep that tan."

"I promise to visit the tanning salon every week until the wedding."

They trotted up to the clearing. "This will make a good place for a house, don't you think?"

"It's wonderful," Casey said. "You'll love it."

"Countess, I told you I'm an Indiana schoolteacher through and through. I'm not leaving Crawfordsville until it's time to retire."

"You can spend your summers in your Wyoming house and your winters in your Indiana house. Other married people do things like that."

"If I'm married, I intend to spend my winters in my husband's arms. Not a thousand miles away."

"You don't think any of them would want to move to Indiana with a cute, perky forty-five-year-old?"

Develyn laughed and led My Maria across the clearing. "Think about it: could you see Quint Burdett living in a white-brick ranchette-style home in central Indiana where the neighbor kid works on motorcycles until two in the morning and the biggest event of the year is the Covered Bridge Festival?"

"Probably not."

"How about Renny? You think that mustang breaker would be satisfied to lead llamas around the school petting zoo at the annual fall carnival? And the only cowboy hats he'd see have pink-dyed duck feathers for a hatband?"

"No, I don't think Renny could survive that," Casey concurred. "How about Coop?"

"Honey, Coop thinks Argenta is a town. He won't build where the cabins are because it's too crowded."

"Are you saying you are going to reject all three of them?"

Develyn frowned. "I just want to take care of my Dee this summer and let everything else fall into place. I might daydream but not too much. Reality keeps tugging me back."

"What is reality?"

"Are you going to get philosophical on me?"

"I promise not to quote Jean Paul Sarte or Rene Decartes, but sometimes it seems the thing we call reality is the fence we construct to guard our world. Self-imposed limits, so to speak. What if we tore down those walls and just said, "Lord, you can do anything you want with me.' What do you think might happen?"

Develyn dropped the reins around the saddle horn, raised her arms in the air, and shouted, "Here I am, Lord! You can do anything you want with me!"

At the sound of her shout, My Maria lunged forward. Develyn tumbled off the back of the horse, landing on her hands and knees in the dirt.

"Oh, that's what would happen?" Casey laughed. "In that case, I don't think I'll do it."

"How can that happen again?" Develyn staggered to her feet and looked at her hands. "I used to have nice-looking fingernails. I haven't had this much dirt crammed in them since Mari Clennen broke her ant farm in the girls' bathroom during the talent show."

Develyn swung back into the saddle. "You know, I will not miss being bucked off."

"You weren't bucked off. You just fell off. My Maria didn't buck at all."

"Did you say that to make me feel better?"

Casey laughed. "No, I just want the story to come out right in the teachers' lounge back in Crawfordsville."

"I have no intention of confessing each time I was bucked or fell off a horse."

"I'm going to tell them. Remember, I'm going to come visit you between Thanksgiving and Christmas."

"You intend to go tattle about everything that happened this summer?"

"I'm going to title my report, 'Ms. Worrell's Summer Vacation.'"

"Hmmm, well, I'm going to try not to fall off again before I go."

"Are you running out of gas?"

170

"What are you talking about?"

"There's a gas can chained to the tree over there."

Develyn looked around. "Oh, that belongs to Hunter Burke. He asked if he could leave it there. It seemed a little strange, but Coop didn't mind."

"It's strange to me."

"That's what I thought. If he needed more fuel, why not carry it on the back of his ATV?"

"The strange part is that gas can has a seam in the middle."

"What does that mean?"

They rode over to the red Jeep can that was chained to an eight-foot cedar.

Casey pointed to the can. "There's a hinge on this side. It opens up in the middle."

"Like some kind of secret compartment?"

"It's not too secret. I spotted it across the clearing."

Develyn swung down out of the saddle and handed the reins up to Casey.

"Can I open it without unlocking the chain?"

"Give it a try."

Develyn unhooked the latch and lifted up the top of the can. "The top's heavy. I think it has gas." She peeked inside. "Oh, my!"

"What's in there?"

Develyn slammed the top back on the gas can. "Bullets."

"What?"

She opened the gas can again. "There are six boxes of .38-special bullets."

"That's for a handgun. Is there a gun too?"

"No, just bullets." Develyn stared across the clearing. "But he did say he was sizing up hunting grounds for later this year. Maybe he wanted to store up some bullets too."

"He's not going to hunt elk with a .38-special handgun. Besides, no one is such a bad shot they need a hundred bullets for hunting."

Develyn mounted up. "What are you saying?"

"You stash bullets where you think you'll need them."

"You think we should tell someone?"

"Tell your Coop. He'll know what to do."

"My Coop. First it was my Quint, then my Renny, and now it's my Coop?"

"You have a possessive nature."

"I've been told that."

"By your other daughter, I suppose?"

"Yes."

"That's the other reason we needed an early morning ride. She wants me to go with her to the doctor. What kind of advice do you want me to give her? Dev, I'm not smart enough to figure out my own life, let alone someone else's."

"Casey, I know Dee's made some mistakes. I just don't want her to compound them."

"You mean like get an abortion?"

"She said she didn't want that, but I don't know what kind of doctor she'll be seeing. I don't want her talked into something she'll regret. If she's pregnant, I'd like for her to find some direction, make some plans to take care of herself and her baby."

"You want me to tell her all that?" Casey asked.

Develyn mounted the paint mare. "No, sweet Casey. Just be yourself and be her friend. No girl needs two mothers."

● ● ●

Develyn showered, pulled on clean jeans and a yellow blouse, and was putting on her makeup when Delaney crawled out of bed. "How are you feeling?"

"I'm OK. Did we get in another argument, or was that a dream?"

"I believe we had a difference of opinion about your dating Hunter Burke."

"Yeah, that's what I thought." Delaney studied her mother. "Mom, do you have any idea what it's like going through life with a cute mother?"

"Thanks, Sweetie. I never thought about it much."

"I can't remember how many people have said, 'Delaney Upton? Are you the one with the cute mother?'"

"Who said that?"

"Or the one I like best: 'So, you're Develyn's daughter. You look just like your father.'"

Develyn studied the oval mirror and used her fingertips to rub cream into the lines around her eyes. "Dee, people always say dumb things. I was always ask, 'Why can't you be more like your mother?'"

"Who ask you that?"

"My mother." Develyn touched up her eyelashes with black mascara.

"Mom, did you ever get elected homecoming queen or prom queen or something like that?"

"Why would you ask that?"

Delaney crawled out of bed and spun around in her extra-long pink T-shirt. "I don't know. I think since Brian lost interest in me this summer, I've been feeling ugly. I'm twenty years old. This is me. I can't pretend any more that when I grow up I'll look like my mother. I'm never going to be as cute as you."

Develyn turned and put her hands on Delaney's shoulders.

"Honey, we will always look different. That's the way God created us. Until the twelve-year-old boys elected me rodeo queen last week, I had never been queen of anything. You've seen my old high school annual. I didn't turn anyone's head with my looks, that's for sure. I was the sassy bulldog who put everyone, especially the boys, in their place."

"You turned Daddy's head."

Develyn hugged her daughter. "Yes, honey, I believe I did, for a while. But that's the point. When the Lord leads you to the right man, you will turn his head, and he will think you're the cutest thing on the face of the earth. And you know what?"

"What?"

"You won't give a squat what anyone else thinks. None of us has to be cute for all men, just for that one man."

"Is that why you fix yourself up so good?"

"Yes," Develyn laughed. "I never know when that one man will walk into my life."

The front door of the cabin swung open.

"And there he is. My prince charming."

"It's obvious that he loves you," Delaney grinned.

"I know. We have this sort of animal magnetism between us."

"You make a lovely couple."

"Thank you, honey." Develyn strolled to the front door. "Uncle Henry, I told you not to open the front door. If you keep doing that, I will not let you sleep on the porch. Now go on."

The short brown burro glanced over his shoulder toward the road but didn't budge.

Develyn stepped to the porch edge and shouted, "Leon, you go home right now. I will not have you harassing Uncle Henry."

Delaney stepped to the doorway.

Cooper Tallon stepped down out of the travel trailer by the corrals. "You need any help, Dev?"

"Morning, Coop," she called out. "No, I can handle this." She stepped out in the yard. "Leon," she shouted, "I will be running Mrs. Tagley's store the next few days. I will not sell you a Little Debbie unless you stop this. Go home!"

A twelve-year-old in camouflage pants and T-shirt crawled out from under Casey's horse trailer. "That ain't fair. Your pony snitched on me."

"Yes, he did. Leon, you are not allowed in this yard unless I am outside. Is that clear?"

"If I stay out of your place, will you give me a Little Debbie?"

"I will sell you one if you have the money."

Leon trudged back down the long driveway, then turned. "Why do you make your old man sleep in the trailer?"

"Mr. Tallon is not my 'old man.'"

"He looks old to me," Leon shouted, then trudged on out toward the road.

"Sorry about that comment, Coop."

"Hey, I am old."

"Mr. Tallon, you are not old."

"Well, that makes two things I'm not," he murmured. "I'm headed for Casper. You need anything?"

"I don't think so. I'll be going in myself later to see Mrs. Tagley."

"I'm going to borrow a truck and skip-loader and clean up that burnt cabin. Are you sure there's nothing more to salvage?"

Develyn stared across the yard to the charred ruins. "I don't think so. Most of it belonged to you. You should be more discreet whom you rent to, Mr. Tallon."

"I reckon renting to you was the smartest thing I've ever done."

"Thank you, sir." Develyn studied the yard, then turned back to the cabin.

She glanced at Delaney. "Where's Casey? I thought she was grooming the horses."

"While you were in the shower, she and Jackson went down to open the store."

Develyn raised her eyebrows. "I'd better get down there."

"Mother, Casey is thirty years old. She doesn't need you to watch her like she was thirteen."

The long, deep sigh caused Develyn's shoulders to relax. "You're right, Dee. Sometimes I just can't stop being a fifth-grade teacher."

"I know, Mom."

"I presume, from your tone, that you're thinking about our discussion about Hunter?"

"Yeah."

"Dee, to be real honest, I'm troubled by him. There are some puzzling circumstances. But I can't explain why I'm so uneasy."

"I'm not troubled."

"Well, I am. But I refuse to treat my beautiful daughter like a twelve-year-old. So the decision is yours."

"That sounds so good to my ears."

"That I'll let you make your own decisions?"

"No, the 'beautiful daughter' remark."

"Dee, I've called you pretty all your life."

"Yes, most all mothers do that. But somehow this summer it means more."

"I'm headed down to the store to check up on . . ."

"Inventory?"

Develyn laughed. "Yes, I'm checking on the inventory of bronze bombshells."

• • •

Develyn gaped over the top of her sunglasses at the brown, large-eared animal that meandered next to her toward Mrs. Tagley's store. "Now, honey, if you stay down at the store today, Leon might try to torment you. If that happens, you just go home, OK?"

Ms. Worrell, it's 8:00 a.m. You've been up for three hours, been riding, and now you're hiking down a dirt road talking to a burro. It's windy yet hot, and there isn't a person in sight. You are in the middle of Wyoming, and the first day of school is less than two weeks away. This can't be real. I'm sure it's a green chile frozen burrito that I got at the mini-mart on my way home, and I'll wake up in Crawfordsville with a really bad stomachache and two naughty cats.

Well, one naughty cat.

The alarm will ring, and I'll . . .

She stopped.

See? There it is . . .

"My cell phone?"

"Hi, Devy, where are you right now?"

"Lil'! I'm on a dirt road in the middle of Wyoming."

"Are you sitting down?"

"On the dirt road? Of course not."

"Is there anyone with you?"

"Uncle Henry."

"Burros don't count as anyone."

"Don't tell Uncle Henry that. What is this all about?" Develyn shoved her sunglasses on top of her head. "Lily Martin, did you get married?"

178

"Not yet."

"What do you mean, not yet?"

"Well, I was asked."

"Oh my, really? Oh, wow. Yes Honey! I'm so excited I could . . ."

"Well, don't do it in the middle of the road. You didn't ask what I said back to him."

"You said yes, of course."

"No, I didn't."

"You turned him down?"

"No. I said I would have to get my sons' approval and . . ."

"They approve, don't they?"

"Yes, they do and . . ."

"So when's the date?"

"Would you let me finish? I told him he'd also have to have the approval of Ms. Develyn Worrell."

"Me?"

"You'd do the same, wouldn't you?"

Ask for Lily's approval before I said yes?

"Wouldn't you?" Lily pressed.

"Oh, yes. I would want your opinion, that's for sure."

"So I want you to give us your blessing."

"I approve, I approve," Develyn giggled.

"You haven't met him."

"Lil, you've been happier this summer than anytime I've ever known you. I hear it in your voice every time I talk to you. I want you to be this happy the rest of your life."

"Sweetie, for the first time in years, I think that dream might come true, but I want you to meet him first."

"I'll be home in a week."

"I know. I thought we might speed that up a little."

"How? Aren't you in Wisconsin with Bart, Terri, and the kids?"

"We're in Denver, Dev."

"What? Denver? We?"

"I told you to sit down. Stewart and I are in Denver. We're going to rent a car and drive up and see you."

"Today?"

"Is it a bad time?"

"Lil', it's a wonderful time. I just can't believe it."

"When we get to Casper, I'll phone, and you can tell us how to find your dirt-road town."

"Lil, this is so great. I could kiss . . ."

"Which cowboy?"

"Uncle Henry."

"Girl, you've been in the wilderness too long."

"Lily, I've been wandering in the wilderness most of my life. But you are the one who is about to cross the Jordan. Are you actually going to stay a few days?"

"Four days, if that's alright. I know you are crowded in Argenta. We'll stay at the Holiday Inn Express in Casper."

"You already made arrangements?"

"One room on the third floor and the other on the second floor, Mama."

"Oh, good. I don't need three daughters to watch over."

"How are the other two?"

"One is back in the cabin trying to decide if she loves me or hates me."

"And the bronze countess?"

Develyn glanced at Mrs. Tagley's store. "She's cozy on the front porch of the store with Jackson Hill, and they are . . . oh, my!"

"Dev?"

"I've got to go, Lil. Call me from Casper."

"Stewart says we might spend some time in Cheyenne, so it could be late."

"Call me anytime. This is so exciting!"

"Me coming to see you, or what's happening on the porch?"

"Both."

8

Jackson Hill rose from his knees and lounged next to the wagon seat on the covered porch.

"Did you lose something?" Develyn asked.

"Look!" Casey pointed to the bench.

Develyn scanned the collage of carved initials.

"There . . . inside the heart!" Casey grinned.

"Oh, J. H. plus C.C.R? Does that mean Jackson loves Credence Clearwater Revival?"

Casey stuck out her tongue.

"How's the store?"

"It wasn't what I expected at all," Jackson said.

"Disorganized?"

"Just the opposite. Mrs. Tagley has charts under the counter about what products should be on each shelf, how many should be there, and what her wholesale price is. It's incredible record keeping. This might be the easiest store in Wyoming to run."

"Good for her." Develyn led them into the store's main room. "She once told me that she writes everything down so she won't worry about forgetting things. She's quite a lady for being ninety-four."

"Her records show she's getting a delivery in the morning from the wholesale outfit in Casper," Jackson explained. "There won't be enough money in the till to pay for it. What do you think we should do?"

Develyn tapped the counter with her fingers like a snare drumroll. "I'll ask Mrs. Tagley this afternoon."

A loud bray from the yard bought all three back to the front door.

"Your watch-burro is having problems," Casey said.

"I'm sure it's Leon. He's decided to torment Uncle Henry. I'll take him back to the cabin and put him in the corrals with Coop's horses."

"Leon?" Jackson grinned.

"Hmmm, I'm tempted. I'm sure you two can take care of the store for a while by yourselves."

"Oh, no more hovering over me?"

"Nope, you're on your own, girl."

"I didn't mind you treating me that way."

"I mind. I need to learn to be different."

A second bray scurried Develyn out on the porch. "Leon, what did you throw at Uncle Henry?"

The dark-haired boy gawked from behind the tree. "A carrot. I thought he looked hungry."

"Uncle Henry does not eat carrots."

"Sure he does, look at him."

The burro licked a dusty carrot off the dirt and began to munch on it.

"Baby, don't put that dirty thing in your mouth!" She dashed over to the startled burro.

"What are you doing now, Ms. Worrell?" Casey called out from the porch.

"Uncle Henry . . ."

"He's acting like an animal. You don't want him to be a fifth-grader, too, do you?"

Develyn folded her arms and ground her teeth. "You're right, Casey, Uncle Henry can eat anything he wants. But I am going to lead him home and put him in the corrals."

An off-key trumpet blasted, and Leon scampered back toward his grandmother's.

Develyn scooped up three dirty carrots and hiked back toward the cabin.

Lord, this is a lot harder than it looks. How do you do it? How do you give all us sinful, rebellious people so much freedom? I have a tough time letting a wild burro eat carrots off the dirt. Or allowing a thirty-year-old woman spend time alone with anyone she wants. How do you sit back and let us do so many questionable things?

Uncle Henry snapped his teeth. She gave him another carrot.

WISH I'D KNOWN YOU TEARS AGO

"Perhaps I haven't been giving you a very balanced diet. I'm not sure I've had one either. Some things will be nice to return to. But then, I don't eat well at home either." She stared at the carrots. "No, honey, I'm not going to eat one of your dirty treats. There is no telling where it came from."

The rumble of a vehicle behind her caused Develyn and Uncle Henry to scoot over to the side of the dirt road. A huge motor home towing a horse trailer and sporting Kansas license plates pulled up beside them. The tinted, electronic window yawned open. A man with a buckskin shirt and raccoon fur hat leaned out.

"Howdy, ma'am. Do you speak English?"

Develyn studied his sunburned face, then glanced at the heavyset woman wearing a calico dress and bonnet. *I have never been asked that in my life.* "Yes, I do."

"Oh, good. I'm Mean Missouri River Marvin, and this mountain mama is Two-Shoes Katie."

The woman in calico rolled her eyes. "I'm Katherine."

"Is this the trail to the rendezvous?" he asked.

"Which rendezvous are you talking about?"

"The Mountain Man rendezvous and black powder shoot."

"Where is it held?"

"On Rawhide Creek at the base of Carter Mountain," he said.

"I'm not familiar with those places."

"It's on the Pitchfork Ranch," Katherine explained.

"Two-Shoes Katie, I told you we weren't going to call it that," the man scolded.

"Marvin, I told you not to call me Two-Shoes until we got

186

to the rendezvous. Until then, I'm an accountant's wife from Topeka."

"Never mind Two-Shoes. She's peeved because she spent yesterday out in the sun gathering genuine buffalo chips."

Develyn glanced over at the lady. "Really?"

"That part is true. Mr. Everything Authentic insisted we spend the day gathering genuine buffalo chips. The man at the Buffalo ranch thought we were crazy, of course."

"We'll be the only ones at the rendezvous with genuine buffalo chips," he boasted.

Develyn swiped her blonde bangs off her forehead. "Well, the Pitchfork Ranch is west of Meeteetse. Go back out to Highway 20, drive up through Thermopolis, then follow the signs. I think you'll turn west right near the creek. That should get you in the neighborhood."

Katherine stood, then pointed to the back of the motor home. "Well, we aren't there yet, and I want some coffee." She glanced out at Develyn. "Would you like a latte?"

"I would love one, if you have some half-and-half. You have an espresso machine?"

"Yes, it helps me keep in touch with reality. You can call me Katie, but leave off the Two-Shoes."

"I'm Develyn."

"Ah-hah! Devil Woman, that's . . ."

"Marvin!" his wife snapped.

He winced when the pointed elbow clipped his shoulder. "Anyway, I can't take the highway. We want to follow Ol' Gabe's trail."

"Old Gabe?" Develyn asked.

"Jim Bridger."

"You're looking for the Bridger Trail?"

"Yep."

"If you continue east along the railroad tracks, this road will turn north. The first dry gulch you cross will have a narrow trail high on the north rim. That path is said to be part of the Bridger Trail."

"Can I drive the motor home down it?"

"I don't think so. There isn't any road."

"I can drive this sucker across any terrain."

"You can't drive an ATV down it, let alone a motor home. I would guess that even Uncle Henry would have trouble in places. Besides, the trail is washed out after . . ."

"Can I hire your Uncle Henry to act as scout?"

She pointed to the donkey. "Uncle Henry is my burro."

"How much you want for him?"

"He's not for sale."

"I'll rent him. Give you five hundred dollars for two weeks. He can lead the way down the Bridger Trail."

"He's not for rent either. I didn't say he knew the trail, just that it wasn't much wider than him in places. You'll need to go back to the highway."

"I didn't drive all the way out here from Topeka just to cruise down a blacktop road. No, ma'am, this is an authentic rendezvous. I'm following Bridger's trail wherever I can."

Katherine appeared at the window. "Hand this down to Develyn."

Develyn took the Styrofoam cup. "Thank you very much."

"Marvin, you heard her. We need to go back to the highway."

"Two-Shoes, we are going on the Bridger Trail. I can feel it in my bones."

"All I can feel is a migraine coming on," Katherine said. "I'm going back to take a nap."

"Follow this road, then turn right just past the first creek?"

"Turn left," Develyn corrected.

"Got it. We're a comin', ol' Gabe, we're a-comin'."

The giant travel home lurched forward in a swirl of thin, yellow dust.

"You know what I'm thinking, Uncle Henry? There are worse things than being forty-five and single. My life seems quite sane and peaceful." She took a sip. "Two-Shoes Katie knows how to make a good latte."

Develyn spied the white Ford pickup the minute she turned up the long dirt driveway to the cabin.

Hunter Burke? What's he doing here at this time of the day? What's he doing here at all? She said she had a date tonight. It is not night.

Develyn tried to pace herself but refrained from jogging.

Why aren't they on the porch? Where is he? If he's in the cabin, this is going to stop, and it's going to stop right now. I don't know this man. Delaney doesn't know him.

She shoved open the unpainted wooden door. "Delaney?"

The shadows of the cluttered room came into focus. "Dee, where are you?"

Develyn breezed through the cabin and back out the front door.

"Delaney?"

She stomped to the white pickup. *They had better not be in that truck. I don't see them, but that doesn't mean . . .* She jerked open the front door on the passenger side, then the extended cab door. When she did, a handgun tumbled to the dirt beside her feet.

She stared at it, glanced around at the empty yard, then picked up the gun. *A 38 special?* When she shoved it in behind the seat, she noticed several rifles.

Are those hunting guns? How would I know what's a hunting gun? Everyone in Wyoming has some kind of gun in their rig.

She eased the door closed and walked back toward the cabin. "Delaney!"

The voice was distant. "Out here, Mom!"

Develyn scurried to the pasture. Hunter Burke and Delaney stood next to My Maria.

"Your mare got tangled in some wire, Mrs. Worrell. I just stopped to get the wire loose," Hunter called out.

"She did?"

Delaney and Hunt strolled back toward the gate.

"It was lucky that Hunt came along when he did," Delaney said.

"Yes, well, thank you, Hunter. I appreciate that."

He tipped his hat that revealed no tan line on the forehead. "No problem, Mrs. Worrell. I was on my way to . . ."

"To see your friend, Billy?"

"Yep."

"Don't let us keep you."

"Mother."

"Honey, I know you and Casey need to go to town. You'll want to change clothes."

"I will?"

"You walk Hunter to his truck. I'll see what you have that's clean."

"Everything's clean. We just bought all new clothes, remember?"

"Oh, good, that should make it easy. Thanks again, Hunter."

"Yes, ma'am." He tipped his hat and sauntered to the white Ford truck.

From the cabin window, Develyn could see Delaney leaning through the open window.

I don't understand this, Lord. Why am I so paranoid about Hunter? It's as if there's a bear prowling outside, and I want to pull my baby to safety.

Develyn felt a deep release when Hunter drove away and Delaney started for the cabin.

"You were rude, Mother. I have plenty of time to get to the doctor."

"I'm sorry for that. And I'm sorry about the clothing remark. I shouldn't have said that. I wouldn't go to the doctor in denim shorts and a tank top with my belly button showing, but you can wear whatever you want."

"Mother, you wouldn't wear anything that exposed your belly button."

"Probably not, but I'm from a different generation." *Maybe a different world.*

"You know what, Mother? I've never seen your belly button."

"Nonsense."

"No, really, you always wear one-piece bathing suits. I do not know what my own mother's belly button looks like."

"Honey, you know me. I'm not comfortable wearing clothes like that."

"I didn't say you had to wear hip-huggers and short shirts. It just dawned on me that I have never seen your belly button."

Develyn chewed on her tongue, then sighed. She untucked her blouse and yanked it up a few inches. "There!"

Delaney giggled. "Wow, I can't believe you did that."

Develyn felt her face redden. "Neither can I."

"You have a cute belly button, Mom."

"Thank you. I've never considered a belly button cute."

"You ought to pierce it and wear a ring."

"Absolutely not. There's no way I'm going to pierce anything else. Not my belly button, not my nose, not my eyebrow, not my anything. The ears were bad enough, but no more."

"Why don't you just come right out and say what you think, Mom? No reason to beat around the bush," Delaney laughed.

Develyn hugged her daughter. "I've never been one to keep my opinions to myself. How about you? What do you have pierced, besides your ears?"

"Do you really want to know?"

"Probably not," Develyn said. "Just tell me that you didn't pierce your . . ."

"I didn't."

"Good."

"Of course you didn't ask me about the tattoo."

"What tattoo?"

"The rose one."

"Do I want to know where it is?"

"No."

"Let's change the subject."

Delaney pulled her hair back. "Why were you so rude to Hunt?"

"Honey, I told you. He makes me nervous. There's something about him . . ."

"You too?"

"No, I get a feeling inside that . . ."

"I know. There's a cool mystery about him. Sort of like a young James Bond, right?"

"What?"

"Oh, my word, are you jealous of me, Mother? Do you like him too? Well, he likes me better, and you just can't handle that."

"That's absurd. I think . . ."

"This is a first. I made my mother jealous over some man."

"This conversation is turning bizarre."

"You are really jealous. Do you know how good that makes me feel?"

"Dee, that is not what I meant. I assure you, I am not . . ."

"Of course not, Mother. It would be too embarrassing to admit. I understand that. I have a hard time admitting all the times I was jealous of you."

"Of me?"

"This might be the most wonderful day of my life!" Delaney declared.

And when you get the doctor's report, it could be the most devastating.

● ● ●

Develyn was standing next to Jackson Hill when Casey and Delaney drove off to Riverton.

"What's the schedule now?" he asked.

"I'm going to have an orange Popsicle. Would you like one?"

"No, thank you. But I do want to look at the picture."

"What picture?"

"Of this guy named Hunter who says he knows me but never stops by when I'm around."

"Oh, yes, I left Coop's camera in Mrs. Tagley's living room yesterday. Get me two double-A batteries."

Develyn started into the store, but Jackson paused.

"What are the rules here? Am I allowed in the store at the same time you are?"

Develyn glanced at Jackson's thin, strong face.

"I must be about the most controlling person you ever met.

I'm sorry for being so bossy. You can come and go in the store as you like, whether it's me or Casey or whoever. I can't believe I told you two some of those things."

"You're a lot like my mother."

"Yes, it's the schoolteacher mind-set, no doubt."

● ● ●

They stood behind the counter inside the store as Dev fumbled to install the new batteries. "OK, let me turn it on. Here."

"That's cute," Jackson grinned. "Hunter looks a lot like Cooper Tallon."

"That's the wrong picture."

Develyn pressed the silver button again.

"There. Do you know this guy?"

"It's David."

"No, his name is Hunter Burke."

Jackson studied the picture closer. "No, it's David Vincent."

"Who's David Vincent?"

"A guy I went to high school with. He graduated two years behind me."

"Are you sure it's him?"

"Oh, it's David."

"I wonder why he changed his name?"

"I don't know. I haven't seen him since he went back east to college. He had a full ride to Yale."

"Hunter had a full scholarship to Yale?"

"I heard he got his master's at the University of Paris."

"This is not the same guy," Develyn insisted. "What did he major in?"

"History. Last I heard he was doing research at some big museum in New England."

"This is definitely not the same guy."

"I haven't seen him in eight years. If that's not David, I don't know who it is."

"I don't believe this Hunter graduated from Yale."

"Then there's no reason to tell you that I graduated *summa cum laude* with a degree in philosophy from Harvard?"

"You did? Jackson, that's . . . that's wonderful."

"No, I didn't. But for a second you believed it. That's my point. You believed it about me but not about him. How do you know the guy who calls himself Hunter Burke didn't graduate from Yale?"

"A point well taken, Mr. Hill. No more stereotypes. But the next time he stops by, I want you around to visit with him."

"Maybe he got that job up in Cody."

"What job?"

"Assistant curator. My mom knows his mother, and she said David applied for some important job at the museum in Cody."

"Wait a minute. You mean to tell me the man hanging around my daughter, the one who stashes gas and bullets out at Coop's springs, the one who showed up mysteriously when we had a flat tire, this guy is a Yale graduate and a museum curator?"

"Does it change your opinion of him?"

"Yes."

"Is he still creepy?"

"Yes, but now he's a highly intelligent creep."

Jackson leaned against the counter. "What do we do now, wait for the lines of customers to flood in? I'll be the bag boy; you can be the cashier."

"I'm going to get my orange Popsicle and eat it outside."

He followed her out the door. "Casey said watching you eat a Popsicle is quite an event."

Develyn plopped down on the bench and tugged off the wrapper. "Oh, she did? Well, I do know how to enjoy every lick. Most people are rank amateurs."

"You don't have to just lick it. You can bite right into it. That way it doesn't spill on your shirt."

"I would have thought a man who graduated *summa summa summa* from Harvard would know better than that."

"I was sick the spring they had the confectionary consumption class," he laughed. "Perhaps you can school me."

"Always happy to enlighten those still dwelling in darkness. What you need to do is take long licks. You put your tongue at the base, near the stick, and lick all the way to the top."

"You never bite it?"

"Never. It kills the taste. You might as well chew an ice cube. And no matter what, you never, ever break it. There is only one Popsicle in a bag, not two."

"But there are two sticks."

"Look at the bag. What does it say?"

"Popsicle."

"Precisely. It does not say Popsicles. For full flavor and texture, the two sticks must remain in the ice until the last possible moment."

"That sounds like a very messy way to eat a Popsicle."

"Oh, it is a dull, boring lad who chooses function over flavor. How terribly sad to be thirty-two years old and never savor the exquisite yet delicate delight of the juice from an orange Popsicle."

"I was culturally deprived."

"And your mother a teacher? Oh, don't tell me she never taught you how to eat peanut M&Ms?"

"I don't suppose you pop them in your mouth and chew them up?"

"Oh, my heart. How could you suggest such a thing? No, my poor, wretched friend, you gently let the hard candy shell dissolve on the top of your tongue, rolling it over and over so you will hit the milk chocolate all at once. Then you let it sit on your tongue and slowly dissolve its cocoa bean juices. Finally, when the peanut is as naked as a baby's bottom, you reward yourself by crushing it between your teeth."

"I won't even ask what you do with an artichoke."

"Oh, heavens, I don't have enough time to teach you that. In some midwest colleges, you can major in artichokes."

Jackson flopped down on the bench beside her. "You don't exactly fit the stereotype of a fifth-grade teacher. You are a really funny lady."

"You know what, Jackson? I would never have launched into that tirade in Indiana. I have an image to uphold. But out here

I get to relax and cut loose. I like it. I don't like being serious all the time."

"Can we be serious for just a minute?" he asked.

"Sure."

"Ms. Worrell, I'd like to ask your permission to marry Casey."

Develyn patted his knee. "You don't need my permission."

"Casey wanted me to ask you. And I wanted to. You see, Casey wants to get married, and I want to marry her. But I'd surely like a third opinion on the matter. What kind of husband does she need, Ms. Worrell?"

"She needs a man who is strong yet gentle. But also very patient, someone with slow hands. Do you understand what I am saying?"

"Is that because of what happened when she was younger?"

"Yes, it is. Did she tell you?"

"She said you would tell me because it made her hurt too bad to have to tell it herself. Was she abused when she was a little girl?"

"Casey was raped by three men when she was about fifteen."

He sat straight up and slammed his fist into his knee. "Did they get arrested?"

"No, Casey was on her own, and there was no one to stand up for her. She was too humiliated to get a physical exam. She is one tough girl, Jackson. I can't think of anyone else I would rather have with me in some dark alley in Chicago. But she needs to be treated with extra tenderness in some areas."

"I think I figured that part out."

"She can be cocky, almost arrogant, aggressive; but inside she's scared of being hurt. Not physically. I'm convinced she'd take on the devil himself face-to-face, but she is scared of being emotionally hurt. Right now she is so scared that she might lose you."

"Lose me?"

"She loves you, Jackson, and wants you more than anything she has ever wanted."

"I love her, too, Ms. Worrell. What worries me most is what if I'm not the best she can do? What if there is someone better for her, and here I am trying to squeeze into her life?"

"She is a bold, fearless woman. She will go anywhere and do anything with you. She holds little regard for material possessions. Jackson Hill, you won't need much to support her at the level to which she is accustomed. But she will need continual assurance of your love. Her bravado is grand, but her self-esteem is low. Be patient."

"Sort of like you eating that dripping Popsicle?"

"Yes, I think so."

"Then you give us your permission?"

"You know I'm not related to Casey. But you two have my unreserved blessing to get married."

"I have one more request. Since Casey doesn't have any family, she's adopted you as a surrogate mom. Would it be alright if I adopt you as a surrogate mother-in-law?"

"Only if you promise never to tell any of those horrible mother-in-law jokes, no matter how true they might be."

"That's a promise."

"If I'm the mother-in-law, you have to bring the kids to see me so I get to babysit."

"Are you volunteering?"

"Yes, I am. Now, when will this wedding take place? Casey hints about waiting until next June, but somehow I just don't believe her."

"We have to get the jobs thing settled," he reported. "I can't support a wife on a wrangler's pay."

"What kind of job are you looking for?"

"It doesn't matter. I want to pay the bills and have lots of time to be happy. I've been chasing dreams my whole life with education, with rodeo, with ranch work . . . Casey is the first dream I've ever caught and the only one that matters. I'd love to be my own boss, but there aren't a lot of positions out there for a Harvard grad, *summa cum laude* in philosophy."

Develyn laughed and shook her head. "You can't fool me again, Mr. Hill." She noticed a drop of orange splash on the porch and leaned over for a long lick. "Let me guess. You graduated from junior college as a secondary education major, took a few classes at the University of Wyoming, then dropped out to be a big rodeo star. How close did I come?"

"You missed it by six hundred miles."

"Six hundred?"

"That's the distance between the University of Wyoming in Laramie and Montana State in Bozeman. But you are right about the major. Do all teachers' kids end up education majors?"

"Mainly those who admire their parents."

"Is Delaney an education major?"

"She was, but she changed it to communications after her freshman year. That was the first of many changes. Jackson, did you ever consider finishing college and getting your teaching degree?"

"Now you are sounding like my mama."

A white Buick sedan with Ohio license plates pulled into the dirt parking area in front of the store. Develyn watched as an older, white-haired man wearing a blue golf shirt, khaki Bermudas, black socks, and shoes emerged from the car and hurried around and opened the door for a woman in crisp white tennies that contrasted with the deep purple slacks and matching short-sleeved blouse. Arm in arm, they sauntered up to the porch.

Jackson stood and opened the door. "Good morning, and welcome to Argenta."

"Thank you. We pulled off looking for a store. This is a store, isn't it?" the lady asked.

"Argenta's finest."

The man grinned and nodded at Develyn. "I told my Barbara that it had to be open because there were young people on the porch eating Popsicles."

"Thank you for the compliment."

The lady offered a soft smile. "When you're our age, every-one is a young person."

As they entered the store, Develyn listened to Jackson's voice. "What can I find for you?"

"We need some of those cold/flu pills that fizz. I saw them on *Oprah* and felt like we need to take one before we get to Yellowstone."

The voices filtered through the screen door. Develyn leaned over to hear the conversation.

"This is a little store, but we do have two different types of pills for that. You may certainly buy that one. The other we have is a couple of dollars cheaper, and the May issue of *Consumer Today* rates it more effective. Buy whatever you are confident in, but my mother says the cheaper ones really work."

"Is that your mother on the porch?"

Develyn flopped back against the wagon seat and chewed on her Popsicle stick.

"No, my mother teaches school up in Sheridan. Every winter she used to get the same colds that the students got, but this stuff has kept her healthy the past couple of years."

"I was superintendent of schools for thirty-one years," the man proclaimed. "Let's take the young man's suggestion."

"Well, I hate to shun dear Oprah. Why don't we buy both, dear? That way we can compare."

Develyn rubbed her tennis shoe on the orange spot on the porch as if that would erase it. *You are a salesman, Jackson Hill. They will be inviting you to visit them any time now.*

When they emerged from the store, the man carried a small plastic bag. The lady toted an orange Popsicle.

She nodded at Develyn. "I haven't had one of these in years."

"They are very tasty."

The man led the way across the dirt yard. "Come along, Barb. We'll walk down to that corral and back for a little exercise."

The woman turned to Dev. "He won't let me eat it in the car. He's afraid I'll drip it on the leather seats. Says I eat them too slow."

"She just licks and licks and licks until she makes a mess," the man reported.

Develyn glanced at Jackson, who stood in the doorway. He shook his head.

●　●　●

She marveled at the number of customers who found their way to Mrs. Tagley's. She had just restocked the soda case when a honk from a large truck brought her out to the porch.

Cooper Tallon drove a dump truck with a trailered skip-loader towed behind. "I thought you might be here," he called out. "Did you pull everything out of the rubble that you want? The rest will be hauled off."

She glanced back. "You are on your own, Jackson. I'll stop back on my way to Casper to see Mrs. Tagley. Be sure and get something to eat for lunch. Help yourself to what's in her fridge. It will all spoil before she comes home."

She trotted out to the truck and could barely hear Jackson's "Yes, Mother."

"Hey, truck driver, can you give a girl a ride?"

"Sorry, lady, I never give rides to purdy women."

Develyn yanked her mouth wide open with her fingers and stuck her tongue out. "Is that ugly enough for a ride?"

"That will work," Cooper laughed. "Come on."

They pulled into the long driveway back to the cabin and noticed Leon running toward them. Cooper stopped the rig, and Develyn rolled down the window.

"I'm going home, and you can't talk me out of it," he cried.

"What's the matter, Leon?" she asked.

"I'm not going to play with him again."

"Play with whom?"

"I went up to let your pony mule out of the pen, and he bit me in the butt."

"Uncle Henry bit you?"

"It hurt."

"I'm sorry, Leon. I'll scold him."

"Tell him I ain't comin' back."

"I'll mention that."

Leon spun around. "Did he rip my jeans?"

Develyn noticed a half-eaten carrot sticking out of his pocket. "No, they are fine."

Leon pulled up his wrinkled red T-shirt and wiped his eyes. Develyn noticed foot-long, parallel scars sliced diagonally across his stomach. She reach into her pocket and pulled out three quarters. Develyn leaned out the window and handed them down. "Leon, why don't you stop by the store for a Little Debbie. Maybe that will make you feel better."

He grabbed the quarters. "Yes, ma'am," he grinned, "I reckon it will."

Cooper eased the truck and trailer into the yard. "I guess Uncle Henry gained a little respect."

"Yes. Did you see . . ."

"I saw."

"Do you think . . ."

"Those weren't scars from surgery, Dev. No one has parallel incisions. But they looked old. Do you know anything about Leon before he came to visit his grandmother?"

"No. I haven't heard a thing. It certainly changes my attitude."

Cooper drove on up the drive. "I reckon all of us have a few hidden scars."

9

The hum of the tires on the highway reminded Develyn of the band warm-up before a concert. Plenty of noise but no discernable melody. She turned on her Eagles CD and listened to half of *Hotel California*, then turned it off.

Maybe it's the caffeine. I'm so edgy. Too many loose ends. In a few days I need to drive home. Home to what? Home to my two cats . . . and my classroom of fifth-graders? No Quint. No Renny. No Cooper. No Casey. No Uncle Henry. No My Maria. Delaney said that she wants to live in West Lafayette, whether she goes to Purdue or not.

Will I just mope around at night and reminisce about summer? Will I go down to Greencastle on Sundays and have their potpie, then drive straight home? Will I vegetate in the living room with the lights out, watching a fake fire in the fireplace?

This summer has made a difference. I just don't know what the difference is yet. So much I don't know.

Lord, I'm not ready to go home. I wish the girls had returned from Riverton before I left. Why didn't Delaney call from the doctor's office? Maybe she just couldn't tell me. Casey could have called. Maybe there are complications. I should have gone with her. I should be there.

But she didn't want me to be.

I am determined to return to Indiana with a good relationship with my daughter.

I'm not putting pressure on you, Lord, but you've got about a week for that one.

Then there is poor Mrs. Tagley. She's outlived her family and friends. I want to encourage her, but I don't have the right words to say.

And I can't go home without knowing what Hunter Burke is up to.

And then there is Cooper. Dear Coop. The more I know about him, the closer I feel. What a joy to live close enough that we could be friends. He would be a great neighbor. He is a great neighbor.

I'm not going there, Lord. It's not about me.

I've got to get my mind off going home. I need to take care of some things today. Right now.

The small, battered, black pickup's headlights blinked behind her. Develyn glanced at the speedometer, then ahead at the hill. *I have no idea why you are blinking those lights.* When her eyes went back to the rearview mirror, the truck was nowhere in sight.

The whine of a small engine turned her head.

He's passing me? Uphill? Over a double yellow line?

A semitruck crested the hill and barreled down on the little truck. Develyn stomped on her brakes and pulled off the road to the right in a cloud of dust.

The small truck swerved south to the correct lane and shot on up the hill. The semitruck veered so quickly to the north that the right wheel lifted off the ground.

"Oh no!" Develyn groaned.

The tires slammed back down on the road. The truck and trailer skidded down the gradual embankment and came to a brake-squealing stop in the sage.

Develyn jumped out and sprinted toward the truck. By the time she reached it, the driver slid to the ground, bent over, with his hands on his knees.

"Are you alright?" she called out.

He stood up and hurried to tuck his shirt in. "Yes, ma'am. Thanks for stoppin'. That's way too close. I thought I was going to lose my lunch."

"I thought you were going to lose a lot more than that."

He looked back up the now-empty road. "What a jerk."

"I have a cell phone. Can I call anyone for you?"

"No, I'm covered. When I relax, I figure I'll be able to drive back up on the road. This old Peterbilt didn't tip over, so I should be able to get on down the road." He stuck out his hand. "I'm Max."

She shook his calloused hand. "I'm Dev."

"Say that again."

"I know it's unusual, but my name is Dev, D–e–v. That's short for . . ."

"For Develyn."

"How did you know? No one ever guessed my name before."

"We met once. I'll be. Can't believe I'd stumble across you out here."

She shaded her eyes with her hand. "Where did we meet?"

"Your sister introduced us."

"My sister?"

"Stef . . . she works at Thelma Lou's in Iowa. It was early summer, or was that last summer?"

"Of course!" Develyn pushed her sunglasses to the top of her head. "Max Knowlton from Tacoma."

"How did you remember that?"

"I don't know. I can just hear Stef calling your name."

"Ain't that somethin'? Was that this summer?"

"Yes, it was. But it does seem like a long time ago."

"Thanks for pullin' over when you did. If you'd held your lane, we'd all be in a pile."

"Have you seen Stef lately?" Develyn asked.

"I had me a chicken-fried steak there two nights ago. How about you?"

"I haven't talked to her since June, but I'll be stopping by in a week or so."

"If you were headin' west, I'd buy you supper in Lander."

"Thanks, Max. If I were heading west, I'd take you up on that. I'm going to Casper to visit a friend in the hospital. Mrs. Tagley is in her nineties and had a heart attack."

"Well, she's got my prayers, and you, too, Ms. Dev. You got a mighty fine sister. She treats every driver special."

"Thank you, Max. I'll tell her."

• • •

Develyn pulled into the first gas station in Casper and filled up the tank.

Well, Lord, you got my eyes off the future, alright. I can't believe the trucker was someone I knew. I don't think I know more than three truck drivers on the North American continent. Why Max? Why did you do that?

Stef? I haven't thought of her for weeks. I will definitely stop back and see her. Delaney will be with me.

I think.

Dev studied the tall gray-haired man who filled the tank of the silver Lincoln with Colorado plates ahead of her.

I think this was the station where I first met Cooper. That seems so long ago too. He invited me to the wild horse auction, and all of this began.

The lady on the passenger's side of the Lincoln fumbled with a cell phone.

They are dressed too nice for Wyoming. They must be from Colorado Springs or maybe Aspen. Her hairstyle reminds me of someone. Maybe my mother, but that's definitely not David.

The gas pump had just shut off when her cell phone rang. Develyn retrieved it out of the front seat. She stared at the back of the woman in the Lincoln.

"Hello?"

"Hi, Devy, we are in Casper now. We didn't even stop for lunch in Cheyenne but drove straight up. I just couldn't wait any longer. How can we find you? We won't need horses, will we?"

Develyn reached into the Jeep Cherokee and retrieved her straw cowboy hat. "Get out of that white Lincoln, Ms. Martin."

"White Lincoln? Dev, where are you?"

"Look in your side-view mirror, Lily girl!"

"Oh, my word . . . oh . . ."

Lily Martin slung the door open and flew out of the car. "Dev? What have you done to my Dev? You're as brown as Cindi Martinez. And the hat?"

"What were you expecting, Ms. Martin, some prissy Indiana schoolteacher type?"

Arms circled arms. The two women hugged and danced and giggled around the gas pump.

"I can't believe this. Look at you!" Lily shouted. "Look at you! You've gone native."

"Me? Me? Look at you." Develyn pointed at the tall man wearing a long-sleeved dress shirt and loosened charcoal gray silk tie.

"You're the one with Mr. Tall-and-Handsome!"

"Honey, how good it is to see you!" Lily tugged Develyn to the startled man.

He rubbed his narrow chin as if trying to decide which entrée to order.

"Stewart, this is my best friend in the whole world," Lily announced. "This is my Devy-girl."

"My word, that explains it." His thin lips broke into an easy smile that made him look more handsome but not younger. "I was expecting . . ."

Develyn pulled off her straw cowboy hat. "You were expecting an eastern schoolteacher?"

He held out his hand. "I'm delighted to meet you at last, Develyn. I don't believe a day has gone by all summer that you were not mentioned in conversation."

"Oh, my, I trust it was most often positive."

"Oh, yes," he murmured. "Most often, it was quite positive. I believe 'Dev is the classiest lady in central Indiana' came up often."

Develyn glanced down at the drips of orange on her jeans. "It's a good thing this is central Wyoming, not central Indiana."

Lily slipped her hand into Develyn's. "I can't believe we were at the same gas station."

"I wouldn't even have stopped here, but I had a near accident on the highway, and I decided to pull in." She looked up at Stewart. "Isn't this something?"

"I find the serendipitous sequence of events quite disarming," he mumbled.

"Don't you love the way lawyers talk?"

"It's been a while since I heard a man speak without a western drawl. I am so hyped that you came to Wyoming," Develyn said. "Have you guys checked into the motel yet?"

"We just drove through town, and I was anxious to phone you. What are you doing in Casper?"

"I'm on my way to the hospital to visit Mrs. Tagley."

"Who's Mrs. Tagley?" Stewart questioned.

"She's the lady your mother's age who runs the store in Argenta," Lily explained. "How is she doing?"

"That's what I hope to find out. She was more depressed than hurting yesterday."

"Why don't you go to the hospital? We'll check in; then we can meet for dinner," Lily suggested.

Before Develyn could answer, an old Dodge truck with a silver, two-horse trailer pulled in beside them.

A small face peeked out the jump-seat window behind the driver. The boy waved as the tall, thin driver scooted out.

"Ivan, how are you?" Develyn called out.

"Miss Dev, seein' you makes me happier than a coyote with a full moon. Is Renny with you?"

"Who's Renny?" Stewart mumbled.

"He's the mustang breaker," Lily whispered.

"No, Renny's in Twin Falls."

"You reckon he'll take that teaching job?"

"I don't know, Ivan. I think he's needed here."

"Right now, you're needed here." Ivan lifted the boy from the backseat and set him on the concrete.

Develyn squatted down. "Hi, Buster."

The little boy hopped from one foot to the other. "Hi, Devy. I've got to go to the bathroom."

"Yes, I can see that."

"Dev, Naomi's in the backseat. Would you watch her while I get Buster inside?"

Develyn looked into the pickup. "Sure, go ahead. Where's Lovie?"

"In Torrington, buyin' some horses."

"Well, hi, honey," Develyn cooed. She grabbed the baby, dressed in a diaper and ruffled pink T-shirt. She waltzed over to Lily and Stewart. "This is Naomi."

"My word, Ms. Worrell, did you adopt the entire state of Wyoming?"

"Now Stewart, Ivan, and Lovie had the mare that dropped the foal alongside the interstate that Renny and Dev had to help with. Remember when I told you that?" Lily said.

"You mean it was true? Things like that don't happen."

"They don't happen in Indiana," Lily corrected. She turned to Develyn. "Speaking of the baby, have you . . ."

"Not yet . . ."

"Did she go . . ."

"Today."

"With . . ."

"Yes."

"How will you . . ."

"She's supposed to . . ."

"When?"

"Any time now."

"Good heavens," Stewart said. "It's like the microphone cutting in and out at the Rotary meeting. Did you two have a complete conversation?"

A horn honked from a mud-splattered black Dodge pickup. The truck made a hard U-turn and bounced up on the sidewalk in front of the mini-mart gas station.

"Hey, Miss Dev, we came to town."

She glanced at the three cowboys in the front seat and one sitting in the back of the truck. "Hi, Cuban, Tiny, boys. How are you?"

"He doesn't look Hispanic," Stewart said.

"He's not," Lily replied.

"Is that your baby, Miss Dev?" Tiny called out from the back of the pickup.

"Boys, meet Miss Naomi. But I don't get to keep her. She belongs to Ivan and Lovie."

"I thought I recognized Ivan's rig," Cuban grinned. "Well, you look good with a baby, Miss Dev."

Holding the baby in one arm, she tipped her straw cowboy hat. "Thank you, Cuban. What happened to your hat?"

He pulled off his black felt cowboy hat and jammed his fingers through two holes in the brim. "Tiny shot it. We was havin' a shootin' contest."

"Did you lose or win?"

"I won," he grinned.

"I don't like losin'," Tiny mumbled from the back of the pickup.

"We got the rest of the week off."

"Is Quint still in Texas?" Develyn asked.

"Who's Quint?" Stewart asked.

"Cowboy number one," Lily explained.

"Yep, he's still down in Austin. But he sent word for us to take the weekend off. We don't have to be back until Monday," Tiny explained.

"Well, good for you."

"He must have changed his mind," Cuban added. "He gave us a list of chores a mile long before he and Lindsay flew off."

"Who's Lindsay?" Stewart pressed.

"Quint's daughter," Lily shushed.

"It ain't like the ol' man to give us that much time off, but we ain't complainin'," Cuban said.

"You want to go to a movie with us, Miss Dev?" Tiny asked.

She stared into the crowded cab of the pickup. "I think Naomi and I will pass. Boys, meet my friends from Indiana. This is Lily and Stewart."

"Don't that beat all. We met someone else from Indiana this summer," Tiny called out. "Who was that, Cuban?"

"It was Miss Dev, Tiny."

"Nah, she's from over in Sheridan, right, Miss Dev?"

"Cuban is right. I'm a Hoosier."

Tiny scratched his clean-shaven face. "You mean you wear those funny hats and drive buggies?"

"Never mind, Tiny. Maybe I am from Sheridan. You boys have a nice vacation."

"Yes, ma'am," Cuban said. "I've worked for the old man over fifteen years, and he ain't never let us off in August before."

"Are you sure you don't want to go to the movie with us? We'll buy your ticket and Junior Mints," Pete called out.

"Thank you, boys, for that generous offer. I need to go to the hospital to visit Mrs. Tagley. She had a heart attack yesterday."

"She did?" Cuban gulped. "No foolin'? Is she at St. Joseph's?"

"Yes."

"She always treated us square when we came to town. Tell her she's in our prayers."

"I'll do that."

Lily walked over and stood beside Develyn and the baby as they drove off. "Does every cowboy in the state know Miss Dev?"

"Of course not, it's just a coincidence."

Ivan and Buster sauntered out of the mini-mart, hand in hand.

"Well, young man," Lily beamed, "did you get your business done?"

"No, I peed right in the john mounted on the wall," he declared.

"Oh, yes, well," Lily stammered.

Develyn tucked Naomi back in the car seat.

"Hope she didn't trouble you," Ivan said.

"Oh, no, Naomi and I are pals."

"That's because you're both Wyomin' cowboy girls," he said. "And that's a whole lot closer than any sorority sisters ever could be."

"Tell Lovie hi for me. Hope she did well with the horses."

"After we get some feed, we're goin' to eat supper at Earl's or Else," Buster said.

"Miss Dev, you and Renny come see us sometime. It's been months since he stopped by for supper."

The Dodge pickup pulled back out into the street.

"You mean you just drive up unannounced at dinnertime?" Lily said.

"If I drove up to Ivan and Lovie's at suppertime, they'd be thrilled to feed me and insulted if I didn't spend the night. It's a different world."

"Are you still coming back to Indiana?"

"Yes, I am. I hear the new principal wants to move my classroom to the back of the building."

"That was one of several suggestions on the memo," Lily reported.

"I suppose I'll have to school him."

"He's from Idaho. You might be more persuasive if you wore that hat."

● ● ●

The lights were off in Mrs. Tagley's hospital room, but the setting sun filtered through the curtains and gave the room a soft glow like a dim fluorescent light.

"Come in, Devy."

"I was afraid you were sleeping."

"That's about all they let me do."

"How are you feeling today?"

"Tired, but they say that is normal."

"Can I get you anything?"

"Did you bring my other cosmetics?"

"Yes, I did."

"Well, turn on a light and help me with my makeup and hair."

Develyn pulled up a chair and dug into the black canvas bag.

"How are things at the store?"

"A number of tourists and the like. Oh, listen, honey, we noticed in your schedule you have some wholesale groceries to be delivered tomorrow. Do you want me to buy them?"

"Yes, and pay cash."

"Do you have a safe?"

"It's in the closet in my bedroom. Write down the combination."

Develyn grabbed a piece of paper. "If you'd rather I didn't get into your funds, I understand."

The elderly lady laughed. "Honey, what am I saving it for? If I have another heart attack tonight, I'm in the arms of Jesus. Why would I care what happens to it?"

"I just want to do what's right. I won't show anyone the combination; but if you don't mind, I'd like to have someone witness and sign a receipt for what I take out. That would make me feel better."

"Sure, Devy. That's fine. Who's helping you with the store?"

"Casey and Jackson Hill, mainly Jackson. He worked at a grocery store when he was in high school and college."

"Did I tell you his mother teaches up in Sheridan? I knew his grandmother. She was the only lady to catch more fish than me down in Wind River Canyon right after they opened the road through there. Those are good folks. Is Cree-Ryder going to marry him?"

"I believe so."

220

"I'll be; that's good. That's the best news I heard since Misti went back to Harold."

"Did you get to watch your soap today?"

"Yes, and it's a good thing. Do you know what that little tramp Tori did?"

"Oh, dear, what?"

"In my day we wouldn't talk like that at a doctor's convention, let alone standing in line at the bank."

Develyn brushed Mrs. Tagley's snow-white hair.

"Who's staying at my house?"

"We lock it up. Would you like someone on the grounds?"

"I've got all that room, and you girls crowded in that cabin. Someone ought to use it."

"We're all settled in."

"How about the Hill boy? Where is he staying?"

"At a friend's near Casper, I think."

"Have him stay at my house."

"That's nice of you. I'm sure he'll take care of things."

"Did I tell you I knew his grandmother?"

Develyn held her hand. "Yes, Mrs. Tagley, you told me already."

"I think I'm forgetting things, Devy."

"It's OK. It will take a little time to recover."

Mrs. Tagley turned her head away. "I don't want to lose my memory, Develyn. It's my life. It's me."

"Sweetie, you just enjoy today as well as the memories. Think of things in the future. Delight in things yet to be. I guess that sounds like a sermon."

She clutched Develyn's hand. "Devy-girl, are you going to marry him?"

"Me? Marry whom?" Develyn stammered.

"There's only one for you. You know that. All the rest was just stalling around until the timing was right."

"You think I should marry a man from Wyoming?"

"It doesn't matter what I think. I'm just reading your heart, and it wants that cowboy."

"But which one are you talking about?"

"You know in your heart which one, don't you?"

"I think I do. But I also think I want to change the subject."

"Just like Chet did today, when Millie asked him about the duffel bag with the black negligee at the beach house."

Develyn rubbed Mrs. Tagley's hands with aloe cream. "Yes, well, I have a question for you. What do you know about Mrs. Morton's grandson, Leon?"

"Besides the fact that he'll steal every Little Debbie he can get his hands on?"

"Yes. Where are his parents? What's their story?"

"It's sad, Devy. His daddy's in prison, and his mother's in a mental hospital. He's being raised in a state home in Cheyenne, but Mrs. Morton gets to have him every summer."

"What's the dad in jail for?"

"Trying to kill his mother."

"That does explain a lot."

"They found Leon next to his mother in the garage. He won't talk about it. If the neighbors had been any later, she would have died. Leon's dad tried to hang her. And he whipped Leon with the rope."

Tears puddled up in Develyn's eyes. "How could anyone do that?"

"Sin is ugly."

"And now Leon has to bear it all inside."

"He's out of control so much of the time. Poor Mrs. Morton doesn't know what to do. She says that someday he'll end up like his father. But I say the good Lord can redeem anyone. Even the likes of Leon Morton. They say at the state home all he does is hide in his room and play video games."

Develyn applied face cream, then foundation cream, then rouge and lipstick.

"How long will you be here?"

"If I don't die in a few days, they'll send me home."

"They said that?"

"More or less."

"You'll need someone to look after you for a while at home. Will Medicaid help with a home nurse?"

"Oh, Devy, when you are my age and have a business all these years with no family to dote on, there's no worry about money. But I don't know who would want to come live in Argenta, even for a few weeks. Besides, a nurse won't want to operate the store. I think I'd just be better off to die."

"Honey, don't say that. People out there need you. They count on you."

"Things change. Within a month I'll be part of their memory like the Argenta Dance Hall. I was quite a dancer in my day."

"I bet you were." Develyn held up the mirror. "There, you look good enough to dance."

Mrs. Tagley studied her image. "Seventy years ago I could turn every cowboy's head in the room. Now I'm just a very tired, very old lady."

"Let me smooth down your gown and raise your bed up a bit." Develyn fussed around the bed for a few moments. "Now you look like the queen ready to receive her subjects."

"Devy, sometimes I wish you lived in Argenta."

"Sometimes I wish it too."

A knock at the open doorway caused Develyn to spin around.

"Cuban? Tiny? Pete? T. J.?"

"Can we come in, Miss Dev?"

"Oh, yes."

One by one the four cowboys, hats in hand, filed into the room and next to the hospital bed.

Develyn stepped back next to the window and watched Mrs. Tagley's eyes light up.

"Boys!" Mrs. Tagley grinned. "It's nice to see you. You didn't have to come visit me."

"Yes, we did, Mrs. Tagley. You've been lookin' after us since we was in high school," Tiny said.

"I don't know how many times you bailed us out when we was busted," Pete added.

"I wouldn't have been able to buy my truck without you loanin' me that money," Cuban said as he stepped back from the bed. "You know, Miss Dev, what this lady did? I was drivin' back from a rodeo in Santa Fe. It was two in the mornin', and some drunks ran a stop sign and plowed into the side of my rig and totaled it. By the time it was breakin' daylight, I was at the phone booth in front of the hospital with about ten bucks to my name. It had cost me over $200 in the emergency room. I didn't know what to do. Mr. Burdett was out of town, so I called Mrs. Tagley at 5:00 a.m. and asked if she could wire me enough for a bus ticket home."

"And she sent you the money for a ticket?"

"I went to Western Union, and there was $25,000 and a note that I should buy myself a new truck, and she'd have some loan papers I could sign when I got home."

Mrs. Tagley waved it off. "Buses are so slow. I knew he'd want to get home sooner than that."

"She paid the doctor's bill when I ran into that baseball bat with my jaw," Tiny said.

"Baseball bat?"

"Victor Slade was trying to empty the Drifter's Social Club."

"Oh."

"Mrs. Tagley, you get yourself well. Knowin' you are there for us helps us keep pluggin' away. We need you in Argenta," Pete insisted.

T. J. just stood against the wall, tears rolling down his cheeks.

Mrs. Tagley glanced at Develyn.

"Whether I recover or not is surely up to the good Lord. Thanks for coming to see me. It perks me up and makes me feel young."

"It does?" Tiny asked.

"Yes, at the moment I don't feel a day over eighty-five."

Pete cleared his throat and stared at the top of his worn brown boots. "I don't think you look a day over eighty."

Mrs. Tagley grinned at Develyn. "You can't beat that cowboy charm, can you, Devy girl? And people wonder why I like living out in ranch country."

When Cuban shoved his cowboy hat on, the others did the same. "We'd better light a shuck, ma'am. You take care of yourself. We'll send some bunkhouse prayers your way."

"Thank you, boys."

One by one they filed by her bed. Each one held her hand, leaned over, and kissed her on the cheek before they left.

Develyn stood by the bed, her arms folded across her chest. "Mrs. Tagley, oh sweetie, those boys need you."

The white-haired lady exposed a sly smile. "I never thought the day would come when looking eighty would be such a wonderful compliment."

"You really sent Cuban $25,000?"

"He paid off that truck in three years. Why does the Lord give us money anyway?"

Develyn's cell phone rang. She stepped out into the hallway.

"Hi, Mom."

"Dee, what did the doctor say?"

"I didn't see her."

Develyn felt her neck stiffen. "Sweetheart, this has to stop. You have . . ."

"Mother, relax, take a big breath. It was not my fault this time. When we got there, we were told that she had an emergency. There was a difficult delivery—twins, and both turned wrong."

"Oh, dear, that does sound critical."

"They asked me to come back in a couple hours. So Casey and I hung out with a friend of hers who owns a pizza place."

"First Stop?"

"Yes, isn't it great pizza?"

"That's not what I want to talk about."

"When we went back, the nurse said the doctor needed to stay with the babies and had to cancel. I got another appointment for the day after tomorrow. Mother, I didn't know what else to do. You can talk to Casey if you don't believe me."

"I believe you, Dee. Sorry I got so jumpy. That's all you could do. How are the babies?"

"Fine, as far as I know."

"What did she have? Boys or girls?"

"I don't know, Mom, a cow is a cow to me."

"Cow?"

"Yeah, the doctor has some cattle and went home at noon to check on them."

"You were talking about cows?"

"Mom, this is Wyoming."

"Yes, I, of all people, should know that. Lily and Stewart made it to Casper already. I'm staying in town and having supper with them here. You and Casey . . . and Jackson are welcome to join us."

"Mother, I told you I have a date with Hunt."

"Yes, well, I guess that slipped my mind."

"We have a bunch of pizza left. Casey says the four of us should just hang out at the cabin. Would that be alright?"

Develyn bit her lower lip. "Dee, you are a smart girl. Do what is smart, OK?"

"Thanks, Mom. We'll go back to the cabin now. Casey said she'd teach me how to throw a knife before the guys come over."

"She's going to teach you what?"

"Mom, you are so fun. Casey told me to say that. She said you'd fall for it. Casey wants to talk to you."

"Hey, Dev."

"Bronze Bombshell, what are you teaching my daughter?"

"Devy-girl, I'm just tryin' to take up the slack for the pathetic Indiana education."

"Thank you for that. Is that why you wanted to talk to me?"

"No, I had an idea. Let's pitch a barbecue for your Lily and her fella. I mean, we all want to meet each other, so why not have a cookout? Kind of a Miss Dev goin' away barbecue."

"Where?"

"At the cabin."

"You mean outside?"

"We aren't going to get a hundred people in the cabin."

"A hundred?" Develyn gasped.

"Oh, how I'd like to see that expression. OK, . . . a dozen or so. It was just a thought. I sort of think I'll have an announcement by then."

"Oh, that kind of barbecue!"

"What do you think? Could we do it tomorrow night?"

"Casey, I think the day after would be better. I don't even know if Coop's got the old cabin site cleaned up. We will need to figure logistics, like getting tables. Then there's the stress of finding the right placemats, matching napkins, and placecards."

"Whoa! For a barbecue?" Casey replied.

"Oh, my dear countess, two can tease."

"You rat."

"Thank you, I've had a good teacher. But we will need a day or so to get ready. Cooking might be problem. Let me check with Coop. He said he always had a company cookout with a big portable barbecue. Maybe he has some ideas."

"Watermelon."

"You want watermelon?"

"There's some for sale at a roadside stand near here. Shall I bring some back?"

"That would be nice."

"How many?"

"Several. We can always sell the excess at Mrs. Tagley's."

"How is she?"

"Feeling a little down, I think. Listen, tell Jackson she'd like him to bunk at her place until she comes home."

"Really? That's cool."

"Alone."

"Rats."

"No, I don't think so. Maybe a spider or two, but I haven't seen any other varmints."

"No, I meant . . ."

"I know exactly what you meant."

"Well, have a nice evening with your Lily and her guy. After we get the melons, me and Delaney and the fellas will stop off at the Dew Drop Inn for a few beers and be home before midnight if one of us is sober enough to drive."

"Casey, I'm not that gullible."

"I know," Casey laughed. "I just said that so you'd feel better."

"Always thinking of me. How kind."

"Hey, that's what good friends are for."

"You know what I was thinking? Having you, Lily, and Delaney here means my three best friends in the whole world are with me."

"Wow, we ought to do something memorable."

"Let's make it a good memory."

"Oh, here's the Dew Drop Inn. And look, it's full of bikers. They must be on their way home from Rally Days in Sturgis."

Develyn laughed. "Well, don't hurt them, honey."

● ● ●

Develyn checked her watch when she turned off the blacktop and bounced down the gravel road to Argenta.

One a.m. I haven't stayed out this late all summer. But it was so fun to visit with Lil. I think I missed her more than I realized. I might have missed her more than she missed me.

230

I like Stewart, Lord. He seems good for her. He's a little stuffy but so tenderhearted to her. That's what she needs. He's so much taller than she is, but then Coop's quite a bit taller than . . .

Why did I think of that?

Lord, maybe I envy Lil a little. In a good way. I'm so thrilled for her. It's just, coming out here, well, it's sort of an impossible dream. Oh, pooh. I don't even want to think about it.

I think Casey's right about the barbecue. It will be a fun way to end the summer. It's like the last day at summer camp. When I think about it, I want to cry.

When she turned up the drive to the cabin, she noticed a light on in Cooper's travel trailer.

She parked the Cherokee and was greeted by familiar big brown eyes when she stepped out.

"Hi, honey," she whispered. "You need to get some sleep." She rubbed his ear, then slapped him on the rump. Uncle Henry trotted off to the shadows.

She paused in the yard. The wind drifted clouds past the half-full moon, like a slow strobe light. The air smelled of sage. It was just a little chilly; she held her arms.

She peered at the trailer. No noise. No movement. Just lights.

Go to bed, Ms. Worrell. One a.m. is not a good time to visit any man.

Of course, Coop is not just any man. Why did Mrs. Tagley insinuate that he was the one for me? One of the privileges of being ninety is blurting out anything you want.

Her arms still folded, she meandered toward the travel trailer.

Coop could be the man. I mean, if the circumstances were different. If we lived in the same area. If we lived in the same world.

I wish I'd have known him years ago . . . tears ago.

I wonder what he was like in his prime?

I don't even know what I was like in my prime.

Did I have a prime?

Maybe it's now.

The metal door of the trailer felt cold to the soft knock of her knuckles.

"Coop?" she whispered.

10

When Develyn got out of the shower the next morning, Casey was braiding her long black hair. "You aren't going to wear it down?"

"It's the moment of truth. Jackson needs to see it this way sooner or later. Did I hear a phone call this morning?"

"Lily called from Casper. She said Stewart woke up with a horrible stomachache. She's going to wait a while and see if he feels better. If not, she'll drive out by herself."

"What about the barbecue?"

"It's all planned for tomorrow evening. I stopped by and visited with Coop last night when I came back from Casper."

"What time was that?"

"You don't want to know."

"Did you go to sleep at all?"

"You don't want to know that either. We had a wonderful talk. But I might need to wear my sunglasses indoors all day. When I get tired, my eyes look like I'm 110."

"Coop sure slicked up the old cabin site. You can hardly see a trace of anything."

"Yes, that's alarming in a way, isn't it? We've spent most of the summer there, and now it doesn't exist anymore."

"Life is fragile, Ms. Worrell."

"I'm going to the store. I don't know when the delivery guy will show up. Mrs. Tagley wants me to pay him in cash."

"Say good morning to the cutest bronze stud in Wyoming."

"You don't mind if I just call him Jackson."

Casey grinned. "Call him anything you want, but he's mine."

Develyn studied Delaney still asleep on the lower bunk bed. "Tell sleeping beauty I'll be down at the store for a while this morning."

"Does she always sleep like that?"

"On her stomach with her rear pouched up? Ever since she was a baby. But don't mention it to her; she will deny it."

"Dev, do I sleep weird?"

"You mean, besides bouncing up in bed, waving a knife, and shouting, 'One more step and you'll be singing soprano?'"

"Yes, besides that? Do I snore or anything?"

"Are you thinking about married life?"

"I don't know how to live with someone else. I mean, besides you."

"Don't worry. You'll figure it out when the time comes.

Sometimes I do hear you tossing and turning, but I sleep so light, I hear my cats turn over."

"Were you always a light sleeper?"

"I think so. When I was young, I was afraid of night noises and insisted on leaving a light on. Then when Delaney came along, I wanted to make sure I heard her if she needed me. Then I tried to listen and find out what time Spencer came home."

"He was out late a lot?"

"Yes, but I wanted to know when he came in, so I could pretend to be asleep."

"Oh, Dev, really?"

"I made a lot of mistakes. That was probably one of them. I didn't have anyone to talk to. According to my mother, marriage was supposed to be perfect. I couldn't admit any problems."

"What would you have done different?"

"I could have confronted Spencer fifteen years earlier and dragged him to counseling."

"You think that would have helped him?"

"I don't know, but it would have helped me." Develyn scanned the mirror. "Do I look like a store clerk?"

"You look too cute to go to the store and see my Jackson."

"I'll leave my sunglasses off. How's that?"

Casey laughed. "That will work."

Develyn grabbed her purse and eased the door closed.

Uncle Henry met her; then Cooper stepped out of the trailer and jammed on his black cowboy hat. "Mind if I hike along with you two to the store? I need some shaving cream. Sorry for the beard this morning."

She reached up to a startled Cooper Tallon and rubbed her fingers over his cheek.

"You're right, you need a shave. Don't you try to kiss me with a beard like that."

"But . . . I won't . . . I didn't . . ."

"Mr. Tallon, you should have spent more of your life around women."

"That's a fact I learned too late."

The Wyoming sky was a thin blue and cloudless. The sun burned yellow-white and cast dark shadows as they strolled out the dirt drive. When they reached the road, Uncle Henry brayed and scooted between Develyn and Cooper.

Coop nodded toward the empty corrals to the west. "Looks like someone's plannin' an ambush."

"Is that Leon? What's he doing?"

"Sitting in the dirt and leaning against the fence."

"I want to talk to him. You wait here with Uncle Henry."

"Yes, ma'am."

Her eyes bored into his rugged face. "Sorry, Coop. I can't seem to keep myself from bossing everyone."

"Did you ever wonder what it would be like to have two bossy people in a household?"

She wrinkled her upturned nose. "No, I don't' think I've thought about that."

Develyn heard him mutter, "I did," as she strolled to the corrals.

"I didn't do anything," Leon called out.

"I didn't accuse you of anything."

"What do you want?"

Develyn plopped down on the dirt beside the twelve-year-old and leaned against the fence. "I don't want anything. You look comfortable. Do you mind if I sit here?"

"Your pony/mule and the old man are waiting for you."

"Yes, they are. You look sad, Leon. Did you get into trouble?"

"Grandma says it's about time I have to go back to the home."

"Summer is about over. I have to go home next week too."

"Do you live in a state home?"

"No, I live in Indiana. Do you know where that is?"

"It's between Illinois, Ohio, Kentucky, and Michigan. It has over six million people, and the capital is Indianapolis."

She hugged his shoulder. "I'm surprised. That's very good."

"I looked it up on a map when Grandma said you were from Indiana."

"Most adults I've met in Wyoming don't know that much."

"I like maps."

"So do I. Aren't they fun?"

"I like to pretend I'm someplace else."

"Leon, where would you like to be?"

"Anywhere people like me."

Develyn shut her eyes for a moment. *That's the wish of every person on this earth, isn't it? Lord, this isn't fair. No boy should live like this.*

"When do you have to be back to the home?"

"Monday."

"I tell you what, between now and Monday, you and I are friends, and I like you. So right here in Argenta somebody likes you."

"You mean that?"

"Yes. Listen, I'm having a barbecue at my cabin, and you and your grandmother are invited. Would you like to come?"

"No one ever invited me to supper before. Are you sure?"

Dear Lord, I hope I'm sure. "Yes."

"All right." He jumped to his feet. "I'll even take a bath."

"That will be nice. But remember, I said tomorrow, not today."

"What time?"

"About six in the evening."

He reached out his hand. "Can I help you up?"

"Thank you, young man."

He dashed past Uncle Henry and Cooper Tallon. "I'm going to a barbecue at her house."

They continued their trek to the store.

"You made his day."

"You know what? In almost every fifth-grade class, there's at least one like Leon, a troubled boy or girl that it takes weeks and months to figure out. They break my heart. Some kids come out of a tough home environment and sparkle. Others seem stunted forever. I can never figure out why that has to be. They are the ones that make me want to continue teaching."

"The difficult kids?"

"When I think about retiring someday, I know there will be many very good teachers to come along and fill my position. Each of them will do a great job teaching the good kids. I've got some great kids. I could put a stack of books and assignments on their desks, and they wouldn't need to see me until spring."

"But the others?"

"Every time I get a student like Leon, I think, *Do the elementary education majors coming out of the university know how to love this one? Would they spend four hours at night making a picture book of motorcycle parts, just to teach Rondell how to read? Would they sit in the dunk tank at the carnival just so Sherri could release some of her anger? Would they come an hour early for three months so that Taylor can conquer his fear of math?* Maybe they could, Coop. But young teachers have young families of their own and busy lives. The ones like Leon need me. And you know what? I like being needed."

"Funny you should say that."

"About being needed?"

"One of the attractions of retiring at my age was to say to myself, *Won't it be nice to get up in the morning and there are no demands? No one needs me to bury a line, make a bid, repair a Cat, or survey a site.* I got excited thinkin' about going a whole day without an emergency. How about a whole week? A month? Then I got to thinkin', What would it be like if no one needs me . . . ever? It's a lonely image."

"I can't imagine you around the house doing crossword puzzles or watching television."

"Nor can I. Maybe I'm too young to retire."

"Or maybe you need a different career." Develyn turned up the walkway to Mrs. Tagley's. "How would you like to own a store?"

"Can you envision me as a store clerk?"

"No, I can't." He followed her up the steps.

"Neither can I."

Jackson Hill popped out of the back room when the screen door banged behind them.

"Hi, Miss Dev, Mr. Tallon. I opened the store early just to see if I'd snag any more customers."

"So how's business?" Cooper asked.

"Three cans of condensed milk, two videos returned, one box of disposable diapers, two dozen eggs, a box of Frosted Flakes, and two Little Debbies, for a total of $17.45."

Cooper searched the aisle. "I didn't know I'd get the whole inventory."

"I had some extra time. What did you find out about that wholesale shipment, Miss Dev?"

Develyn shoved her sunglasses in her purse. "Mrs. Tagley wants to pay for the shipment in cash, so I'll get the money out of her safe."

Cooper sauntered up with a red can of shaving cream. "And just how much is this?"

Jackson grinned. "It's $2.67. I read the inventory after I went to bed last night, trying to get some sleep."

"Tough to sleep in a new bed?" Develyn asked.

"Usually I can sleep anywhere. But I got to thinkin' about a purdy black-haired girl, and well, I figured I needed a diversion."

"Well, the purdy, black-haired girl was dreaming of you."

"Isn't she the sweetest lady you ever met?"

Develyn glanced at Coop, then back at Jackson. "Casey is a jewel."

Cooper counted out the money. "Now, that sounds like your wholesale truck."

Jackson stepped to the porch, than glanced back.

"You help him unload and check the invoice," Develyn called out. "Cooper and I will get the money."

"It takes two to pay a bill?" Cooper asked.

She took his hand and tugged him to the back room. "You afraid of going back here with me?"

"Maybe you are the one who should be afraid," he grinned. "Jackson isn't the only one that had a tough time sleeping last night."

"That's because that neighbor lady kept you awake with her incessant talking."

Mrs. Tagley's bedroom smelled of antique dust and lilac perfume.

"Where are you taking me?"

"You old bachelors get real nervous fast, don't you? Mrs. Tagley has some sort of safe back here. I want someone to sign for what money I take out. You're the witness."

"You brought me back here for a signature?"

"Disappointed, huh?" Develyn swung the closet door open. "Now, all we have to do is find the safe."

Coop stuck his head in. "The whole closet is a safe."

Dev stepped around Cooper and stared. "That's the biggest safe I've ever seen in a house."

Cooper pointed at the faded white letters on the black safe. "Natrona County Bank, Argenta, Wyoming."

"How did she get this into her bedroom closet?"

"I imagine they built the closet around the vault."

"Why would she need a vault this size?"

"To keep her inventory of Little Debbies, perhaps. There's the dial. I assume you have the combination."

On the third try, they heard a deep click. Cooper shoved down the handle and swung open the heavy door.

"It's too dark," Develyn announced.

"I bet she has a battery-operated light up here somewhere." Cooper fumbled for a moment and then clicked a switch. The carpeted interior of the safe lit up.

Develyn stared in. "I can almost stand up in here."

"She is one neat old lady. She's got antiques covered with blankets and shelf after shelf of shoe boxes. Those must be yearly invoices. Look, 1996, 1997 . . . each is labeled."

"Where do you think her cash box is?" Develyn asked.

"Look for a little metal box."

"You check behind the blankets. I'll sort through the shoe boxes."

"Well, well, Dev, darlin', look at these." Cooper pointed to the far wall.

"Guns? She's got four old guns?"

"Five. She's got four Henry rifles and a Winchester 1873. This is incredible."

Develyn scooted over next to Cooper. "Is that good?"

Cooper plucked up the nearest rifle. "Good? I've got one Henry I bought a couple of years back."

"What did you pay for it?"

"Twenty-five thousand."

"For one gun? Does that mean she has $100,000 worth of guns in here?"

Cooper plucked up the next gun. "Oh, my, an engraved Henry." He went down the line looking at each one. "This one is martially marked. It was used in the Civil War. I've never seen anything like this."

"What are those little cardboard tags?"

Cooper turned over the tags and studied the faded pencil marks. "This one says 'Don Hillard, Rafter H, $30 and groceries, June 4, 1936.' She bought them during the depression."

"You mean, she took advantage of their poverty."

"Just the opposite. They probably couldn't get five dollars for these back then. They didn't make any bullets for them anymore, so they were useless wall hangers. She pawned them, and they never came back for them. Here's another. 'C. H. Hall, 2 cases of Lucky Strikes, August 20, 1938.'"

"And she kept them all these years?"

"What a cache," he hooted. "I haven't got this excited since I saw you at that Casper gas station."

"You play with your toys, honey. I still need to find the cash box."

"Here's an octagon-barrel '73 first model with a set trigger. It's engraved and still has a little blue . . ." Cooper shoved the gun at her. "Look at those words on top of the barrel."

"That's nice scrolled engraving. I think that font is called Regality II."

"These were done by hand. Read those words."

"'One of One Thousand.' Is that good?"

"Devy, this gun alone is worth at least $100,000."

Develyn read the faded tag attached to the lever. "'P. Moyes, for 1927 Model A, broken crankshaft.' Are you telling me she has over $200,000 in just five guns?"

"I'd write her a check in a heartbeat for $200,000, if she wanted to sell."

"So would I, but my check would bounce."

"Mine wouldn't."

Develyn dropped to her knees and searched behind the shoe boxes. "Where is the cash box?"

"Look at the shoe box with this year's date."

Develyn pulled down the blue Reebok box and slid back the lid. "Yes," she called out. "No."

"No money?"

"Full of money. Neatly stapled one hundred dollar bills."

Cooper leaned over her shoulder. "Ten in a bundle?"

"Yes, but look at all of them."

Develyn laid them on the carpeted floor of the safe. " . . . thirty-five, thirty-six . . . forty-one. Coop, she's got $41,000 cash in a shoe box."

He grabbed the box labeled for the year before. "This one has more."

"The boxes are full of money? Oh my word . . . all in $100 bills. There's got to be a million dollars in here," Develyn whispered.

"Let's get out of here and get the door locked," Cooper suggested.

Develyn grabbed a one-thousand dollar bundle, then shoved the other boxes back on the shelves. Without saying another word, they locked the safe, closed the closet, and scurried back into the store. She shoved the bills into her pocket and laced her fingers on top of her head.

"Cooper, did we really see all that?"

"That's incredible, Develyn. Don't tell a soul."

"No, no, you're right. That's between Mrs. Tagley and the Lord, and we aren't supposed to know."

Jackson Hill stuck his head in the door. "Hey, did you find the money?"

Develyn closed her eyes, then sighed. "Oh, we found the money."

●　●　●

Casey puttered around in Mrs. Tagley's kitchen cooking lunch while Jackson shelved the inventory and waited on customers. After one trip home to stir up Delaney, Develyn leaned back on the bench seat in front of the store with an orange Popsicle held in front of her.

245

A white Ford Taurus with Delaware plates pulled up. Two couples in their sixties climbed out and stretched their arms and legs.

A fluffy white poodle scampered up to Develyn. "Well, hello young man, who are you?"

"General Patton," one of the ladies called. The dog spun around and scampered back.

With the windows cracked open and General secured, both couples ambled for the store.

A lady in a purple-flowered blouse nodded, "Hello."

Develyn tipped her straw cowboy hat. "Howdy, folks, welcome to Wyomin'. You got yourself a mighty fine dawg there, ma'am. Mighty fine. Kind of like husbands, ain't they? You find one that will mind you, and you jist keep him forever, even if you got to lock him in the car."

"Sarah, don't you just love that western drawl?"

"That's something you have to be born with," the other replied.

One of the men held open the screen door for the others. "Say, is this a shortcut to Yellowstone?" He pointed at the gravel road in front of the store.

Develyn stood, pushed her hat back, then took a long, slow lick on the Popsicle. "Yessir, it is. Jist go down here to where those twin cedars used to be and take a right turn up that dirt road. Go about, oh, fifteen or twenty miles, and you'll dip down to find Miller Crick. It shouldn't be too deep this week. The road slants off to the northwest and is kind of steep in places. You'll want to turn left right back at the stone foundation for the old Windmill Ranch. Now, it don't look like much of a road, but in ten miles or so, there's dirt wide as a chicken coop."

"A chicken coop?"

"Now that brings you to the oil fields. But don't let all them 'keep out' signs slow you down. As long as your rig keeps movin', you have as much a right there as the next guy . . . well, almost, anyway. Follow that straight west for about twenty more miles. There are several gates across the road. Just make sure you close them after you get through, and whatever you do, don't let the cows out."

"That's quicker?" he gasped.

"It's shorter. I thought you said shorter. The quickest route is to go back out to the blacktop and follow highway 20."

"I think we'll stick with the pavement."

"That's a fine idea."

They had just entered the store when the woman named Sarah stuck her head back out. "Are those Indians in there?"

"Yes, ma'am. We call them Native Americans. The woman is of mixed descent from the Cree tribe, and the man is pure-bred Crow."

"They seem rather . . . chummy."

"They do?" Develyn grinned. "It's a cultural exchange program, I'm sure."

The screen door had just slammed when a long silver Lincoln pulled up next to the white Ford. Dev jogged up to the rig, licking her Popsicle.

"Stewart is still ill," Lily reported. "He sends his regrets."

"I'm sorry, honey. Would you like a lick?" Dev held out her orange Popsicle.

"I think I'll pass. So this is Mrs. Tagley's? It's just like you described it."

Develyn waved her hands. "And this, Ms. Martin, is Argenta, Wyoming. Isn't it wonderful?"

Lily shook her head. "Others dream of Paris or Florence or Jerusalem, and you dream of . . . "

"Anyone can dream of Paris, but only a select few dream of Argenta."

"Yes, I can see why."

The door swung open. Casey led the Delaware folks out onto the porch. Each carried a bottle of water.

"Lily!" Casey boomed.

The dark-haired woman standing in the dirt yard spun around and glanced at the woman with the thick black braid hanging down her back to her waist. "Casey?"

Cree-Ryder jumped the steps, and the two women met in the yard and hugged. "Yes, yes, yes," Casey called out as they danced around in the dirt.

"Casey, I'm so glad to see you!"

"Old friends, I presume," the lady wearing purple flowers said.

Lily released Casey. "No, we've never met before."

"Oh, well, I suppose that's western hospitality." The two couples circled the yard just as a rusted black Ford pickup parked behind their car, and three cowboys piled out and marched straight at the store.

Each tipped his hat and repeated the greeting: "Howdy, Miss Dev."

Develyn licked on the dripping Popsicle. "Howdy, boys."

"We came to town for supplies."

"Mrs. Tagley's in the hospital. Casey will take care of you."

"You ain't packin' guns and knives, are you, Cree-Ryder?"

"What do you think?"

"You boys missed the boat," Dev called out. "Casey's going to marry Jackson Hill."

"That's good news for us," one of them called out.

"He's a braver man than me," the blond cowboy said.

"Which ain't sayin' a whole lot," another added.

"I say," one of the men from Delaware called out. "We seem to be hemmed in. Could I ask someone to move the truck?"

"Go shopping, boys. I'll move it."

"Thanks, Miss Dev."

Develyn drove the truck to the side of the Lincoln, and the people from Delaware dusted back out toward the highway.

"They left the key in the truck?" Lily asked.

"Lil, that one doesn't have a key, just an on and off switch. Who would want to steal it?"

"I suppose I overreacted when I locked the Lincoln."

A cowboy riding a buckskin gelding rode up to the tree in front of the store. A brown burro trotted up to him.

"Here comes my baby!" Develyn called out.

"Which one?" Lily asked.

"The burro!" Dev laughed.

Uncle Henry ran right up to Develyn and leaned his head on her shoulder. The cowboy swung down to the ground and led the horse over to the ladies. He held out his hand. "You must be Miss Lily."

She shook his hand and peered over the top of her sunglasses. "If you aren't Mr. Cooper Tallon, I'm going to be terribly embarrassed. I'm Lily Martin; I teach school with Dev."

He tipped his hat. "You can call me Coop, ma'am. Indiana schoolteachers are a purdy bunch, aren't they?"

Lily laughed. "That does it. I'm moving to Wyoming."

Develyn stepped over to them. "Lily's friend, Stewart, is feeling sick today and stayed in Casper."

"My tentative fiancé," Lily corrected.

"Tentative?" Cooper asked.

"He has to pass Dev's inspection."

"I like him. Marry him," Develyn blurted out.

"You hardly met him. You have to wait a few days and then tell me."

Develyn put her arm around Lily's shoulder. "You know, I've been trying to get her married off for years. She's so reluctant to leave home."

"Me? Oh, no," Lily protested. "Coop, can you believe how hard it is for me to try to land this blonde a date?"

"Indiana men are dumber than I thought." He pushed his black, beaver felt cowboy hat back. "I'm riding out to the springs this mornin'. I saw the cars down here and figured one might be Miss Lily."

Develyn and Lily stood by the cottonwood in front of the store and watched Cooper ride north across the rolling sage toward the cedar ridge.

One of the cowboys banged open the door and stomped out on the porch holding two videos. "Miss Dev, which do you like better, *Tombstone* or *Wyatt Earp?*"

"*Wyatt Earp.*"

He lumbered back into the store. "I told you!"

Uncle Henry wandered over to the Lincoln and rubbed his ear on the side-view mirror.

"Baby, you get back over by your tree. I don't want you to damage Lily's rental car."

The burro gawked at Develyn.

"You heard me."

He plodded back to the shade of the lone cottonwood tree.

Lily shook her head. "Looks like you have Wyoming all organized, Ms. Worrell. They mind you like everyone at Riverbend."

"Yeah, right."

They stepped up on the porch, and Lily studied the initial-carved old freight wagon seat. "So this is your famous bench from which I have often received a phone call?"

Develyn licked the orange Popsicle and plopped down.

"Come on, Lil, sit a spell."

"Ms. Worrell, I don't believe I've ever sat a spell, but I'm willing to learn how." She sat down beside Develyn.

The three cowboys exited, grocery sacks in hand.

"You know, Miss Dev, if we had one more purdy gal, we could have ourselves a dance."

The shortest one, wearing the largest silver belt buckle, shifted his sack of groceries from one arm to the other. "Miss Dev makes us take off our spurs and boots when she dances with us."

"I heard that," Lily said.

The old pickup lurched down the road.

Lily leaned back against the bench. "This place is exactly as I pictured it. But still, it seems so unreal. This is the twenty-first century. Don't these people know that?"

They heard an off-key trumpet blast and a shout. "Leon, you get back here!"

Uncle Henry's ears shot up, and he trotted down the dirt road to the west.

"What was that?"

"Mrs. Morton sounded the Leon-is-loose warning, and Uncle Henry is going home."

Casey and Jackson Hill stepped out on the porch.

"Lily, this is my Jackson." Casey took his arm. "Isn't he the yummiest guy you ever saw in your life?"

"*Yummy* is the exact word I was thinking of." Lily offered her hand.

Jackson's dimples framed his smile. "Under this brown skin, I'm turning red."

"When's the wedding date?" Lily asked.

"We have to figure out some future jobs and things first," Casey said.

"It's nice to meet you, Miss Lily. I need to go stock some shelves." Jackson retreated to the store.

Casey plopped down on the bench next to Lily. "Where's your man?"

"He has a stomach problem this morning and needed to stay at the hotel."

"Where did you guys eat in Casper?" Casey asked.

"At Zapatos," Develyn said.

"Did he eat the Sonora Steamer?" Casey inquired.

Lily looked startled. "Yes, he did."

"Don't worry," Casey shrugged. "Everyone gets sick with that one."

"They have something on the menu that purposely makes customers sick?"

"Yes, but it's tasty."

"They should put some kind of warning on the menu."

"Then no one would eat it. He'll feel better once he . . . expunges it. Most of the people I know just jam a finger down their throat and barf it up afterward."

"But how can they get away with making people sick?"

"I guess no one ever complained. No one's ever sued."

"Stewart is a lawyer. That could change."

"I'm sure Mrs. Gomez would refund his money. She's a very nice lady."

"But . . ." Lily stammered.

A young girl about ten years old, barefoot and wearing a long-sleeved dress that hung straight to her ankles, ran down the road to the east.

"Hi, Miss Dev, I'm in a hurry."

"Be careful, Sierra," Develyn called, then turned to Lily. "She's the other orange Popsicle fanatic in town."

"It's called SOD," Casey blurted out. "The Sisterhood of Orange Drops."

A deep, male voice called out from inside the store. "Casey, babe, I need your help."

She turned to Develyn and Lily. "Ladies, it just doesn't get any better than this." Casey scurried into the store.

Sierra sprinted back carrying something in her hand.

"Cap gun?" Lily quizzed.

"I don't think so." Develyn waved at the girl. "Everything OK, Sierra?"

"Snake in the outhouse. Can't stop now."

"What did she say?" Lily gasped.

Sierra darted around the house west of the store. "I believe she said . . ."

A loud explosion, and a shout, "Yes!" interrupted them.

" . . . there was a snake in the outhouse."

"They still use outhouses?"

"When the septic tank is full."

Sierra hiked back to the store with a revolver in one hand and dragging a dead, three-and-a-half-foot rattlesnake. She plopped it right up on the porch.

"I got him with one shot."

Lily slid her feet back under the bench, hugged herself, and rocked back and forth. "Get it away," she croaked.

"I'll skin it for you if you'd like to make a belt, Miss Dev.
But I can't let you have the meat 'cause I promised that to
Mr. Lanley. He let me borrow his gun."

"I'll pass on the belt, Sierra. I don't have anything to wear
it with. But, thank you very much."

"What's wrong with her? She looks green?"

"This is my friend, Lily, and she ate at Zapatos last night."

"I bet she had the Sonora Steamer. That's what I always
order."

"After you take the gun and snake to Mr. Lanley, stop back
by and I'll buy you an orange Popsicle."

"Thank you, Miss Dev."

When Sierra and the snake were out of the yard, Develyn
patted Lily's knee. "Relax, honey. That's only the second snake
I've heard of in town all summer. Usually they have more."

"Is that meant to comfort me?"

"Welcome to the frontier, Ms. Martin."

11

Lily held a glass of iced tea and surveyed the bare dirt patch that stretched out like a garden plot waiting for spring seeds. "You spent the summer right here?"

Develyn strolled up beside her. "That's where my cabin was until last week."

"There is no trace of it."

"Coop cleaned it up and hauled it away yesterday. He's very good at what he does."

Lily raised her eyebrows. "I imagine he is."

"Heavy construction equipment."

"Oh, that. I imagine he's quite strong for an older man."

"Don't let that age factor fool you. He can pick me up by the ankles and hold his arms straight out with me dangling down like a fish."

"He what?"

"You know, if he wanted to."

"He dangled you upside down by your ankles?"

"I needed to recover something."

"Your sanity?"

The two women meandered over to the fence.

"I like your horse."

"Isn't she pretty? I think she knows she's good looking."

"Does she have that arrogant attitude like Silena Lipman?"

"Yes, that's it. She torments Uncle Henry something awful."

"Just like your cat, Josephine, treats Smoky."

"Very similar. Will there be anything left in my house, or will the monster cat have destroyed it all?"

"She seemed to have calmed down ever since the neighbor boy took her for a walk."

"You don't walk cats."

"Don't argue with success."

Delaney drifted out of the cabin, a towel wrapped around her head. She wore sandals, khaki shorts, and a dark blue halter top.

Develyn could see no extra piercings or tattoos.

"Hi, Lily. Isn't Wyoming wide open and wonderful?"

"It certainly is wide open. I forget the world isn't closed in by trees like back home."

"Mom, do you think I can find some conditioner at the store? Mine was lost in the fire."

"You can use mine."

"I need something a little, you know, for softer, finer hair."

"That's a nice way of saying it," Develyn said. "Lil, did you ever wonder what shade our hair really is under all this coloring?"

"I know what color mine would be, Devy-girl, and I don't intend to go there. Ever."

"Can I take the Cherokee?" Delaney asked. "I just polished my toenails."

"Sure, honey, the keys are in my purse on top of that pile on the table. Lil and I are goin' to walk down to the corrals where this whole adventure began. Did the four of you have a good time last night?"

"Sure. Didn't Casey tell you?"

"I forgot to ask."

She watched Delaney scoot back into the cabin. "I think that means the conversation is over."

Develyn and Lily ambled down the lane. Uncle Henry tagged behind.

"Dev, after spending the summer in a one-room cabin with a roommate most of the time, you'll be lost in your big house back home."

"It's funny, I came to Wyoming to slow down. To think things through and to find a simpler life. From where I am now, Indiana seems like the quiet, uncomplicated life."

"Could it be you take the stress and busyness with you?"

"That's a happy thought. But it's a different kind of activity. I've had less time to sit and ponder all my problems. I've been happier here. But I've also had more times I was scared to death. I've helped more people and had more people help me.

I know for a fact I've had more men flirt with me . . . in a nice way . . . than eight years of high school and college. And in the past nine weeks, I've doubled the number of men who have ever kissed these lips."

Lily giggled. "Now we are getting to the good part. Who is the best at kissing?"

"The verdict is still out. One of the contestants has yet to submit his entry."

"You haven't kissed Cooper yet?"

"Not really. I mean . . . just a peck on the cheek or a brush across the lips in greeting. The kind of thing you do with your brother."

"I have never brushed my lips across my brother's," Lily insisted.

"You don't have a brother."

"Good point."

They paused at the road, then turned west toward the corrals.

"I should have saddled up My Maria. We could have ridden down here."

"I'm not anxious to ride large animals, but I do want to get a picture of Ms. Worrell and her horse."

Uncle Henry brayed.

"And her burro," Lily added.

A trumpet blast caused Develyn to turn. Leon raced toward them. He was barefoot and stepped lightly across the dirt and gravel.

"Is he wearing just a towel?" Lily asked.

"I believe so."

Uncle Henry hid behind Develyn.

"Leon, what are you doing?" she called out before the boy reached them.

"I spied you over here and wanted to tell you that I'm gettin' me a bath."

"That's very good. You do remember that the barbecue is not until tomorrow?"

"Yes, ma'am, Miss Dev. I'll get another bath tomorrow. I just wanted to practice."

"That's very commendable. Now go on home so you don't get your grandmother's towel dirty."

When he turned around and trotted back to the house, Lily burst out laughing.

"Leon!" Develyn called. "You should wrap the towel all the way around you."

"I don't think he heard you. That reminds me. Did I tell you the latest about Dougie Baxter?"

Develyn still faced the Morton house when the champagne-colored Cherokee rolled down the dusty drive and took a hard turn east toward the store.

"Did my daughter still have that towel on her head?"

"And the halter top."

"She can't go out in public like that."

Lily stared up and down Argenta's one empty dirt road. "Maybe she doesn't think of this as going out in public."

"You don't go to the store like that . . . ever."

"We don't go to the store like that. When was the last time you were in West Lafayette in the summer?"

They turned toward the corrals. "That is one goal I don't think I've accomplished yet this summer, Lily. I wanted Dee and me to find the relationship the Lord wants for us . . . and to come to peace with it. I find no peace with my daughter bouncing her barely covered chest out in plain view."

"I've been praying for you too, honey."

"Thanks, Lil. I know I can count on you. You're my rock. You always have been. You've saved my life on more than one occasion."

They stopped by the fence and glanced in at the empty arena. "I think you exaggerate a bit, but thanks. So this is where Miss Dev made her grand entry into cowboy life?"

"Casey and I sat right over there, where the board is smooth. See that big dirt clod out there? That's where that paint monster mare slammed my face into the dirt. I was ready to jump on a plane and fly home right then and hide in my livingroom the rest of the summer . . . or the rest of my life." She put her arm around Lil. "I didn't exaggerate about you saving my life. I remember one January driving back from the science convention in Wheaton during an ice storm at night with a three-inch ice cap on the highway. I was in tears, thinking about Spencer, about Delaney, about my hopeless situation. I got down to the river where there are all those curves and cliffs, and I said, 'Lord, I just can't take it. This life is too hard for me.' And I thought about stepping on the gas and ending it all."

Lily hugged her. "Oh, honey, I'm so glad you didn't."

"*But*, I thought, *not before I talk to my Lil. I need to say good-bye to her face-to-face.*"

"I don't remember."

"It was the time the monster cat ate my date palm and barfed all over the bedspread and in my clothes closet. By the time I ran her to the vet and cleaned the house, the depression had lifted. There were several other times. It's you, sweet lady, who has been my rock."

Lily wiped the corners of her eyes. "We have been there for each other. It's important to have someone who cares."

"Yes, everyone needs that."

"Of course, if I'm honest," Lily grinned. "I'll have to admit that I hang out with you because you are so young and cute and a stud magnet."

Develyn burst out laughing. "Oh, that's the joy of having older friends. I can forever be young. But a stud magnet? In Indiana?"

"I suppose one has to be a man of steel to be attracted to a stud magnet. There aren't many of those in central Indiana."

They sauntered east toward the store. "Lily, we tease each other a lot. But before this summer, I haven't had a legitimate date in Indiana since I was at Purdue."

"You had illegitimate dates?"

"I had several boring encounters that I couldn't wait to escape."

"Remember that young bull rider in Louisville? He took one look at you and said, 'Oh, thank you, Jesus, I must be in heaven.'"

"Is that the lad who was knocked unconscious when the bull slammed into his forehead?"

"I believe it was."

"He's also the one who, when asked what day of the week it was, said 'September.'"

"OK, so he was a little delusional, a tad mixed up."

"Speaking of mixed up, what did you say about Dougie Baxter?"

"Oh, so you did hear."

"Did you figure a way to keep him out of your class?"

"I didn't figure it out. But Mr. and Mrs. Baxter did."

"Did they put him in private school?"

"No."

"They aren't going to try to homeschool him, are they?"

"Oh, no. They took Ms. Worrell's advice."

"You mean they are really going to keep him back a year and let him mature?"

"Yes, they are."

"I can't believe it. Someone did something right. That's wonderful."

Develyn noticed several pickups parked in front of the store.

"Hold onto your wonders, Dev. It gets more bizarre. The Baxters came in and demanded that Dougie be kept back a grade and placed in Ms. Worrell's class."

"They can't do that. School policy states that a failed student has to have another teacher."

"Dougie insisted. His parents claim you're the only teacher who treats him decent."

Develyn waved her hands as if warding off an improper advance. "Decent? You call twenty-six detentions decent? They can't do this to me. No teacher should ever have Dougie Baxter more than once. I won't let this happen."

"I wanted to tell you in person. I knew you'd handle it well."

"Can't they put Dougie in Brian's class?"

"Brian told them he'd take the junior high opening if Dougie Baxter was in his class."

"Lisa hasn't had a turn."

"Lisa said she would go on maternity leave."

"She's not pregnant."

"I don't think that's the deciding factor."

"Ms. Martin, there is no way . . ."

An off-key trumpet blast silenced her.

"Was that for Leon?" Lily asked.

Develyn looked east and rubbed her temples. She chewed on her lip, then shook her head. "No, I think that blast was for Dougie."

"Dougie?"

"I think the Lord's using Leon to prepare my heart for Dougie Baxter . . . again."

"You mean you aren't going to protest the placement?"

"No," Develyn signed. "I won't."

"You are amazing, Ms. Worrell."

"Not hardly. But I am learning a few things this summer." She and Lily continued to walk toward the store. "Of course I might need to borrow Casey's brass knuckles and handcuffs." Develyn waved her hand toward Mrs. Tagley's store. "What are all those rigs doing here?"

"Rigs?"

Develyn pointed ahead. "At the store."

"Rush hour? Lunch break?"

"Break from what?"

Several men lounged in the shade of the sole cottonwood tree. Others spread across the porch. Most held white-bread sandwiches in their less-than-clean hands.

A big man with a thick beard pointed at Uncle Henry. "Hey, lady, does he belong to you?"

"Yes, he does."

"Well, you've got a fine lookin' . . ."

"Mister, the future of your children and your children's children depends upon the next word out of your mouth," Develyn growled.

"Yes, ma'am, you've got a fine lookin' burro."

"Thank you, his name is Uncle Henry."

Another half dozen men stood in line at the counter with a busy Jackson Hill. "See if you can help the girls in the back," he called out.

Develyn led Lily to Mrs. Tagley's kitchen. Casey and a T-shirt-clad Delaney were making sandwiches. "What's happening?"

Casey rubbed her broad, brown nose. "You're the carrot lady. Open another bag. They get three of those little carrots each. They started working on the state highway, and the crew drove back in here looking for lunch."

"Jackson made them a deal, Mom. They get a lunch meat and cheese sandwich, chips, three carrots, and a soda for six dollars. They love it. They said to sign them up for two weeks at least."

Casey waved across the table. "Lil, grab another variety box of chips from that aisle near the door. Jackson said these lunches cost us around $2.88, so we can double our money with a little work."

"Some of the guys even tipped us," Delaney added.

Casey grabbed another hunk of lunchmeat. "Until Dee put on the shirt."

Develyn studied her daughter's T-shirt. "Where did you get a shirt that says, 'Argenta, Wyo. POLICE DEPT'?"

"Under the counter."

"Your hair looks . . ."

"Casey combed it out for me in a hurry, and I just pinned it back."

When the last of the highway workers left, Develyn and Lily scouted for trash outside while Casey and Delaney cleaned the kitchen. All four sprawled on the front porch when Jackson strolled out.

"Listen to this. They spent $214.81."

"That's more than six dollars each," Develyn said.

"Most had more than one sandwich. Lots took a candy bar and another soda for later. Even with leftover bread and mustard and all, we made $111.12."

Dev shook her head. "I've never known anyone so quick to calculate profits."

"Jackson is good at that," Casey said.

"I spent a lot of time stocking shelves at Albertsons, so I would figure how much profit per item. It runs in my head. Listen, I was thinking. What with a highway crew every summer, and BLM crews, and firefighting crews, and oil crews . . . we ought to cater lunches. Take them right out to them. I think we could keep a lunch profit going most all summer and into September. We'd need two people running the store, so one could deliver, but it would increase profits." He glanced around at the ladies. "You know, if the store was ours, and all."

Casey rubbed her nose and grinned.

"I almost forgot. David came by this morning," Jackson announced.

"You mean Hunter Burke? Did he stop by before or after Miss Purple put on the T-shirt?"

"Mother."

"Before she came up," Jackson said.

"Why the name change?"

"He did a lot of New England theater work while at Yale. That was his stage name. He just kept using it."

"What did he want from you?"

"To talk to my boss. He wants to rent the entire string of horses up in Glacier Park to take some Japanese tourists on a trail ride. He works for the museum in Cody and arranges cross-cultural events."

"Really?" Delaney pressed. "Sounds like a very responsible position, doesn't it, Mother?"

"OK, I'll grant you that. An actor?"

"Couldn't you just see him playing James Bond or someone like that?" Delaney questioned.

Develyn bit her lip and refused to glance at Lily Martin.

● ● ●

"I told you I don't ride large animals," Lily sputtered.

"You don't ride small ones, either, so what does that mean? I'm not having my best friend come all the way to Wyoming to see me and not ride my horse."

"If I had known this, I would have stayed away."

"What a wimpina."

"And your point is?"

"You are going to ride, Lily girl."

"I'd rather not."

Develyn tightened the cinch on My Maria, then pulled herself into the saddle. "I'll tire her out a little first."

"Great! Have a nice afternoon. I'll see you tomorrow."

"Lily!"

"Perhaps I'll go catch some rays with Dee." She motioned to the shaded dirt in front of the cabin.

"No, she needs some quiet time. She's studying the Purdue catalog, trying to decide on a major."

"She's changing again?"

"She thought about changing to nutrition, but it has too much chemistry. She was trying to avoid taking a class with Mr. Corvette from South Carolina."

"So what does that leave her?"

"Today's debate is between child psychology and drama."

"A sudden interest in acting?"

"So it seems. I'll be right back. Let me stretch her legs out."

Develyn turned My Maria north and dug her heels into the paint horse's flanks. The burst of speed slid Develyn against the cantle, but she leaned forward, gripped with her knees, and refused to grab the saddle horn. The wind whipped at her straw cowboy hat, but it stayed put. Develyn found the rhythm and was soon rocking back and forth.

"We haven't had many rides in the past few days. Summer is almost gone. Casey will take real good care of you and ride you some. I'll be back next year and . . ."

She turned the galloping horse east with a slight touch of her knee.

"That's the same speech I gave Brownie thirty-five years ago. But I have more motivation this time. I want to see you and Uncle Henry, and Casey and Jackson and their little one. There is no way that girl won't have a baby nine months after they get married. I'll want to see how Renny is doing and check on Quint and Lindsay . . . oh, and Mrs. Tagley."

Develyn circled My Maria and galloped toward the waiting Lily Martin. "And, of course, Cooper. Mrs. Tagley thinks he's the one. I know she does. And to tell you the truth, I do too. He's the right one at the wrong time. If I were twenty-one and he were thirty-one, if there had been fewer mistakes, fewer tears . . .

"But his family can't have girls. That's the strangest thing I've ever heard of. And that means no Delaney. You see what I'm saying, honey. The right man at the wrong time. Rats."

In a fog of dry, yellow dust, Develyn reined up and spun My Maria one full circle before dismounting.

"Wow, Ms. Worrell, I'm impressed. I can't believe you've learned that much this summer."

"My Maria is a good horse, just a little snotty." She handed the reins to the shorter, dark-haired lady. "Your turn."

"No. Really, Dev."

"Let's ride together. You get on, then I'll swing up behind."

"Oh, no, I don't know how to steer. You drive. I'll ride behind."

"OK."

"What did I do? Did I just agree to ride your horse?"

"Come on, Lil." Develyn climbed back into the saddle and reached her hand down.

With a grunt, a giggle, and a groan, Lily made it up. She wrapped her arms around Develyn's waist.

"Take it slow, Ms. Worrell. I have a sick man back in Casper who wants me to marry him. I don't want to croak yet."

"You're not scared, are you?"

"This is fast enough."

"Fast? If she went any slower, My Maria would fall asleep."

"What's that noise?"

"She needs a lube job."

"What?"

"It's my cell phone, Lil." Develyn dug in her pocket. "Kind of breaks the ambience, doesn't it?" She plopped her hat on the saddle horn and shoved the phone to her ear.

"Hello?"

"Hi, Miss Dev, where are you?"

She studied the sky. "I'm out for a ride near Argenta. Where are you, Quint?"

"I'm still in Texas, but I'm thinking I should fly home. Do you know what's going on at the ranch? I've been trying to reach someone since six this morning. There's no one there."

"Of course there isn't. You gave them the weekend off."

"I did?"

"I saw Cuban and the boys in Casper yesterday. He said you gave everyone a few days paid vacation before fall work begins."

"I did no such thing."

"He said you left a message out on the message board in the hanger. I'm sure Cuban wouldn't make that up."

"I didn't do any such thing, but I agree, Cuban wouldn't make it up. That's strange, isn't it? I'm flying home."

"How's Lindsay?"

"She got the job and just rented a furnished condo. Her boss and wife are taking her out to supper to introduce her to the other staff."

"How's Daddy doing with all that?"

"I was doing fine until this ranch exodus thing."

"Anything you want me to do?"

"If you see the boys, tell them to get back to the ranch. I don't want to leave it vacant. You riding with Casey?"

"My friend Lily came to see me, so we're out for a ride."

"Tell Miss Lily that I had a nice talk with Alberto Rogers. He's the president of the Texas Bar, and he knows her Stewart. He says he's truly one of the finest gentlemen in the profession. So I give her permission to marry him."

"I'll tell her. Bye, Quint."

Develyn prodded My Maria to a trot.

Lily clutched tighter. "What are you doing?"

"That was your friend, Quint."

"My friend. I've never met the man."

"But you talk to him often?"

"On several occasions. We have a mutual friend."

"Hmmm, and you didn't bother telling me?"

"You didn't ask."

"Well, your pal Quint Burdett, says that the president of the Texas Bar gave your Stewart a five-star rating. So your friend Quint says to go ahead and marry him."

"Goody."

"I can't believe that. You getting chummy with Quint."

"He's a very nice man, Dev. Miss Emily was one lucky lady. Where were guys like that when we were young?"

"Riding horses in Wyoming, I suppose."

"Can we slow down now?"

"You need a change of pace?"

"Yes, please."

Develyn kicked My Maria, and she broke into a gallop.

"Dev!" Lily screamed.

"I thought that was reverse."

"I want off right now!"

"You'll have to jump. Try to land on your feet and keep running."

Develyn reined up and slowed My Maria. "Oh, Lily, admit it. You like the wind in your face and leather slapping your rear."

"Now that I've lived through it, I suppose it was alright. Can I get off now?"

"Just one more thing, then we better get to the cabin. There's a thunderhead blowing this way. It will dump rain."

Develyn tugged the reins back and brought her leg over My Maria's head.

"What are you doing?"

"Time for you to ride solo."

"Oh, no."

"You can't say you rode a horse if you haven't been on one by yourself."

"I can lie."

"You cannot. When you ride by yourself, you set the speed."

"I can go slow?"

"Very slow."

"Well, just for a few feet maybe."

Develyn slid to the ground and gave Lily the reins. She grabbed the paint mare's headstall and led her across the prairie. "See how nice that is?"

"It is rather fun."

"All right. When we get back to the corral, I'll grab my camera."

"Hmmm. Perhaps I could borrow your hat."

"I knew it!" Develyn shouted.

"Is that your phone again? Or did I do something wrong?"

Develyn turned loose of the headstall. "You're on your own, sweetie. Hello?"

"Hi, Devy-girl."

"Wait . . wait, what do you mean, I'm on my own? I don't want to be on my own."

"Pull back on the reins gently and say 'whoa.'"

"Whoa."

"Not you, Renny."

"Devy, who are you talking to?"

"Lily came to see me. I'm letting her ride My Maria."

"Lily is there? That does it. I'm headed back to Wyomin'. Tell Lily darlin' howdy for me."

"I suppose she talked with you on the phone too. Hmmm. Now, Mr. Mustang Breaker, what did you decide about the job?"

"It's a dream job, Dev. Good pay, summers and holidays off. They have a great apartment above the indoor arena. Expenses paid. Nice folks. The president of the college came to talk to me. It's one of those deals a guy only stumbles into once in his life."

Develyn watched as Lily nudged My Maria to a trot. Somewhere to the west she heard thunder, but it was still sunny above.

"So you're going to take the job?"

"I turned them down, Dev."

"What? Why?"

"I spent forty-two years not being tied down by my work. I like the freedom. I'm going to get a phone call some mornin' before daybreak that Lloyd and Denise's cattle are stranded in a November blizzard up in the Big Horns, and I'll be hundreds of miles away giving some eighteen-year-olds a pop quiz in elementary equine production. You're right, Dev. I can't do that. It would eat at my soul."

Develyn's voice softened. "I think you're right, Renny."

"I owe that to you. You could see what I was really like."

"You are my hero, Renny. Not a silver screen actor or a sports star. Not even the rodeo star with a world championship buckle. But you're my hero. No matter what danger I faced, you'd be the first one I'd want with me."

Lily circled the horse and headed back.

"Renny?"

"Thanks, Dev. You're the most special friend. I don't know what's up ahead for you. Don't know if, or whom, you'll marry. But ask him if I can have permission to call my Devy-girl ever' once in a while, when I can't beat the melancholies and need to hear your voice."

"I don't need permission from anyone. Day or night, cowboy, you call me. When are you headed back?"

"Right now. I'm in Burley, Idaho, gettin' some gas."

"We're doing a barbecue for Lily and her Stewart tomorrow night. Anyway, you can come?"

"I'll be there. Count on it."

"It will break my heart if you aren't."

"Darlin', did you ever dream about what it would have been like?"

"Yes, but I'm too old, remember?"

"Too many years and too many tears."

"But you will always be my Renny. You know that, don't you?"

"Yes, I do. Hey, the trip wasn't a complete waste of time. Guess who I ran across in Twin Falls?"

"Meg Ryan?"

Renny laughed. "Janie DeFore is in town. She's doing PR work for Dodge Trucks."

"Is she an old friend?"

"She hated me for four straight years while she was in high school."

"Does she still hate you?"

"Nope."

"What does this mean?"

"When she's in Sheridan next week, I promised to buy her some supper."

"Is she . . ."

"Yep."

"Has she been . . ."

"Nope."

"Does she have . . ."

"Nope."

"Do you think . . ."

"I don't have a clue. That's up to the Lord, I reckon."

"Whoops, the thunderstorm is getting closer. I don't want another cabin to burn down. Talk to you tomorrow."

"Your cabin burned down?"

"Now you will have to come see me."

"Yeah, I surely will, Miss Dev. Bye, darlin.'"

"Drive careful, mustang breaker."

Lily rode straight at her. "Dev, do something! She won't mind me."

"Spin her a few times, then get off. She's scared of lightning."

"So am I!"

"Turn her head and spur her."

Lily kicked My Maria's flanks. The mare galloped toward the corrals with Lily screaming "No!" at the top of her voice.

Develyn jogged after them. *I said turn her head first, then spur her. If you fall off and break your neck, I will be very angry with you.*

Lily's feet bounced free from the stirrups.

Hang on, girl! Hang on!

Develyn stumbled but kept upright as she raced after the galloping horse. Raindrops slapped her face as the cloud opened up to a downpour. My Maria slowed to a trot then halted at the corral gate. Develyn huffed her way up to them.

Lily banged down off the horse, staggered two steps back, and stumbled to her rear on the moist prairie dirt.

Develyn pulled Lily to her feet. "Are you alright?"

"Alright? Alright? I'm wonderful!" Lily screamed into the

crashing thunder. "I'm alive. I lived through it." She danced around the sagebrush. "Yes! Yes! Yes!"

Develyn grabbed her shoulders. They both danced to the rumble of the thunder. Rain streaked down their faces.

"I'm alive, Devy."

"Yes, you are."

"And I'm going to marry Stewart."

"Yes, you are."

"And as soon as I can, I'm going to buy a horse."

Develyn stopped dancing.

Like an empty bucket, the rain stopped all at once.

The cloud blew west.

The sun broke through.

"Lily Martin's going to buy a horse?"

"I loved it."

"But you said you thought you were going to die."

"That's the part I loved the most."

12

"And that's why I say, at our age, it's risky trying something new like this." Stewart tugged at his tie as if his collar was too tight.

Develyn sipped ice water from a crystal goblet. "You presented an excellent case, counselor. But your strongest point is also your weakest."

"Our age?" he murmured.

"Yes. At our age we're prone to follow logic and reason as if it's a divine command."

"It pays good dividends," Stewart boasted.

"I agree," Develyn continued. "And that, too, is your weakness."

Lily turned to Cooper. "Your honor, I'm confused."

"My word, are we spoiling a fine meal arguing over legal technicalities?" Stewart asked.

Cooper wiped his mouth with a green linen napkin. "I believe the counsel for the defense still has the floor."

"Thank you, your honor," Develyn said. "I would now like to present my closing arguments. The honorable prosecutor, Mr. Stewart Lawrence, Esquire, has made it clear that the proposition under consideration should be rejected because, first, it is imprudent at our advanced ages to engage in such a risky venture, and second, sticking with logic and reason would be a better financial investment. Is that correct?"

"Sounds quite convincing," Stewart concurred.

Develyn tapped on the water glass with her spoon. "And it is my contention that at our advanced and decrepit age . . ."

"I resent that remark," Lily smirked.

"We have few opportunities to follow our hearts and dispose of that stinking logic and reason. I say that if we do not follow our hearts now, if we let this grand opportunity ride into the western sunset, never to raise its magnificent head again, we will regret it the rest of our lives."

"No matter how short that might be," Lily added.

"Yes." Develyn triumphed. "The mind has an uncanny ability to overcome defeat, but the heart rejected aches forever."

"Do you think she had too much flambé sauce?" Stewart chided. He glanced around the restaurant at other patrons who were listening to their discussion. "Perhaps we've all had too much flambé sauce," he whispered into his napkin.

Develyn stood up. "And for my concluding argument . . ."

"Good heavens, Ms. Worrell, be seated," Stewart pleaded.

She glanced over at Cooper Tallon. He pointed to her empty chair.

She plopped down. "As to the idea that logic pays the best dividends, Mr. Prosecutor is correct. This can be an expensive change of life. But that's my point. At our age not a one of us needs more dividends. Most of us have life so structured that right now our dividends will outlive us. Is that not true, Mr. Prosecutor?"

"Objection," Stewart puffed.

"Objection overruled," Cooper replied. "Answer the question."

"Yes, I believe my dividends will outlive me."

"So we do not need dividends. We do not need a boost of financial stability. What we do need is adrenalin. We need something to make our hearts race and our spirits soar. We need a reason to get up in the morning and hurry home after work. We need to know someone is depending on us and longs to see our face. Someone who doesn't care if it's a bad hair day. Someone who doesn't mind if our socks don't match our earrings. Someone who doesn't care if the kid pharmacist always gives us the senior citizen discount. We don't need dividends; we need love fulfilled!"

Soft applause broke out in the restaurant.

"Good grief," Stewart murmured.

"Dev presents that good of a case?" Lily asked.

"Heavens, no. A second-year law student could shred it, but everyone in this room is staring at us."

"If you go anywhere with Dev, you get used to that," Lily said.

Develyn elbowed Cooper Tallon. "Your honor, what is your ruling?"

"The court is recessed while the bench ponders the verdict."

"I'm not used to judges pondering a verdict," Stewart said.

"In Wyomin', there's no *g* on the word *ponderin'*," Cooper corrected. "In renderin' my verdict, the fact that the prosecutor is from a foreign land will not affect my decision."

"That's very judicial of you," Stewart replied.

"When can we expect a verdict, Your Honor?" Develyn asked.

Cooper stabbed his meat. "When I have finished my steak."

"You only have one more bite," Develyn prodded. "Hurry up."

"I will not rush the last bite of steak. It's the most important bite of the evenin'."

"Why is that, Your Honor?" Lily asked.

"Because, dear lady, it is the last bite of steak I will have until . . . "

"Tomorrow?" Develyn interjected.

"Yes, until tomorrow. That means the moist, succulent, sweet juices of this medium-rare ribeye must soothe my pallet for many hours, if not days. This one little bite, and the memory thereof, must sustain me through many toils and snares."

"Coop, eat the last bite of meat," Develyn snarled.

He jammed the morsel into his mouth.

"Now, we want a verdict, and we want a verdict right now," she demanded.

Cooper rapped his spoon on the table. "Court is in session. Having carefully reviewed all the evidence in this case . . ."

"What evidence?" Stewart protested.

"Quiet in the court. I have examined all the evidence, or lack thereof, and come to this conclusion based on Cowboy Rule #14 established in the case of *Sissy McClain vs. Josiah 'Three Fingers' McClain,* August 4, 1872, Ft. Laramie, Wyoming Territory."

"What is Cowboy Rule #14?" Lily asked.

"Never, ever, stand between a girl and her horse. This court rules in favor of the defendant. Lillian Suzanne Martin retains legal permission to purchase a horse, as long as it's a decent breed and not one of those insane thoroughbreds."

"Yes!" Develyn jumped to her feet.

Lily danced over to Develyn. "I won!" They slapped high fives, then plopped back down in their chairs.

Stewart Lawrence pulled his linen napkin completely over his head until his face was covered. "I appeal," he mumbled.

"Appeal denied."

"I appeal the denied appeal."

"The appeal of the denied appeal is denied. In fact, everything you say between now and midnight is denied. Court dismissed."

"Stewart doesn't take defeat well," Develyn mused.

"He never loses," Lily shrugged.

"If you three don't mind, I'd prefer to shrivel up and crawl into this hole-in-the-ground by myself."

"I can hardly wait to get home and start horse shopping," Lily said.

"What if you get bucked off and break a leg?" Stewart grumbled from under the napkin.

"Then you'll just have to carry Lily in your arms everywhere you go," Develyn said.

He pulled off the napkin and winked at Lily. "I can live with that."

"So can I," Lily beamed.

● ● ●

Cooper's diesel engine growled in harmony with the rain-sprinkled blacktop as they rolled west on Highway 20.

"I didn't quite hear all of that," Cooper said. "Too many years running heavy equipment without ear protection."

"I'll scoot over, Mr. Tallon. But that's the most pitiful begging I've ever heard just to get me to sit next to you."

"What did you say?"

"Hmmm, you are very sneaky for an old bachelor."

"You've got to be sneaky to survive to be an old bachelor."

"Well, Stewart's bachelor days are over."

"I like him. He's a good guy in his own stuffy Indiana way."

"Are you saying people from Indiana are stuffy?"

"If you, Lily, Delaney, and Stewart are representative of the Hoosier State, well, there must be lots of fine people back there."

"Every state has its share of saints and jerks."

"And some states have more than their share," he laughed. "I reckon Jackson Hill's bachelor days are over too."

"I can't tell whom I'm happier for, Casey or Lily."

"This marriage thing is spreading like an epidemic."

Cooper flipped on the windshield wipers, though there was barely enough rain to warrant it. The approaching headlights turned south. The yellow line on Highway 20 soared at them like a volley of arrows fired in unison with the thwap, thwap, thwap of the windshield wipers.

Develyn tugged at her diamond stud earrings. "The talk of marriage killed the conversation."

"Sorry, Dev. Can I be honest and just blurt something out?"

"Of course." *Just don't crush me too much, Mr. Tallon.*

"I would dearly love to pull this rig over to the side of the road, kiss you, and ask you to marry me. But I can't. There are too many doubts runnin' through my mind and heart."

"Such as?"

"I don't know which are more important. I have no doubt that I love you. I reckon any fool can see that. But even if for some unexplainable reason you loved me, you have your life in Indiana; and I have my life here or somewhere. I'm not even sure. You've got to take care of your Delaney. You came off a tough deal in your marriage, and I don't have a clue if I even know how to love a woman the way she should be loved. I'm ten years older than you, and that bothers me a lot. Not that we'd be incompatible but that you'd be stuck nursemaidin' an old man. I wish, Dev, it was years ago we had met, when we were young and impetuous and had the future to share and learn together. Anyway, all of this is rather foolish talk for an old man who's not sure of how you feel. Man, I'm glad it's dark in here. This is the most personal conversation I've ever had with a lady."

Develyn clutched his thick, strong arm. "Coop, if things were different, I'd have you pull over, and I'd kiss you and ask you to marry me."

"You'd ask me?"

"Honey, this is the twenty-first century. But I'm confused about all those things too. I'm wired to teach school. I have a commitment to the kids of Crawfordsville, Indiana. My twenty-year-old daughter still needs me. I know the present seems so complicated, and the distant past simpler. In the right time at the right place, years ago, lots and lots of years ago . . ."

"I got to admit one more thing."

"Do I get to find out more about Cooper Tallon?"

"No, you know all about my workaholic, boring history. But I have to admit that I'd have a nervous breakdown asking you to marry me, so to skip that part is a great relief."

"You more scared of me saying yes or no?" she teased.

"Either."

"While we are ponderin' our complex lives, I'll just have to come up with a good answer that will put your mind at ease, providing the time is ever right for you to ask me to marry you."

"Are you sayin' that when the Lord's timing is right, you aren't exactly opposed to the idea?"

"That's a good way of putting it. In the Lord's timing, I'm not exactly against the idea of getting married."

Cooper laughed. "That makes me feel better, I think."

"I suppose it doesn't sound like unbridled enthusiasm."

He patted her knee. "We understand each other, Dev."

She squeezed his arm. "Yes, we do, Mr. Tallon."

He passed a slow-moving semitruck and pulled back into the westbound lane.

"So, Ms. Develyn Gail Upton Worrell, what do you reckon we should do now?"

"I think you should pull the truck over right now."

"And ask you to marry me?"

"No, I think tonight we ought to just stick to the kissing part."

Cooper Tallon bounced the truck to the right shoulder of the road, slammed on the brakes, and killed the engine.

● ● ●

Develyn poked her head through the rails of the corral fence. "He looks lonely."

"Brownie is in there with twelve other horses. How can he be lonely?" her brother insisted.

"I don't care. He misses me. I can see it in his eyes."

Dewayne grabbed up a rock and slung it out on the sage-covered prairie. "He's going to miss you a whole lot more. Daddy says we're leaving as soon as Mama comes back from Mrs. Tagley's."

Develyn pulled her head back from the rail and stared toward the cabins. She shaded her eyes from the early morning sun. "I like Argenta, Dewa. Do you?"

"Not as much as Crawfordsville. I can't wait to play baseball. Some day I'm going to play second base for the St. Louis Cardinals."

"Why don't you root for the Cleveland Indians, like Daddy does?"

"Because they never win, that's why. Come on, let's go."

"I need to talk to Brownie alone."

"You'd better hurry. Mama told you to say your good-byes last night."

"Brownie and I are too good of friends to say good-bye only once."

Develyn crawled between the rails and brushed her hand off on her khaki shorts. She noticed three orange Popsicle drops on her pink T-shirt. As she approached the remuda, the big brown one shuffled her way.

She rubbed the scar on his ear and walked him to the rail.

"Brownie, I want you to behave yourself this fall and winter. You eat right and get plenty of exercise. Don't stay out in the blizzards and get sick. And sometimes when you dream, dream of me, OK? Because I know I'll dream of you.

"Mother says I talk a lot, and maybe I do. But most times I talk about silly things so I won't have to talk about important things. You're my best friend in the whole world because you let me talk about important things. You are a very good listener. Mother says I'm not a good listener, but that's not true. I hear everything she tells me, even the part that doesn't make any sense."

She laid her cheek against the gelding's nose.

"Being with you is so peaceful. I like you. I like me when I'm with you. I don't always like me, Brownie. Sometimes, like when I'm around the girls in my class like Gloria or Kathy or Diane, I don't like me at all.

"Now I told you I'm coming back next summer. I'm going to talk Daddy into letting me stay for four weeks instead of two. And we will ride every day. I'll groom you and brush you and tie pretty ribbons in your tail.

"I was kidding about the ribbons. Dewayne says boy horses don't like ribbons. And I know you are a boy horse. Sort of."

"Devy-girl," Dewayne hollered, "Mama says hurry up."

Develyn hugged the horse's nose. "I love you, Brownie."

Dewayne grabbed her shoulder and shook it.

She clutched the horse tighter. "I love you very, very much."

"I love you, too, Mom. Now wake up. It's Uncle Dewayne, and he only has a few minutes to talk."

Develyn sat straight up in the dark, stuffy cabin. In the shadows Delaney shoved her cell phone at her. "You might want to step out on the porch where the reception is better."

"Dewayne?"

"Your twin brother, remember?"

Develyn shuffled out to the soft westerly breeze on the moonlit, uncovered porch. "Dewa?"

"Hi, Devy-girl. Man, it's good to hear your voice. No one in the world is allowed to call me that but my little sis."

"I'm only six minutes behind you. Remember that. Where are you?"

"I'm in Kuwait. Where are you?"

"Wyoming. I told you about coming out to Argenta, didn't I?"

"I can't believe you actually found it."

"Are you OK?"

"What time is it there?"

"I don't know. The middle of the night. And you?"

"It's noon here. Hey, are Mom and David back from Austria?"

"Yes, but they went to Wisconsin to Aunt Harriet's. Uncle Leland had another stroke. Why do you ask?"

"Devy, I had a little accident."

"You fell?"

"How did you know that?"

"You fell off a cliff?"

"No, our chopper was landing on the aircraft carrier, and it crashed about fifty feet into the deck."

"Oh, no."

"Tom Green was killed in the explosion. A couple of others were injured bad. I was lucky."

"You didn't get hurt?"

"I busted both ankles, that's all."

"That's all? It sounds horrible."

"I'm on my way to Germany for surgery. I should be in the states by September. I'll be home by Christmas. I'm getting out, Devy."

"Out of the Navy?"

"Twenty-five years of this is long enough. Hope I'm doin' the right thing, sis."

"Dewa, you do what the Lord wants you to do. But your little sis is going to be thrilled to have big brother around."

"Only six minutes older. Did you really dream about me falling?"

"Yes, several days ago, Dewayne. Twins are close. You know that."

"My time's up with the satellite phone. Call Mom for me. I might not get back on until after the surgery."

"I will. I love you, Dewa."

"I love you, Devy-girl. Kiss the cowboys and be happy. You deserve it."

Develyn sauntered to the edge of the deck and gazed into the Wyoming night. Uncle Henry waddled over to her.

"Hi, honey. You know what? The Lord blessed me with a great brother and a great dad—and if I will let my pride loose, a great mother too."

● ● ●

Develyn and Lily loitered in the shadows of the cotton-woods and studied activity taking place next to the cabin.

"It looks like a circus is coming to town. That's a huge awning," Lily said.

"Coop said the guys at Wyoming Tent and Awning rented that one for the same price as the smaller one. This size uses steel cable to tie it down instead of ropes. We might need it."

"How many you expecting?"

"No more than a couple dozen, that's for sure."

"You mean, you invited everyone in town?"

"Just about," Dev laughed.

"That awning will hold a couple hundred. Shelley Nagle's daughter, Wenonah, set up an awning like that at Turkey Run for her wedding. Over three hundred attended, but not all were under the awning all at once."

"Wenonah got married? You didn't tell me that. I should have sent a present."

"We gave them a nice crystal serving bowl."

"We did?"

Lily took her arm. "I put your name on it, and you owe me $36.75."

"How nice of Ms. Worrell to remember one of her students."

"I thought so." Lily studied the yard. "That's quite a crew Coop has."

"I'm glad Stewart can help out. Leon's been here since 6:00 a.m."

"He does know the party is tonight, doesn't he?"

"Yes, he's a little hyped, which, for him, is quite normal."

"Dee's pitching right in too."

"She wants to keep busy so she won't worry about the doctor's appointment."

"What time is Casey taking her over?"

"Right after they feed the road crew."

"Do you want to take the Lincoln to town?" Lily asked.

"Oh, no, we need the space to bring home the supplies. Are you ready?"

Lily studied the clouds. "Do you have lightning storms every afternoon?"

"Most times there's little rain and plenty of thunder."

"Is that plane circling around?" Lily asked.

Develyn spotted the silver and blue Cessna. "That's Quint's. Actually, it's Lindsay's plane, but I suppose he didn't want to leave it in Texas. Let's go over to the landing strip and see what he wants."

"He probably wants Miss Dev."

Develyn stuck out her tongue at Lily.

● ● ●

Develyn and Lily leaned against the Jeep as Quint Burdett strolled toward them.

"Oh, my," Lily confided. "I had no idea he was so tall and so handsome."

"Ruggedly distinguished, don't you think?"

Lily giggled. "I want to have his baby."

"I can't believe you said that."

"I didn't. It was a postmenopausal anomaly."

"Howdy, Miss Dev, and this charming lady has to be Miss Lily."

When he reached down to hug Lily, he plucked her off her feet. Her arms went around his neck.

"Mr. Burdett, we finally meet," Lily gasped.

"Call me Quint." He lowered her down and hugged Develyn. "Hi, darlin'."

She hugged him back and kissed his clean-shaven cheek. "How was your flight?"

"Fine. Just can't figure out who would want to leave that fake note for the boys. I never leave headquarters unoccupied. Mom and Pop Gleason went to Billings to watch their grandson in a baseball tournament. I knew that, but having the crew take off, that troubles me. I can't wait to get up there."

"You haven't been home yet?"

"I was just flying over Argenta to get to the ranch and noticed a big white awning or tent over at the cabins."

"Only one cabin left," she reported.

"Yes, that's what I heard. Anyway, when I saw the awning, I naturally assumed someone was having a wedding. And, well . . ."

"You needed to find out if your Miss Dev was getting married behind your back?" Lily asked.

"I suppose that was it."

"It's a long story. It's just a barbecue I'm having, and Coop thought we needed a place that was out of the rain. I really hope you can come. Cuban, Tiny, and the boys are invited too."

"Yes, well, if I can figure out what is going on, I will try to make it. I'd better get on up to the ranch."

"Call me when you find out anything. I'm curious too."

Quint had just turned to head back to the plane when

Develyn spotted a white Ford truck bouncing down the gravel road into Argenta.

"Quint, do you know a man name Hunter Burke?"

"He's the new assistant curator at the firearms museum in Cody."

"I wasn't sure of his position."

"I met him last month. He knows his Winchesters."

"What do you mean?" she asked.

"He came out to the ranch last month and took some pictures of my One of One Thousand, Winchester 1873."

"Why?"

"The museum is trying to locate, take pictures, and identify every one made. Why do you ask about him?"

"He just drove by on the road."

"Dev thinks he's a crook," Lily blurted out.

"Why on earth would you think that?"

"It's very subjective. And I'm not as sure now. I'd appreciate it if you'd check on the safety of your One of One Thousand before you phone me."

"You don't think he'd . . ."

"Burke's hanging around the cub, and mama bear suspects everyone," Lily added.

Develyn and Lily got back in the car and bounced over to the gravel road.

"I can't believe you turned Quint down. That might have been the dumbest move since Hugh Grant refused Julia Roberts in the movie *Notting Hill*."

"Lily, there is more to life than money, good looks, and a charming personality."

"Whatever it is, I can live without it," Lil teased.

"Are you having second thoughts about dear Stewart?"

"No, I'm not. Quint's out of my league but not yours. Julia and Hugh got together at the end of the film. Maybe there is hope for you."

● ● ●

They returned to Argenta with supplies and were still unloading when the dimpled cowboy with blond hair curling out from under his black hat walked straight up to Lily Martin, hugged her, and kissed her on the lips.

"I say," Stewart Lawrence muttered as he stepped closer.

"If you aren't Lily Martin, I'm going to be in big trouble."

"And if you aren't Renny Slater, we'll both be in big trouble."

Develyn stepped between them. "I see you met my Lily?"

Slater stuck out his hand. "Stewart, no offense, I hope. Miss Lily and I have talked on the phone a number of times. I feel like an old family friend. I expect congratulations are in order."

"I didn't think . . . yes, thank you. This is my first view of cowboy hospitality."

"I take it I'm a little early?" Renny asked. "What can I do to help?"

Develyn grabbed him by the arm. "Go ask Coop. He insisted on hosting everything. It sort of ended up being a

going-away party of sorts. Although I don't intend to leave
until Sunday afternoon."

Renny circled his arms around Develyn. "Indiana is lucky.
They get Miss Dev for the rest of the year while the rest of us
can only hold her in our dreams."

"Oh, brother, I'll be so glad to get away from this gooey
cowboy charm," Develyn chided.

Renny shrugged and winked at Lily. "She is one tough lady.
I knew that the first day I met her when she got back on that
paint mare after being bucked off."

Develyn stepped out of his arms. "As I remember it, I left
the arena in tears."

"Yeah, but you rode out on your own horse." He sauntered
over to where Cooper Tallon tossed wood onto a long, raised
barbecue grill.

"I can't believe Renny," Lily laughed. "He's the real live
stereotype, isn't he?"

"He's the real deal, honey. Renny's every little cowgirl's
dream, right down to his bow legs and soft heart."

"How did you find him?"

"Don't you remember? I was sitting on the bench in front
of Mrs. Tagley's eating an orange Popsicle. He stopped out in
the road, remember? From fifty feet away and with his dark
glasses on, I looked twenty-five instead of forty-five. It was a
mistake that didn't take him long to figure out."

"But he stuck around anyway?"

"Lily, if a gal had to go through life with only two or three
friends, you'd want one of them to be Renny Slater."

"No wonder you sounded happy when you phoned me."

"That's not true. I remember some panicked calls to you. But it has been a good summer."

Leon ran up to her. "I got to go home and change. I got my shirt dirty."

"Why don't you wait until right before the barbecue starts and then change? Just in case you get dirty again."

"Yeah, I'll do that. Did you know that we have ten watermelons?"

"Yes, Lily and I just brought them back from town. They were having a sale on Green River watermelons."

"If twenty people show up, we all get half a watermelon. I ain't never had half a watermelon."

"If twenty people come, I'll be shocked."

"When I get my driver's license, Mr. Tallon said he'd teach me how to drive a dump truck."

"That will be wonderful."

"He said he might need a boy to do chores for him next summer. If I come back to Grandma's, he'll give me a job."

"Gives you something to look forward to, doesn't it?"

"Yep. I ain't never had nothin' to look forward to. I got to go. Coop needs me."

Leon bolted back to the awning.

"Dev, he doesn't seem like the Dougie Baxter type to me."

"Lil, that kid changed overnight. This is remarkable."

"Maybe Dougie will change overnight."

Develyn looked into Lily's green eyes.

They responded as a duet: "No."

● ● ●

Develyn was sorting a pile of dirty clothes when the cell phone rang. She stepped over to the window when she answered it.

"Miss Dev, have you seen good ol' Hunter Burke?"

"Quint, what is it?"

"Someone decided to steal my One of One Thousand."

"Oh, no."

"Someone who knew where it was. Someone who knew how to get the crew to town so no one would be around. He left the other guns. He just took the one gun."

"And you suspect Hunter?"

"When I called the museum, they said they fired him two weeks ago."

"What for?"

"He photocopied a bunch of private documents for his personal use."

"That's strange. But it doesn't mean he took the Winchester."

"I know. But he is the last one to look at it, besides family. Maybe he told someone. The sheriff's here now and wants to talk to Burke."

"I'll keep an eye out."

"Miss Dev, I might not get down to the barbecue. I'm waitin' on Cuban and the boys. The only chance of retrieving that gun is to catch him quick. It looks like whomever took my gun cut across the pasture on an ATV."

"A four-wheeler? Quint, do you know where Cooper Tallon's spring meadow is on Cedar Creek?"

"I used to lease that from him."

"We were up there when Hunter came by and asked permission to store a gas can for his four-wheeler. He claimed to want to scout out the southern Big Horns before hunting season. But besides gas, he left several boxes of bullets. Revolver bullets."

"You thinking that's a part of his route?"

"I don't know anything, except he really did leave gas and bullets there."

"On second thought, I might come down that way. Tell Cuban and the boys to wait for me there."

"Quint, I'm so sorry about this."

"Me too, Dev. The gun's worth a $125 grand, but it's the sentimental value that gnaws at me. Miss Emily gave it to me on our twenty-fifth wedding anniversary."

"Doesn't Mrs. Tagley have some old guns like that?"

"She used to. I sold them all for her."

"When was that?"

"Years ago. Her husband bought up old guns during the depression. He ended up with three hundred. He just kept them in a back room at their house. Well, about 1980 Mrs. Tagley wanted to clean out the room and use it for a storeroom. So I took them to a couple of gun shows and sold them—mostly all Winchester 1894 carbines. Quite used, as you can imagine. The only other One of One Thousand in Wyoming is owned by Dr. Bob Simmons in Jackson. He has his on loan this summer to some museum in Japan."

"What should I do if I see Hunter?"

"Call the sheriff's office and stall him as long as you can."

"Johnson County or Natrona County? I had that problem once before."

"It won't matter this time. Place him under citizen's arrest if you have to."

"I don't think I could do that."

"Have Cree-Ryder do it. There isn't a man in Wyoming that isn't afraid of her."

"There's one. And he's going to marry her."

"Casey married? Ranch hands all over the basin will sleep better knowing that. Now what time's supper?"

"Around six o'clock."

"Me and the boys will be down your way. Whether we can stop and eat will depend on what happens with this investigation."

● ● ●

"You didn't tell Quint that Mrs. Tagley had a 'One of a Thousand' in her safe?" Cooper asked.

"I feel funny mentioning anything in her safe. If she never told anyone, I shouldn't either. Buy why would someone steal Quint's gun? Wouldn't it be almost impossible to resell it? You said it has a serial number, and everyone knows that it belongs to him."

"I'm sure there is some collector, somewhere, that would jump at the chance to own it, even if procured illegally."

"But he can't advertise that he has it."

"No, but if he was on the museum staff, he might have contact with those looking for such a gun."

"I don't like Hunter, but I can't believe he'd do that."

They watched Casey and Delaney drive up and park in the shade of the cottonwood, away from the other vehicles.

"You're right," Coop said. "Innocent until proven guilty."

"You talking daughters or gun thieves?"

"Gun thieves," he replied. "Now go on and visit with her. Just let me know the verdict when you get a chance.

Dev strolled over as Casey got out of the driver's side of Jackson's truck.

"Come talk to your girl, Mama. I'm going to the store to check on my man."

Oh, Lord, my little Dee. Oh, give us strength, dear Jesus.

Develyn scooted into the truck and rolled the window halfway down. Delaney's shoulders slumped. She twisted several damp, rolled up tissues in her hands.

"Honey, what did you find out?"

"Everything," she whimpered.

"Tell it all to me, Dee. I want to know."

"Mom," Delaney cried. "I'm so sorry, Mom."

As Develyn hugged her daughter, tears flooded both faces and dripped to their blouses.

"Baby," Develyn sobbed. "It's OK. Whatever it is, it's OK. We'll get through it together, you and me. You cry all you want, and I'll cry with you."

Develyn rocked her daughter for several minutes.

"I'm so sorry, Mom . . . I'm so sorry."

"Baby, it's OK. Tell me what you are sorry about? What did the doctor tell you?"

"I wish I'd listened to you and we had gone to Maine together."

"That choice is long gone. The Lord will help us with the choices we have now."

"I was so stupid," Delaney sobbed. "I was stupid for not realizing your pain when Daddy cheated on you. I was stupid for blaming you for his heart attack. I was stupid for giving in to a guy that didn't want me all that much. I don't want to be stupid anymore."

"If you can learn that when you're twenty, you'll be twenty-five years ahead of me. Tell me what the doctor said. What kind of smart decision do we make from here?"

"I'm going to try not to cry, Mom. I'm a grown woman. OK, here goes. She said I was pregnant."

"You are?"

"That's why I missed my period. And then, when I got back home to Indiana, I had a miscarriage and lost the baby. Oh, God, I hurt all over."

Develyn held her daughter and wept.

Delaney heaved a breath. "How many miscarriages did you have?"

"After my sweet Dee was born, I had at least four, honey. Four that I carried long enough to know I was pregnant."

"Did you feel like you wanted to die when you found out?"

"Every time, baby. Every time."

"I really hoped I was not pregnant. I know I sinned, and I know the Lord can forgive me."

"He has forgiven you."

"But if I was pregnant, I was prepared to accept the consequences. So in some way I was prepared for either option but not this. If I hadn't sinned, the baby wouldn't have died."

"Honey, we can't play God. But I do know how you feel."

"How did you survive your miscarriages, Mom?"

"Time, and prayer . . . and friends . . . and David."

"Grandma's David?"

"No, the Lord's David, in the Bible. When the first baby was born to David and Bathsheba, it lived only a short time. After the baby died, David went on with life. He told people that someday, he could go and be with the baby, but the baby could never come and be with him. He needed to let go of his grief and take God's next step for him."

"Mom, the doctor said that due to the scar tissue and all, I could miscarry other babies."

Develyn hugged Delaney and sobbed. "It's OK, honey. It's OK. The Lord will take care of you."

"But you're crying, Mom."

"We can cry because we hurt, but that doesn't mean we aren't trusting the Lord at the same time."

"What am I going to do now?"

"You're going to go out and live your life, Dee. Accept God's forgiveness, and let him heal your hurts."

"You think I should go back to Purdue?"

"Whatever you decide, I will support you. It's your life, Dee. You make the decisions."

"You mean that?"

"Yes, I do."

"What would you do if you were me?"

"I wanted to be a teacher since I was ten years old. I have never wanted anything else. So, of course, if I were you, I'd finish college and teach. But you aren't me. That's the point."

"Are you going to tell anyone?"

"I would like to tell Lily and Coop. I take it Casey knows."

"Yeah, she cried with me all the way home."

"Would it be alright if I told Coop and Lily?"

"Yes. How about Grandma?"

"No, I will not tell Mother. You may tell her if and when you think it's the right time."

"I don't think I will."

"That's fine."

"I don't feel like a party."

"Why don't you go take a nap in the cabin? We have a couple of hours before everyone shows up. If you feel like it, come out and join us. If not, sleep in."

"What will you tell them?"

"That you aren't feeling well."

"Mother, I invited Hunter to the party. Was that OK?"

"That's OK, honey."

"I don't want to see him now."

"I'll talk to him."

"Mom, I've got something to confess."

"What, Dee?"

"Hunter came by last night, and I visited with him. I was afraid you'd get mad if I told you. Casey and Jackson had to run to Casper for some supplies for the state highway workers' lunches, so they dropped me off here. Hunt was waiting for me."

"I'm surprised Ms. Cree-Ryder left you here without a chaperone."

"She didn't know he was here. He parked his truck behind Mrs. Tagley's and walked over here."

"Why did he do that?"

"He said he liked to camp back in those trees."

"Camp?"

"I think that just means sleep in his truck. We sat behind the cabin on that old log and talked for several hours."

"You just talked?"

"Yes, Mom, I'm not a slut."

"I know you aren't, baby. I'm sorry if it sounded that way. What do you know about him?"

"He's angry and bitter. Did you know the museum fired him? That's why he was sleeping in his truck."

"I just heard that today."

"He found some of the inventory of old guns missing, and when he took those facts to his superiors, they fired him. He claims they are trying to cover up someone stealing some of the deluxe firearms."

"If he was treated wrong, he should take his case to the authorities or to the newspapers."

"They threatened him if he did. He said they would accuse him of the theft and get him arrested."

"He told you all of this?"

"Yes. He seemed to be rambling on and on. He wanted to go to Paris, maybe the Riviera. He said I should go with him."

"He got fired, has to live in his truck, but he wants you to go with him to Paris?"

"I think he was just angry and rambling on and on."

"What did you tell him?"

"I told him I wasn't going with him anywhere, but he could come see me again when he was not angry and bitter."

"That's good thinking."

"He kissed me, Mom."

"Oh?"

"He acted like I was easy. He did try to touch me, but I told him that's where I kept one of my knives. That's when he left."

"You said that?"

"Yeah, Casey taught me."

"Casey taught you how to say things that scare men away?"

"No, how to carry a knife where no one knows you have it."

13

Cooper Tallon hammered the triangle. All those huddled under the awning drew close to the huge, wood-fired barbecue. "I think the hostess should say a few words. So I present to you, Ms. Develyn Gail Worrell, who came here an Indiana schoolteacher and will go home a genuine Wyomin' cowboy girl."

"Coop, I'm not going to give a speech. That would be like saying we may never see each other again. I took thirty-five years to come back to Argenta. I'm never going to make that mistake again. Coop's right. I'm part Wyoming. Mrs. Tagley thinks I always have been. I'll be back. So this is just a party and not some big teary going-away thing. And if I have to say any more, I'll cry, and my makeup will smear, and that could frighten all of you."

"Are you goin' to talk all night, or do we get to eat?" Renny called out.

"Mr. Slater, that's one thing I love about cowboys: they aren't very subtle."

"Subtle don't fill the belly, Miss Dev," Renny shot back.

"Line up behind Leon," Develyn instructed. "He has been helping us set up since 6:00 a.m., so he gets to be first. In fact, he's been holding his plate in his hand for almost an hour."

●　●　●

Develyn nibbled on the sweet, tiny carrot sticks and plowed them through a paper plate of onion dip. A procession of people scooted up next to her to visit.

Lily grabbed her arm and led her to the pile of barbecued pork. "I think there are more than twenty people here. Leon counted forty-four, but that included Uncle Henry."

Develyn stabbed a slab of meat lathered with thick red sauce. "You know what, Lily? Argenta has fifty-one people. I've been here almost eight weeks and haven't met half of them until tonight. Oh, we nod or wave but never visit. I should have done this the first night in town. Do you see that man over there with the gray ponytail? He used to be a professor at Notre Dame."

"He's from Indiana?"

"No, he's originally from Layton, Wyoming."

"Where's that?"

"I don't know, but he said it's smaller than Argenta."

"Well, the party's going to get bigger. Mr. Be-Still-My-Heart Rich Rancher is here."

"Quint?" Develyn looked up to see two Quarter-Circle-Diamond pickups bouncing up the road. She watched as Uncle Henry shuffled over to meet the new arrivals.

"Does your watch-burro park cars too?"

"No, he's the unofficial greeter and official mooch."

"The boys are headed for the food line, and Mr. Burdett is coming toward his Miss Dev," Lily said. "Think I'll mosey over to Stewart."

"You don't need to leave."

"Oh, yes I do."

Burdett held his black cowboy hat in hand as he sauntered up. A tight grin rode on his narrow lips.

"Quint, did you find Hunt?"

"Miss Dev, this is embarrassing."

"Oh?"

"After you called, I dispatched the deputies up to Cedar Creek to pick up the trail. The sheriff insisted that we search the ranch one more time to make sure the One of One Thousand wasn't there. We tore the place apart for an hour and called the sheriff back. He reported all they found up at Cooper's was an empty gas can and tracks headed north. So he and the deputies lit out after them trying to catch up before dark. He figured if the thief made it to the Big Horn Mountains, it would be too hard to follow."

"So what is the embarrassing part?"

"The boys wanted to come to your barbecue anyway. Tiny likes his food spicy, so he brings his own hot sauce. When he went to the pantry to retrieve a jar of hot salsa, there it was on the top shelf."

"The gun?"

"Yes. We figure Mom and Pop Gleason pulled it down from over the mantle in my office before they left and jammed it out of sight."

"So you aren't missing anything?"

"Nothing that I can discover."

"That's great, Quint. Makes me ashamed to blame Hunt so quick."

"Yeah, and I sent the sheriff and three deputies into the Cedar Hills all the way to the Big Horns, and I can't reach them on the phone."

"Oh, dear."

"Yeah, this will cost me next time they are raisin' money for new search and rescue equipment."

●　●　●

Develyn weaved through the crowd of guests. Most were dressed in old jeans and clean shirts.

Leon, with his shirt well-dripped in barbecue sauce, sat across the makeshift table from Delaney.

"Dee, I'm glad you felt like coming out," Develyn said.

"Leon insisted. He said it was the best party he had ever been to in his life."

"Your daughter is purdy smart for a girl," Leon announced.

"Oh? What makes you say that?"

"She told me how to get to Level 14 in RaiderQuest."

Develyn glanced at Delaney. "And how did my daughter learn how to get to level anything in a video game?"

"Coed dorms and a crowded rec room," Delaney said.

"I like your daughter," Leon blurted out. "She's just like you . . . only different."

Delaney laughed.

"That about sums it up, doesn't it?" Develyn added.

Casey waved her over to where she and Jackson sat across from Lily and Stewart.

"What is this quartet planning, a double wedding?"

Lily grinned. "Yes, we're trying to figure out where to hide our knives in a wedding dress."

"Oh, my, you have been around Cree-Ryder too long." Develyn turned to Jackson. "Mr. Hill, welcome to the party. You put in long hours at the store today."

"I was studying the utilization of space. All those tall old shelves take up room. If we had twelve-inch shelves instead of sixteen-inch shelves, and if we went six feet high instead of five, we could add three shelves. That would mean room for approximately 27.6 percent increase in inventory."

Develyn stared at his narrow brown eyes. "Mr. Hill, you were born to run a store."

"It's more fun than leading packhorses down the trail by their nose." His eyes widened. "I forgot. Mrs. Tagley phoned. She wants you to call her at the hospital."

"How was she doing?"

"I couldn't tell, but she sounded cheerful enough."

"That's good."

"But she had a lawyer there drawing up her will," he said.

"Oh, my. Yes, well, I'd better go call."

Develyn toted her cell phone past the dirt yard full of pick-ups to the tall cottonwoods by the driveway. The sun sank behind the distant western mountains, but the evening was still bright. Uncle Henry followed her.

"Baby, you are hovering around even closer tonight. Do you sense that I have to go home soon?"

She found a signal and waited to go through the visitor's desk, then the nursing station. Mrs. Tagley's voice sounded weak but relaxed.

"Thanks for calling, Devy. I just had a nice visit with Becky Oliver's youngest son, Ben. He's been an attorney around Casper for thirty years. I wanted to update my will."

"You plan on needing it?"

"I don't plan on ever needing it, but those who are left after me will. Honey, I want you to be the executor of the estate."

"Me? Why me?"

"I need a cowboy girl with Wyoming in her eyes."

"Mrs. Tagley, that's an honor, but maybe the attorney . . ."

"Nope. You are the one I want."

"I'll be happy to do whatever you want me to, but I'm going home to teach school in a couple of days."

"You can fly out to execute the will. I've made provisions for your plane fare. Please, honey."

"I'll do it, Mrs. Tagley."

"I knew you would, Devy. Next time you come to the hospital, young Ben will have copies to sign. It's nothing complicated."

"That's fine."

"I want you to have all my books. I probably have every book written on the history of Wyoming. Many of them are first editions. You can keep the ones you want and donate the rest to a library. You, being the schoolteacher, will know how to make the best use of them."

"Well, thank you very much."

"Devy, there's some cash in that big safe. Never did trust the banks much after the crash of '29 wiped us out. I'd like the hospital children's wing to get that."

"I didn't know they had a children's wing."

"They don't. But they will have. There's quite a bit of money in there. I stopped adding it up when it got to a million."

"That's very generous of you, sweetie."

"Now, here's the fun part. The Hill boy and Miss Cree-Ryder have been doing a good job, I hear. He phones me every evening to tell me the receipts. So I want to give the store to them."

"Really?"

"With provisions. They have to be married. I will have no one living in sin in my home. And they have to keep the grocery store open in Argenta for twelve years. At that time the business, inventory, and property belong to them."

"Oh, my, that's wonderful. I can't wait to tell them."

"And then my guns. I have a few old ones."

"I noticed them the other day."

"I want to donate them to the Firearms Museum and the Buffalo Bill Historical Center in Cody. I already made some contact there."

"Who did you contact?"

"A nice young man named Hunter Burke. He's the assistant curator there. He stopped by to evaluate them. They wanted to authenticate everything for their records. He loved the guns. He must have spent an hour in my safe looking at them."

"When was that?"

"Two weeks ago, I think. It was the day Lydia caught Tippi in the hall closet wearing a leotard."

"I'll come see you tomorrow."

"Could you bring me a bottle of Dr. Bull's Female Remedy? No one in here seems to have heard of it."

"OK. Is there anything else you want?"

The older lady's voice softened. "I want to see Jesus."

"Mrs. Tagley, you hang in there."

"I'm tired and worn out, Devy."

"I know, honey. You get some sleep."

"Just one thing I want to know."

"What's that?"

"It's Cooper Tallon, isn't it?"

Develyn stared across the yard at the crowd at the barbecue.

"I believe you're right, Mrs. Tagley."

"The only time I missed it was with Lydia."

● ● ●

Some folks left when the thunder hit around 8:30 p.m.

Everyone else dashed to their rigs when the deluge hit an hour later.

With a plate of half-eaten onion dip, Develyn strolled up to Cooper. "Cowboy, this was a wonderful party."

"I like the way the downpour sent them all home. I'm tired."

"You worked all day."

"And you worked the crowd like an aspiring politician."

"Was that a compliment?"

"You have a lot of social graces, Dev, ones that I lack. I suppose that's why they make an impression on me."

"Coop, you are a rock. I like that."

"A silent, heavy lump that doesn't move?"

She poked his ribs. "You're so dependable. Always there. Quiet, yes, in a wonderful way, and so supportive."

"Some folks call that backward or shy."

"I don't feel like I have to entertain you. I know I can't impress you, so I can just be myself. That feels good."

"Where's your girl?"

"She drove Leon and his grandmother home. Leon wants to show her something about his video game."

"She really took to him today."

"Maybe it's the mothering instinct that got all stirred up."

"My prayers are with her. No matter who's at fault, that's a rough deal."

"Thanks, Coop. Did you hear about Casey and Jackson getting Mrs. Tagley's store? She said there was no reason for them to have to wait until—well, she said, wait until she croaks. She's going to lease it to them for a dollar a year, and they pay all the taxes, utilities, and insurance."

"Where did they go?"

"Jackson wanted to take Casey up to visit with his mom in Sheridan and tell her the news. They asked me and Dee to run the store until they get back."

"Lily and Stewart left rather early."

"They went with Quint and the Quarter Circle Diamond boys. Quint invited them up for the night. Lily decided it was her one chance to see the big house at the headquarters."

"I can't imagine Stewart agreeing to something so spontaneous."

"I think he does what Lily wants. Aren't they a great couple?"

"Yes, they are. Hope they don't get stuck in the mud going into Burdett's."

"The sheriff and deputies are stuck in the mud somewhere too."

"You know, ever since you told me about Quint's gun being found, I've been ponderin' that scene. Something's not right," Cooper said.

"But nothing is missing."

Cooper pulled off his black cowboy hat and scratched the back of his neck. "What if it's a diversion?"

Develyn stared into his narrow eyes. "What do you mean?"

"The sheriff and everyone else is concentrated up north. What if that was just a ploy to lead them away from the true crime?"

"You mean the real robbery will happen down here?"

"It could be that the gas can was just a plant. All that talk about renting Jackson's pack string could have been used to get the authorities to think someone was headed for Canada. Even though Burdett's gun is worth over a hundred grand, if a person knew they were available, it would be better to steal Mrs. Tagley's guns. Why bother with one if you can grab five of them? Besides, everyone knows Quint has that one, but no one knows about Mrs. Tagley's. They would be much harder to track."

"Forget the guns," Develyn said. "If he was plotting to steal the guns . . . and stumbled across the cash . . . he'd leave the guns and take the million instead."

"Or take both." Cooper nodded. "Now that Mrs. Tagley is in the hospital, who would know what's missin' from her safe?"

"And if she happened to die." Dev's hand covered his mouth, "it would be the perfect crime."

She tugged on his arm. "Mr. Tallon, would you accompany me to Mrs. Tagley's to check her safe?"

"You think Burke's already been there?"

"Everyone in town was here. Tonight would be a good opportunity."

"We'll take my rig. It's still sprinkling."

As they approached the Sweetwater Grocery, Develyn waved her arm. "Go around back and point your headlights at the cottonwoods."

"What are you looking for?"

"Delaney said Hunt claimed to be camping back there the last couple of nights. Maybe he was sizing up the place."

"Nothin's there now."

"Well, just a thought." Develyn motioned for him to park at the rear of the house. "Let's go in the back door."

"That lightning earlier knocked out some lights. Do you have a flashlight?"

"Yes."

"Door key?"

"Yep."

"The combination to the safe?" he asked.

"Yes, sir." Develyn stood on her tiptoes and kissed his cheek. "Is there anything else you want?"

He lifted her chin with his fingers. "Yes, ma'am, I reckon there is." He kissed her on the lips.

"Will it wait?" she murmured.

"As long as it takes."

"You mean that, Coop, don't you?"

"Dev, I'm good at waitin'. But I got to know what I'm waitin' for."

She slipped her arms around his waist. "Did you know I'm falling in love with an older gentleman?"

"Did you know that an older gentleman has never heard a woman tell him that?"

She opened the back door and stepped inside. She flipped the switch. "No electricity."

"The storm must have hit a transformer. Turn on your flashlight."

Develyn surveyed the back porch with the tiny beam.

"Something's wrong," Cooper said.

"Nothing looks out of place."

"Didn't you say Dee went over to Leon's to teach him about a video game?"

"Yes."

"And she didn't come back yet?"

"What are you insinuating?"

"Look over at the Miller's double-wide . . . they have lights. What I'm saying is that Leon has electricity and so do the Millers, but not the store." He waved his hand in front of the beam. "Over there."

Develyn jumped. "What?"

"Walk over to the circuit breakers."

They scooted through the shadows.

"Throw the handle up," he instructed.

"Lights!"

"What does that mean?"

"Someone's been here and wanted to be in the dark."

She grabbed his arm. "Are they still here?"

"I think they are gone. And all those valuable rifles will be gone too."

They scampered to the bedroom and into the large closet. "It's not blown up," she declared. "Someone with the combination opened it." Develyn spun the chamber. "Rats, I went too far."

Cooper rubbed her shoulders. Stiff thumbs kneaded her back. "Relax, Dev. Whatever is stolen is gone. Two minutes won't make a difference."

Cooper reached in and flipped the switch. Develyn stepped inside. "There's something over there." She pointed at the blanket-covered items against the door.

Cooper pulled back the blanket and snatched up a gun. "It's them. Dev, these are the Henrys."

"They are all here?"

"Yep. And the One of One Thousand is here too."

Develyn pulled open several of the shoe boxes. "The money's here too. I was just dreaming all this up." She stepped back outside the safe into Mrs. Tagley's lilac-smelling bedroom. "The deputies are out in the mud. Quint was panicked, and we ran around frantic for nothing. Good grief, how did I let my mind get this carried away?"

Cooper turned off the light in the safe, closed the door, and spun the dial. "But the circuit was off. Someone threw that lever. And someone did tell the Quarter Circle Diamond boys to take off for the weekend. Something is going on."

"And Hunter Burke knows what."

"I think we need to get an orange Popsicle and ponder this," Cooper suggested.

"Oh, yes!"

"Out on the front bench."

"They are kind of messy. Is that what you mean?"

"I'm in a bedroom with a pretty lady, that's what I mean. I'm not that old."

"Good, Mr. Tallon. I'm counting on that."

The rain had stopped. Argenta was lit by moonlight breaking through the clouds. Develyn plopped down next to Cooper on the freight wagon bench on the front porch. "I thought you wanted an orange Popsicle too."

"We are going to share that one."

"Oh, no, Mr. Tallon. You have to learn that there's one thing I will not share. This is my Popsicle. Get your own."

"OK." He plucked it out of her hand, snapped it in two, and handed her half.

"I can't believe you did that," she gasped.

"I think it's about time you tried something different. This way you can take those long licks, enjoy it, and finish it before it drips all over your shirt. Then we can go get another one and do it all over again."

"But that only works if you have a friend to share it with."

"You have such a friend."

"Do you intend to be here every time I want a Popsicle for the rest of my life?"

"Sounds like a good goal to me, doesn't it?"

Develyn took a big, deep sigh and let it out slow. "Yes, Coop, it sounds like a wonderful goal. Are you available for the rest of your life?"

"Are you proposing?" Coop laughed.

"I'm just finding a Popsicle partner."

"In some places of the world, that's like being engaged."

"How about Natrona County?"

"I'm afraid so. It's a tradition."

"Well," she giggled, "if it's a western tradition, so be it."

"Do we know what we are doin'?"

"I'm sitting on a porch on a rainy night in Wyoming eating half a Popsicle with a man I've known eight weeks, saying I will marry him some day if I can teach school in Indiana and he can be a Wyoming cowboy and we can figure out how a marriage like that can work."

"And I thought we were talking about Popsicle partners," he gulped.

"Hmm. Men. Are you trying to break the engagement?"

"No, ma'am, I'm just worried that when daylight comes, you'll regret promises made while under the influence of an orange Popsicle."

"Popsicle promises are the best kind. They last forever."

Coop put his arm around her shoulder. "Dev, this isn't a joke to me."

She laid her head on his arm. "Nor me, Cooper Tallon. You're the most peaceful, comfortable man I've ever been with. You bring me something I've never had. Deep, deep contentment. I like it. I want it for a long, long time."

When the Popsicles were gone, they continued to sit on the bench and talk.

"Well, Miss Dev, do you think I ought to get you home?"

"I think we should talk and talk and talk and let me fall asleep right here with your arm around me."

"I've pondered that myself."

"Oh? And just what else did you ponder?"

"I believe a crime was committed by Mr. Hunter Burke. We just can't figure out what."

"That's what you are thinking?"

"Dadgumit, Dev. You are a beautiful lady, and it wouldn't take but a blink for my thoughts to run away with me. I have to think about something else. I'm going to do this right, Ms. Worrell. Are you sure all the money was in the safe?"

"I looked in a half-dozen of the boxes."

"Let's go check out the others."

● ● ●

With the safe again open, Cooper waited out in the bedroom under the single lightbulb fixture. "Bring one out here."

Develyn pulled off the lid and shoved it toward him. "See, still crammed with . . ."

He pulled the top bills off the stack.

"Paper? Plain old paper?"

"These aren't real." Cooper turned over the bills to a blank side. "These are photocopies on top and white paper on the bottom. He did it. He stole Mrs. Tagley's cash!"

Dev scooted back into the safe, then hollered, "They are all that way!"

"We were right. Quint's gun was the diversion. He wanted to steal Mrs. Tagley's guns, but when he discovered the cash, he left the guns."

"But it's her money. It will be the children's wing of the hospital some day. He can't do that."

"He just did."

"We have to call the sheriff."

"Can't reach him until he gets out of the Big Horns."

"Then we're going to catch him ourselves. I will not let him get away with this!" Develyn ranted.

"How are we going to catch him? We don't know which way he went."

"He didn't go north. That was all a ploy. If you were going to get out of this country in a hurry and didn't want to be on the blacktop, which way would you go?"

"South through the oil fields. A man could drive to Utah though those oil field roads."

"We're going after him."

"There is no way to catch him. He had a two- or three-hour head start."

"But it was pouring rain. You can't go fast on those roads in the rain. The wind has been blowing for an hour. The roads are drying up. Maybe we can gain some speed on him."

"We won't know which roads."

"The biggest one south. That's the right one. Do you know your way around these oil fields?"

"I laid a ten-million-dollar pipeline through them."

"Then let's get going."

"Dev, this sounds impossible."

"What do we have to lose? We will be inside the cab of the truck talking for the rest of the night. That's OK, isn't it?"

"You've got very good logic."

"So are you going to marry me for my logic?"

"That's one reason. Not the one I'm thinkin' of at the moment but a definite consideration."

"Mr. Tallon, should I be worried about being in a truck with you tonight?"

"No more worried than I am."

• • •

Within twenty minutes of bouncing south down still-muddy dirt roads, Develyn was completely lost. "I don't know if this was a good idea."

Cooper pulled off to the side of the road.

"What are you doing?"

"Looking."

"At me?"

"At that mess by the side of the road. Someone was stuck there tonight. See the ruts? Piles of mud where someone was digging? Someone was in a hurry to get back on the road."

"An oil field worker?"

"Nope. They'd all know better. They'd just pull over and take a nap. An hour after the wind picks back up it will be dry enough to drive out of any ditch."

"It could be Hunter."

"Could be, but we're still miles behind him."

"For Mrs. Tagley's sake, we've got to try."

• • •

They crested a pass and dropped into a small basin. Even in the night shadows, Develyn spotted a familiar sign. "Coop, have you ever heard of one of those gas field warning sirens going off?"

"A few times. They have drills like fire drills at schools, I reckon."

"What are you supposed to do if you hear one?"

"Get to higher ground in a hurry. The gas will hover like invisible ground fog. You're supposed to drive out of the danger area as fast as possible using the ascending roadway. I've never been out here when an honest leak occurred. Don't think I want to, either. One time, Blamey Jim's pals played a trick on him when he was out in the sage. Well, let's just say Blamey Jim took a Cabela's catalog with him to the sage and read ever' page before he returned. Anyway, T. Clark tripped the alarm on the gas field, and ol' Blamey came runnin' out of the sage, with his . . . well, sorry, Dev. I don't usually tell my stories to ladies."

Develyn laughed. "I get the picture."

When they bounced over a slight rise, Develyn waved her hands. "Stop!"

Cooper slammed on the brakes.

"What is that in the road?"

"Part of an old recap tire, I imagine." He started to roll forward.

"Wait, Coop, I'm serious. It's a kill strip. One of those took my tire out last week, and Hunter Burke showed up five minutes later. I think it fell out of his truck and he came back to retrieve it. He was in a hurry to load it up."

Cooper parked the truck in the middle of the road and hiked out to the dark object in the shadow of the headlights.

She watched as he pulled off his hat and stared. Develyn scurried up to him. "Was I right?"

"You were right, Ms. Worrell. This means either Hunter knows someone is following or expects someone to follow. That means it might be dangerous to keep going."

"Coop, do you know how to trip the gas field alarm?"

"There isn't much to it. T. Clark showed me how. Why?"

"What do you think Burke would do if the siren went off now?"

"Is he dumb or smart?"

"Very, very smart."

"Then he'd drive up the nearest incline and get out of the gas field."

"Where would the oil people come from to check out the leak?"

"From the south. Hunter won't want to run into them because they will question him and record his license plate number. Are you saying we should set off the alarm and see if we can force Hunter back here?"

"It's a thought," she said.

"We could get in big trouble if we get caught."

"We could get in big trouble if we just park in the dark and smooch."

"Maybe that kill strip would be helpful," he grinned. "We'll leave it, that way he won't be suspicious if he drives back this way." He took her hand and led her back to the truck.

Cooper Tallon rumbled the black Dodge truck back up to the top of the grade next to the gas field warning signs. "Well, Miss Dev, let's see what happens."

Cooper shorted out some wires and soon had the annoying roar of the sirens churning across the central Wyoming night.

"They're louder than I thought," she called out. "Sort of like tornado warnings back home."

"What did you think they would be like?"

"Maybe like an alarm clock. What do we do now?"

Cooper studied the drying mud on the road. "Figure out a way to stop his truck, if he does come this way."

"Do you have a plan?" she quizzed.

"Yep. It worked before."

"Where?"

"In a John Wayne movie," he replied.

● ● ●

Develyn studied the roadway in the dark shadows. "Tell me again how this works."

"My truck blocks the road. Those boulders and the warning sign barricade the north side. I'll be stretched out on the ground like I'm injured to stop him on the south. When he gets out, I'll jump him."

"And I step out from behind the sign and wave this at him?"

"That is a 38/55, half mag, saddle rind carbine. It will set Burke down in a hurry. He knows his guns. Are you sure you are up to this?"

332

"All I have to do is wave a gun. You have to lie in the mud and hope he doesn't run over you."

"He won't."

"I wouldn't put it past him."

"I would. It would throw the truck alignment out. He'll stop to drag the body into the ditch."

"And if I have to shoot this?"

"Fire one shot over his head, then cock it quick and point it at him. Dev, I don't think you'll need to. I'll have him pinned down by then. I've got some plastic ties for binding . . . Looks like someone's coming. Sure hope it's Hunt."

She stepped behind the sign. "I hope he doesn't run over my cowboy. Doesn't this plan sound amateurish?"

"We are amateurs," he replied.

"Point well taken."

Cooper sprawled in the drying mud in front of his diagonally parked truck. "Just in case something goes wrong here, I love you Develyn Gail Upton Worrell."

The approaching headlight bounced up and down on the approaching dirt road. "I love you too, Cooper . . . Cooper . . ."

"Worthington."

"Your middle name is Worthington?"

"Yep. You want to call off the engagement?"

"No, I love you too, Cooper W. Tallon."

Develyn held her breath when a white Ford slid to a stop. *It is Hunter Burke.*

The driver didn't get out but backed up the truck and headed straight at the boulder next to Develyn.

Is he coming over here? That's not what we planned. He's going to roll the boulders away instead of the "dead body."

With headlights on high beam, the truck stopped. Hunt slammed on the brakes and hopped out of the truck wearing a red bandanna over his mouth.

"This is just what I need," he mumbled as he stooped down and gripped a granite boulder the size of a large watermelon. "First a gas leak, now this guy is passed out. I can't believe this."

Lord, help me.

She jumped out in front of him. "Maybe you can believe this!" She pointed the carbine at him.

"Mrs. Worrell? What are you doing here? It's a bad dream." He continued to roll the rock. "No Indiana schoolteacher is going to shoot me. Besides," he hollered above the siren, "you don't have a clue what's in my truck."

"You have a million dollars cash that belongs to Mrs. Tagley," Develyn yelled. "And you greatly underestimate the teaching profession."

With the carbine lodged in her shoulder, she pulled the barrel inches to the left and blasted the left tire of Burke's pickup.

The explosion of the gun and the tire drove Hunter Burke to his knees with his hands up. As Develyn cocked the lever, Cooper slammed Hunter's face down in the mud and yanked his arm behind his back.

"Son, never rile a Wyomin' cowboy girl."

14

D evy, it's time to go."

"I don't want to go."

"We've got to go home now."

"I want to stay here forever."

The tall, thin man with a dark brown butch haircut stooped down and hugged the ten-year-old. "The Lord gave us a precious gift this summer: a busted water pump, ruptured radiator, and a parts store that got the order wrong twice."

"Why was that a present, Daddy?" Develyn whimpered.

"That's how he guided us to Argenta. All those problems led us here and kept us here. Now it's time to go home."

"Why can't I take Brownie to Indiana?"

"Sweetie, we've been all through that. Besides, Brownie is a Wyoming horse. This is his home. He belongs here."

"So do I, Daddy. I can't leave. I just can't. Why don't you understand? I've got Wyoming in me now, and I can't leave."

"Devy, your mind is filled with prairie and sage and horses. I'm sure part of your heart will always be here. Do you know what?"

"What?" She sobbed.

"You get to take every one of those memories with you."

"But they are only in my mind."

"And your heart. That's the good part. What does Mama do with all the pictures she takes on one of our trips?"

"She puts them in an album," Develyn sniffed.

"How often do we take them off the shelf and look at them?"

"Hardly ever."

"Now you see what I'm saying?" Mr. Upton continued. "Wyoming won't be in some faded scrapbook. It will be in your heart every day of your life. And just think, every night you can let your heart just ride through those memories over and over."

"But, Daddy, I might forget. What if I forget about this summer and Brownie and Mrs. Tagley?"

"Devy, you'll have some bad days. We live in a world that sometimes treats us mean. But even on those days, you can run away to Wyoming, to your memories of this dirt-road town. Do you really think you will forget Wyoming?"

"No, Daddy."

"So come on, honey, get in the car. Mama and Dewa are waiting."

Develyn rubbed her upturned nose with the palm of her

hand. She glanced down at the spots on her yellow blouse. "Can I have an orange Popsicle?"

"Mama said you can't have them in the car. But I think when we stop for lunch in Cheyenne you can have one."

He hugged her and kissed her cheek. "It's time to go, Devy."

It really is time to go.

Develyn shoved her sunglasses on top of her head. *Well, it's not the cabin we stayed in thirty-five years ago. It's not the cabin I spent the summer in, but it's just as difficult to leave. Lord, if I had to repeat one summer over and over, it would be this one. Thanks.*

Casey Cree-Ryder burst through the cabin door, waving her left hand. "Look, look, look! Is that the most awesome diamond ring or what?"

"Oh, honey, it's gorgeous!"

"It belonged to Jackson's grandmother and then his mother. She insisted that I take it. Dev, I never thought I'd be engaged."

"Jackson is one lucky guy, honey."

Casey slipped her arm around Develyn's waist. "Hearing that means more than you know. You were the first person in my life that made me glad I'm me."

"And Jackson is the second?"

"Yeah, and he's cuter than you."

"Are you disparaging my pathetic white skin again?"

"Hey, I like your farmer tan. But Devy, never go out in a two-piece bathing suit."

"Thank you for the advice, countess. I'm thinking of wearing a paper bag over my head."

"A brown paper bag?"

Develyn stuck out her tongue. "Now, Ms. Cree-Ryder, are you sure you want to take care of My Maria and Uncle Henry?"

"Yes, yes, yes. I know the mare is a pill. I'm used to temperamental horses. But I'm not sure Uncle Henry can survive without his mama."

"Coop said he will help you."

"Yes, he said I can live in the cabin until me and Jackson get married. He's going to pull a trailer back to the springs so he can work up there."

"Have you set a date for the wedding?"

"Not really, but whenever it is, you have to be the matron of honor."

"Casey, that will be one of the most joyous days ever. All teasing aside, you are a great friend."

"Let's go outside, Dev. Others are waiting for you, and I'm about to cry."

Delaney relaxed on the porch, her feet hung over the edge. Leon perched next to her. When he saw Dev, he jumped up, ran over to her, slapped her on the arm, then ran down the lane toward his grandmother's.

"I love you too, Leon," Develyn hollered.

"I know," he shouted back.

Dee walked over to her mother. "I think that's the best he can do, Mom. I think he wants to hug you, but he just doesn't know how."

"I know, honey. Touch is a powerful statement. Leon has just never experienced tenderness. Right now, it's beyond him."

"Mom, I laid awake most of last night thinking about it. I decided I'm going back to Purdue."

Develyn slipped her arm around her daughter's waist. "Oh, that's good, Dee. I'm happy to hear that."

Delaney slipped her fingers into her mother's. "I want to teach."

"Are you serious? What happened to the drama major?"

"I decided I want to teach kids like Leon."

"That's a wonderful goal."

They walked hand in hand over to the Jeep Cherokee.

Develyn bit her lip, then stared across the pasture. "I can't believe I'm leaving again."

"Again?"

"I left when I was ten, remember? I was just thinking about that day. I think a person shouldn't have to relive a sad day. Of course, it was different back then. I remember the lecture Dad gave as we left town."

"You miss Grandpa, don't you?"

"Yes, I do. And you miss your dad, don't you?"

"Is that OK, Mom? Are you alright with that?"

"Sure, baby. No one can take the place of a girl's daddy. I'll make you a promise. I won't ever say anything negative about your father again."

"Some things are changing, aren't they, Mom?"

"Dee, this summer has changed almost everything."

"Oh, good," Delaney laughed. "Are you going to get a tattoo?"

"Some things will never change."

"Do you want to see my tattoo?" Delaney asked.

"Why don't you just tell me where it is?"

"Out loud?" Delaney gasped.

Develyn bit her lip. "I don't think we want to go there. Did you get all your things put in the Cherokee?"

"Hey, I forgot to tell you that Lily called." Casey tucked her clean white blouse into her Wranglers as she scampered across the porch. "You were in the shower. She said call her back whenever you get time."

"So their flights went fine?"

"She said the church is available on October 1."

"So they have set a date?"

"Is that cool or what?" Casey licked her fingers and mashed down her black bangs.

"I've never been a matron of honor before, and this year I get to do it twice," Develyn grinned.

Casey wound her long braid on top of her head. "Maybe I should put my hair up?"

Delaney made a face. Develyn wrinkled her nose.

"Then again," Casey grinned, "maybe not."

With packages in hand, Cooper Tallon stepped out of his trailer and strolled up. "Dev, I know we said our good-byes last night . . ."

"You call 3:30 a.m. 'last night'?" Delaney laughed. "In five more minutes Casey and I were going to turn on the spotlights."

"We had the buckets of cold water already poured," Casey added.

Cooper rubbed his square chin, then glanced down at the packages. "I wanted to give you a couple of presents."

"You didn't need to," Develyn protested.

"This one, I didn't need to . . . it's just a fun project." He handed her a small, heavy gift sack. "I found it in the ruins of your cabin. It was broken, but not melted, so I restored it. I figured it must hold a memory or two."

Develyn reached into the sack and tugged out a round, brass object. "My clock? You fixed my clock?"

"It seemed to be stuck on 12:20. So I cleaned it, straightened out the dent, and got it running again."

Develyn sucked in a breath and held it. "You certainly did, Mr. Cooper Tallon."

"Why are you crying, Mom?" Delaney probed.

Tears rolled down her cheeks, and she watched the ticking second hand. "Because it feels good to get my clock running again."

Casey wrapped her arms around Develyn. "I've got to get to the store. Jackson needs me. Doesn't that sound wonderful? You and Dee are stopping for free going-away Popsicles, right?"

"Yes, we are. We'll see you there." Casey piled into her old truck and fogged dust down the drive.

Cooper slipped his arm around Develyn.

"By the way, Renny Slater stopped by around daylight but didn't want to wake you up."

"That was thoughtful, but this is one time I wouldn't have minded."

"He was in a hurry. He said a band of wild horses broke out on I-25 north of Douglass, and the state patrol begged him to come down."

Develyn shook her head, then ran her fingers though her short, blonde hair. "I bet they did. That's my mustang breaker. I don't think Wyoming could survive without Renny Slater. There is no one quite like him."

"He said he'll see you down the road."

She laid her head on Cooper's chest and closed her eyes. "This is tougher than I thought," she murmured.

"I can sit in the car if you two need to kiss some more," Delaney said.

"No," Cooper insisted. "I want you here. I've got another present for your mama to open, and I want you to see it too."

The big gift bag had several envelopes.

"Start with this one."

Develyn read the card slowly.

"Sometimes I wonder if you really know how much you mean to me. I wonder if you know how often in a day my thoughts turn to you. Do you know how I like to watch you, listen to you, tease you . . . love you? You came into my world and changed my life. I am grateful to the Lord for the changes."

"Wow, that is a wonderful card, Coop."

"I meant ever' word of it."

"What were those words he wrote at the bottom?" Delaney asked.

"It was just a personal note," Develyn explained. "Just a quote from a country song."

Delaney grabbed the card and laughed. "'There ain't nothin' about you that don't do somethin' for me.'"

"Open the dadgum present," Cooper blushed.

Develyn stared at the contents. "Airline tickets?"

Delaney peered over her shoulder. "For Thanksgiving week."

Develyn kissed Coop's cheek. "Oh, honey, what a wonderful present. Now I know when I'm coming back."

"Mom, there's more than one ticket." Delaney prodded.

"Oh, there's one for you, Dee! How generous. And two for Mr. and Mrs. Stewart Lawrence? This is going to be a wonderful Thankgiving. The newlyweds get to come too. And tickets for my mother and David?" She tried to pry into Tallon's gleaming steel-gray eyes. "You are flying everyone to Wyoming? I don't understand."

"I figured we'd all like to attend Casey and Jackson's wedding." He winked at Delaney.

"So that's when the date is. I wonder why she didn't tell me. Oh, yes, we will want to come and . . . wait, I mean, my mother and David aren't exactly the Wyoming type, honey."

"I think you are wrong. I'm sure they will want to come." He handed her a small gold box.

"Is this?" Develyn gasped.

"I think your mama will want to attend her daughter's wedding."

"Oh yes!" Develyn kissed Cooper's lips. "When did you do all this shopping?"

"I started plannin' it the night we caught Hunter Burke. I told you I had personal business in town yesterday. Well, a wedding ring and mushy cards is about as personal as this ol' cowboy gets." He put the palms of his hands on her cheeks and kissed her back.

"Now do you want me in the car?" Cooper asked.

"No," Develyn insisted. "We need a chaperone." She opened the box and kissed Cooper again. "But, honey, we haven't got this figured out yet. I'll be in Indiana for almost nine months of the year, and you'll be in Wyoming. How will we do that?"

"Dev, it will work out. Maybe it's taken me all summer to figure out, but if I can only have you part of the time for now, that's far better than any other option I've ever had. If I can only have you here in our big Wyoming log home three months of the year, we'll just have to pack four times as much fun in every day we're together. I'll get to Indiana as often as I can. You come out here when you can. Can you live with that, Miss Dev?"

She slipped the ring on her finger and pressed the ticking clock against her chest. "Yes, sir, Mr. Tallon, I believe I can."

More from award-winning author
Stephen Bly!

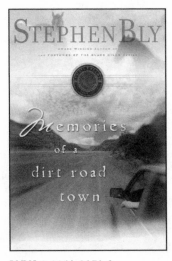

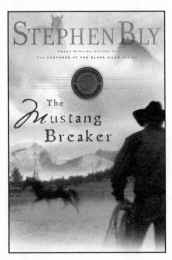

ISBN 0-8054-3171-3
Trade paper, $14.99

ISBN 0-8054-3172-1
Trade paper, $14.99

Don't miss *Memories of a Dirt Road Town* and *The Mustang Breaker*, books one and two in the Horse Dreams Trilogy.

Look for the classic Western series, the Fortunes of the Black Hills, the epic story of the Fortune family's struggles and triumphs in six action-packed novels about faith and destiny that spans several generations.

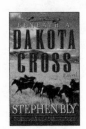

The Fortunes of the Black Hills series:

Beneath a Dakota Cross 0-8054-1659-5
Shadow of Legends 0-8054-2174-2
The Long Trail Home 0-8054-2356-7
Friends and Enemies 0-8054-2437-7
Last of the Texas Camp 0-8054-2557-8
The Next Roundup 0-8054-2699-X

BROADMAN
&HOLMAN
PUBLISHERS

Available at your favorite bookstore or visit www.broadmanholman.com for more information.